SHADOWS IN THE DEEP

THE DURAND CHRONICLES: BOOK ONE

LARK BRENNAN

BARKYBOY PRODUCTIONS

ALSO BY LARK BRENNAN

To my brilliant husband Steve,
who makes every day a romantic adventure!

1

Fat Dog Harbor, The Grenadines

"Can't you harass somebody else for a change?" Bodie Flynn muttered at the ancient Obeah woman shaking a mummified bird claw at him from the end of the dock. Every time he came to shore she materialized on the beach to curse at him. Sometimes she threw shells.

He had no idea why, and after three years the routine was getting old. Turning his back on her, he rammed the business end of the faded red hose into the tank of his sailboat and turned on the water.

Where was Joshua with his supplies? He adjusted his sunglasses and scanned the break in the line of palm and papaya trees along the stark white beach. Bodie would get his own provisions if it wasn't for his little *infirmity*. In the mid-afternoon sun, the translucent globes and shapes he saw hovering above the sand could have been reflections off the water. But they weren't. And they waited to torment him.

The fiberglass sailboat wasn't what he would have

chosen. The stark white hull and minimum of teak trim made it indistinguishable from the larger bareboats chartered to tourists throughout the Caribbean, which was the point. The last thing he wanted was attention. Still, a sleek, classy vessel would have made his exile more endurable.

His fifteen-year-old part-time assistant was twenty minutes late. Not that it really mattered. He had nowhere to go and nothing in particular to do. And that was becoming a problem. He was sick and tired of his own company and bored to death of sitting in the harbor of Fat Dog Island, a.k.a St. Nowhere.

The hum of an engine broke the peace. He searched the sky to the west until a seaplane appeared above the mountain tops, circling low over the cove, the island's only harbor. The height of the surrounding hills created wind currents that made landing tricky. On the other hand, the seas outside the bay were rough with a strong current and landing there was impossible. Either way, the island's geography discouraged casual visitors by air or by sea.

The seaplane approached from the mouth of the harbor, coming in low and slowing. Bodie chuckled to himself. "Good luck, cowboy."

The first wind shear hit the plane, lifting a wing so suddenly most pilots would have found themselves flipped over. Not this guy. He steadied the craft and continued his descent. The next freak gust came from the other direction just as the plane skimmed the water. With a lurch, a pontoon sunk into a wave, nearly sending the plane nose first into the water before the pilot compensated and glided the craft across the choppy bay to the end of the pier.

Bodie shook his head. "Either damned good or damned lucky."

The pilot cut the engine, climbed onto a pontoon and

tied the plane to a cleat on the far end of the pier. All Bodie could see was the guy's height—six feet at least. Only when the pilot leapt onto the dock did he see him clearly. And *he* was most definitely a *she*. A young, long-legged brunette striding down the dock in his direction.

This did not bode well. He bent to untie the bow line.

"Going somewhere, Bodie?"

His heart sputtered and started pounding. Nobody knew where he was or even that he was alive. Well, almost nobody. He straightened and turned to face her, expecting his height—all six-feet-seven-inches—to intimidate her. Instead she grinned.

"You *are* Bodie Flynn, aren't you?" She planted her fists on her hips and her tone was less friendly now.

"Never heard of him."

The woman wore a tailored uniform of crisp white shirt and khaki shorts. The dark aviator glasses were a little disconcerting but her body was worldclass—slim, athletic, and feminine in all the right places.

A slim eyebrow cocked over the Ray-Bans. "*Really*? You mean there's another Talos IV in Fat Dog Harbor?" She glanced down at the line he hadn't quite untied. "I came from the British Virgins to see you, so don't even think about blowing me off."

Which was exactly what he was going to do. He folded his arms across his chest. "You've wasted your time and fuel."

"I was told you could help us. I'm head of the Marine Mammal Research Foundation. Some whales we've been tracking have vanished. Their GPS devices went silent in the Puerto Rico Trench."

Fear's icy fingers gripped his lungs. Who was this woman? "Sorry. Can't help you."

She removed her Ray-Bans and fixed him with a blue-eyed stare. "I'm Lex Durand, Mark Durand's sister."

And with that, Bodie's peaceful life shattered around him like a plate glass window strafed with machine gun fire. Mark Durand. The man who'd saved his life. The S.O.B. who owned his soul. He swore under his breath.

She chuckled. "Mark has that effect on people. I, on the other hand, am quite reasonable. How about we talk over lunch? My treat. I'm famished."

He eyed her suspiciously and slid his Durand Tech communications device—ComDev—from his pocket. "You won't mind if I verify your identity."

"Have at it," she said and waved at the ComDev.

He snapped a photo of her and sent it to Mark Durand with a two word message: *Your sister?*

The reply came back instantly. *Yes. Help her.*

He glared at the screen, tempted to tell Durand to stick it. Except he needed Durand Tech's resources, not to mention the cash flow.

The rattle of a makeshift cart on the wooden dock announced Joshua's arrival.

"Hey, boss," Joshua said as he pushed the cart to a stop next to the Talos. "You got company." He grinned at Lex.

"Josh, this is Ms. Durand. Would you please show her where she can get lunch?"

The kid nodded and motioned for Lex to follow him. "There's a nice café on the square or a beach bar that serves fresh fish."

She stayed put. "If you won't join me, can we get something brought here?" She pulled some bills from her pocket.

Josh shrugged. "Whatever you like."

Bodie was trapped. This woman wasn't going to be put

off easily. "Right. Josh please get a couple orders of fish and chips from Manuel."

"No fish for me," she said, "Salad, fruit, chips would be great."

"Sure." Josh reached for the money, glancing at Bodie for approval.

Bodie shook his head. "Put it on my account and get yourself some lunch, too."

The kid winked at him. "Right, boss."

"Thank you," she said as she flashed a friendly smile.

Bodie grabbed a couple canvas bags from the cart and stepped onto the deck of his boat. "I need to stow these. You might as well come aboard."

———

BODIE DUCKED INTO THE COMPANIONWAY, and Lex wondered why a man his size would live on a sailboat. A glance was all it took to size up the vessel. A production boat, sixty feet and so common in the islands it was almost cliché. She noted the spotless deck and the neatly stowed gear, signs of a good sailor.

His head popped through the hatch. "Come on in out of the sun." He wasn't smiling, but he wasn't barking at her. In fact, his tone held resignation. "How about some iced tea?"

"If it isn't too much trouble."

A snort. "No trouble, ma'am."

She stepped into the companionway and descended the narrow stairs, blinking until her eyes adjusted to the dimmer light. "Geez. This is..." She gaped around her.

"Unexpected?" he offered.

She nodded. Instead of the cramped quarters of a charter sailboat, this space had been custom designed for a man

Bodie's size to move around in. In place of cheap veneers and vinyl, the finishes were mahogany, teak, and leather. "From topside this looks like a generic charter boat. I don't get it."

He leaned back against the counter of the galley. "Nothing to get."

"I guess if you want to blend in, a charter bucket's the way to go."

He removed his sunglasses and pinned her with an all-too-familiar silver stare. Her stomach lurched. Shit. Bodie Flynn was a revenant. Even in the Durand world revenants were rare and mysterious. Bodie's eerie gaze drifted down her body and up again. He half-smiled, flashing straight white teeth. "You'd rather be the center of attention."

"Not at all."

"Flying around the Caribbean in a souped-up seaplane is low key?"

Luckily he didn't know just how high tech it was. No way was she jumping to his bait. The fact remained Lex needed his expertise.

"Can we just start over?" she asked. "Mark told me you might be able to help me find my whales. The foundation will pay you for your time and expenses. Will you help us?"

"I'm willing to listen, but there's nothing I can do that a decent technician can't. GPS systems aren't that complicated."

"Fair enough." She accepted a glass of tea from him and slid into the tan leather seat. While she took a laptop from her backpack and booted it up, Bodie poured himself a glass and sat across from her. He set his drink on a cardboard bar coaster and rested his elbows on the mahogany table, flashing three intricate hieroglyphics tattooed on the inside of his forearm. She stared at the delicate symbols, transfixed by a mystical quality that pricked her psychic senses. Quickly, he lowered his arm, covering the ink.

Lex took a deep breath. "Three years ago the Marine Mammal Research Foundation began a program to track the movements of humpback whales and bottlenose dolphins in the Caribbean and Atlantic. The devices use the most advanced GPS technology available and in some cases digitally record physical, audio, and ambient data that we download periodically." She left out her telepathic debriefing of the animals to clarify the data. Even her team didn't know about that.

"Maybe the batteries ran out. Not unheard of," he said.

"Not these batteries."

"K-3s?" The comment was thrown out casually, as though he'd said Duracells.

"Yeah. K-3s."

His chuckle startled her.

"What's so funny?"

"You want my help but you're leaving out important pieces of information, aren't you? The only way I work is with all the facts. Anything else is a waste of my time and yours."

All the facts. Like he'd believe them if he knew. "I'll give you what I have starting with our data on the humpbacks' disappearance in the Puerto Rico Trench."

Two clicks brought up a 3-D image of the depths of the trench.

"What are we looking at?" he asked.

"A whale's journey at about 200 feet. The software creates the visual from the data in the recorder."

"What's with all the color? At that depth everything looks blue."

"The software corrects to actual color to help us identify plant and animal species."

His fingers drummed on the tabletop as if itching to get at the keyboard. "Can you zoom in and out? Look side to side or from different angles?"

She suppressed a grin. He was a computer geek after all. "Sure. Like this." A few demo clicks of the mouse and a half dozen keystrokes later, she slid the laptop in front of him.

Without hesitation he took over, long fingers flying across the keys. While his attention was glued to the screen, she studied him. What ethnic mix had resulted in this man? High cheekbones, a chiseled jawline, and a sensual mouth that twisted in concentration. And she'd bet that tan wasn't just the tropical sun. Yes, Bodie was a genetic puzzle and definitely attractive in an über-masculine sort of way.

"Okay, so you have good software," he said without even looking up. "That it? Because I can't see what this has to do with a faulty GPS system."

She pulled up a second file. "The journey you just watched was recorded five days ago by Poseidon's recorder. Poseidon was our first humpback subject so we were excited to be able to follow him in real time." She typed in coordinates, angled the screen so Bodie could see it. "Now this next part is fifteen minutes after the footage you just saw, a couple kilometers from where the first part was recorded."

"What am I looking for?"

"Just keep watching."

A moment later the wall of the trench in the newer video began pulsating, a rhythmic undulation like the breathing of a living being.

"What the hell is this?" he muttered.

She didn't answer.

The pulsating increased. Lex's heart caught the cadence

and its echo pounded in her ears. She knew what was coming. In slow motion the visual angle dove, showing Poseidon's perspective as he plunged deeper. The vortex caught him like an underwater tornado, spinning, sucking him down, down, down into blackness. The screen went blank.

Bodie exhaled loudly. "Damn." He rose and crossed to the galley. He popped the cap of a Heineken and took a long pull on the bottle. "I don't know what Mark told you, but I can't find your whales."

2

———

"I was laughed out of M.I.T. My work was dismissed as delusional."

From the frown on Lex's face, Bodie deduced her brother hadn't told her anything about him, not even his cover story. Figures. The S.O.B. tended to omit a lot of mission critical information. Based on the footage he'd just seen, what Lex was asking him to investigate was no GPS failure.

"Yo, Talos. Fat Dog Catering has arrived!" Josh called from the dock.

"Lunch." Bodie swept a hand toward the stairs.

Lex didn't move.

He shrugged, took a couple plates from a cabinet, three bottles of water from the fridge and headed up the stairs to the deck.

"So who's the babe?" Josh unloaded foil-covered paper plates from a cardboard box onto a foldup table in the cockpit. He wiggled his eyebrows.

"Trouble. Don't let her looks fool you."

He caught a movement in the hatchway. She'd heard his comment. Why couldn't she go away and leave him alone?

She flashed a dazzling smile at the boy. "Thanks for delivering lunch. It smells delicious."

Josh grinned and gawked at her. "Happy to do it."

Bodie uncovered the plates. "We have fish, chips, johnnycakes, coleslaw, tomato and cucumber salad, mango slices. What'll you have?"

After slipping her aviators back in place, she filled a plate with salad, fruit, a johnnycake and a hearty helping of fries.

Josh joined them as they ate and asked Lex question after question about her plane. Bodie watched her from behind his Oakleys. She used her utensils like a European, reminding him she was a rich girl—a very rich girl—and Mark Durand's sister.

"So did you play basketball?" she asked.

For a moment he didn't realize she was addressing him.

Josh proudly answered for him. "San Antonio Spurs. The NBA."

Bodie shifted on the bench and popped a chip into his mouth.

She studied him. "Really?"

"My eight-game career consisted of mostly pine-time and ended in a six player pile-up that destroyed both my knees." That at least was true. For some reason he felt compelled to add, "Fortunately my contract said they had to pay me for two more years and my agent had insisted I get disability insurance. So I went to grad school."

"M.I.T.? Impressive for a jock."

Actually Princeton, but M.I.T. was his cover story. "Some of us can read and write."

She picked up a piece of mango with her fingers and

slipped it in her mouth. "Where did you go for your under-grad degree?"

He was saved from lying by the clatter of four boys running down the dock toward the seaplane. "Hey, guys, look but don't touch," he called after them.

The adolescents ignored him, one climbing onto a pontoon.

Lex rose, muttering in French under her breath. "Kids are going to be kids. I don't want anyone to get hurt."

"Finish your lunch. I'll take care of them." Josh leapt onto the wooden dock and headed for the boys.

Lex started to follow and Bodie caught her arm. "Let him handle them. He's good with kids. They respect him." Her skin was warm and smooth. He released it.

She watched as Josh ordered the boys off the plane. "He seems like a good kid."

"Yeah. And smart. He wants to learn and has turned out to be a damned good assistant. Better than some of the grad students I had assigned to me."

"And I bet his family needs the money."

"He lives with his grandmother." Just like Bodie had. "Good woman but it's a poor island."

"Are you going to help him go to school?"

He shrugged. "We've talked about it. There's no Fat Dog U and he's lived here all his life. Going off island to school would be a culture shock at best."

"You choose to live in the middle of nowhere, the kid should get a choice."

He swallowed a bitter laugh. Like he'd live in Fat Dog Bay if he could live anywhere else without getting himself killed. "If he wants to go to college, I'll see what I can do."

"He will," she replied. "So tell me more about what happened at M.I.T."

A bead of sweat ran down the back of his neck and under his t-shirt. Which version of the story would she buy?

Leaning back, Lex planted the heels of her boat shoes on the bench not two feet from his thigh. "I'll know if you lie to me," she said. "It's one of my talents."

Right. He'd become an expert liar in the last three years. "I discovered the secret of turning iron into gold?"

"Quit the games, Bodie. I saw your face when you watched that video. You saw something. I want to know what happened to my whales and Mark asked you to help me."

Commanded him to help her. Every cell in his body wanted to take the leap, to tell someone who might get it about his current work in spite of the likelihood she'd laugh at him. "How open are you to unconventional theories?"

She smiled. "Very."

He took a deep breath. She *was* Mark Durand's sister and Durand had financed his research. "I invented a monitoring system that senses the strength and nature of a certain kind of natural energy."

"I get the strength part but *nature* of the energy? What does that mean?"

"Energy can take all kinds of forms—kinetic, thermal, gravitational, sound, light, electromagnetic and so forth. The energy my system measures is... well, more like psychic energy." He waited for her to laugh. She didn't.

"Psychic energy? Can you elaborate?"

"It's energy that fuels consciousness, mind," he hesitated. "Soul. I know it sounds far-fetched."

"You've discussed this with my brother?"

"Durand Tech funded my research."

She stood and his heart sank. It was what he expected but the disappointment still smarted.

"I need to move Silverbelle," she said. "Where's your mooring?"

"Port of that barge." He pointed to the only other large vessel in the bay. "You can tie up to the barge and I'll meet you there."

"Good. I'd rather have this conversation where we won't be overheard."

"Nobody's listening..."

Lex nodded behind him and he turned to find the Obeah woman waddling down the dock toward them.

"There's no way she'd understand what Ph.Ds. at M.I.T didn't."

"No, but we need to move. Her magic isn't anything you want to mess with," Lex said. "But I'll bet you already know that."

Lex stepped up onto the dock, and stood directly in front of the Obeah woman. She slid off her sunglasses. Neither woman moved. Several seconds of this unearthly stare-down went by, then the Obeah turned and hurried back toward the beach.

3

"Mess with me, will you?" Lex muttered as she strode toward her seaplane. After dealing with vicious Parisian socialites, no Obeah woman could scare her off. Lex had sensed her magic, and though it was potent for sure, it was far from truly sinister. Certainly nothing formidable enough to challenge the powers of a Durand.

Bodie was another matter entirely. It couldn't be a coincidence that he was a revenant and somehow mixed up with Mark—although she didn't dare breach the taboo subject of revenants with her brother. She pulled her ComDev from her pocket. "Call Mark."

His line didn't even ring before the call went into voicemail. Like the rest of the technology she used, her ComDev was far more advanced than any smart phone commercially available. It worked anywhere on the planet and probably in space for all she knew. Unfortunately, she still couldn't get her brother to answer unless he wanted to.

Josh shooed the boys aside to let her pass.

"Thanks," she said. "Would you push me off the dock?"

"No problem."

He untied the lines from the rusted cleats and tossed them to her. She climbed into the plane and he pushed it away from the end of the dock. A musical note from her ComDev signaled a new text message. She glanced at the screen and saw a single character from her brother: *?*

Eloquent as ever. At least she had his attention.

She typed, *Who is Flynn? Really.*

A moment later he responded. *Genius.*

Interesting, but didn't begin to answer her question.

What does he know about the Durand?

Only public intel on family.

And yet Bodie had a ComDev like hers and operated on K-3s. And he was a revenant. Her fingers flew across the screen. *Can I trust him?*

No response appeared for several seconds. She shifted in the pilot's seat, annoyed at not being able to talk to Mark. He sent her here, she deserved an explanation.

Then his message appeared.

You decide x

"*Merde.*" She should decide? Great. The sister of another man might read the final x as shorthand for *kiss*. She knew better. X was Mark's shorthand for over-and-out, end of subject, finis. Decide herself, huh? For once she wished her telepathy worked with humans, not just animals. No, maybe not. He'd made it clear he wanted her gone.

The barge, which had appeared to be a rusty old piece of junk from across the bay, looked much less disreputable up close. The rust was reddish paint and the twisted fans on the roof were wind generators. Someone had put a great deal of creativity into camouflaging the vessel, but why? Fat Dog Island had no tourist industry to speak of and even private sailboats bypassed it for Union Island or the Tobago Cays.

The Talos IV glided to the far side of the barge and

Bodie hurried to the bow to hook the mooring line. In a smooth motion he flipped the line over a cleat, bringing the boat to a stop. With the grace of a dancer he moved along the starboard deck securing lines and positioning bumpers to prevent the barge from damaging the lighter vessel.

She watched him work, admiring the play of muscle stretching the gray t-shirt across his broad back and shoulders. Everything about the man was blatantly physical, from his striking good looks to his athlete's body. Not that any of that affected her. She was here for one reason—her brother had called Bodie a genius, and she desperately needed his help to find out what happened to her whales. But, damn, the package that genius came in was hard to ignore.

"Would you throw me a line?" she called to him as she floated up to the barge.

Five minutes later she stood on the deck inspecting black patches that looked suspiciously like small solar panels. "Why all the camo?" she asked.

He ignored her question. "What did you do to the Obeah woman?"

"Trade secret."

He straightened, leaned against the wall of the cabin and surveyed her skeptically. "What trade would that be, the wicked witch's guild?"

"Very funny."

"Why did she haul ass when you gave her the evil eye?"

Like she was going to explain *that*. "I'll make you a deal. You give me a tour of your barge and I'll tell you."

"Nope."

"Come on, Bodie. What're you hiding? I've seen messy bachelor pads before." She reached for the handle of the cabin door.

His hand shot out and caught her wrist before she could turn it.

The strength of his calloused grip on her arm sent a thrill of electricity through her and her senses went on high alert.

"I said no," he growled. "Antagonizing strange men can get you in a lot of trouble."

"Not a problem. I'm strong enough to take care of myself."

His hold on her relaxed and his thumb brushed the sensitive inside of her wrist. "I'm much stronger."

And she was highly trained in hand-to-hand combat. Still, she'd never fought an opponent his size. Not that his tone suggested he was looking for a fight. On the contrary, and her traitorous body was totally on board. Her skin burned under his work roughened palm. This was no timid academic, nor was he one of the accommodating yacht-club set.

"Fine. You keep your secrets and I'll keep mine. Shall we get down to business?"

"My data's on the Talos." With a sweep of his arm he gestured for her to precede him. "After you, princess."

Princess, huh? He had no idea.

"The aft cabin is my office," he followed her. "The data's back there." He ushered her into a surprisingly roomy space complete with some of the most sophisticated electronic equipment she'd ever seen. Three screens lined one wall, each displaying a colorful map of a section of the Caribbean.

"Don't you worry about the humidity damaging your electronics?" she asked.

"No."

For the first time, she noted the silence. No generator?

The cool air indicated the presence of a highly efficient air-conditioner and the computers and screens required a substantial amount of electricity. "How many K-3s does it take to run all this?"

He picked up his ComDev and tapped in a code. A moment later a control panel unfolded from a mahogany cabinet. "Four large K-3s and a little invention of my own." Pulling out a stool, he seated himself in front of the console. "You understand how the K-3s store solar, heat, and wind energy?"

She nodded.

"My booster multiplies the output. Handy when you have to be self-sufficient."

She studied him with renewed interest. If it ever became economically feasible to mass produce Mark's K-3 batteries, there were still practical application issues. Her seaplane was a revolutionary design hybrid that flew on electricity, but she still needed fuel to power take-offs and landings. If Bodie had a booster... the implications were staggering. "Does Mark know?"

His good humor vanished, replaced with a fierce scowl. "Your brother owns the patent and in exchange, I have all this."

As much as she loved her brother, she wasn't blind to his many faults. Greed, however, wasn't one of them. He'd sent her to Bodie for a reason and that was the only issue she intended to deal with right now.

"Tell me what this energy of yours has to do with my missing whales," she said.

"Ah, yes. The whales." He began typing on the keyboard in front of him and the map on the center screen shifted and zoomed out.

Lex studied the oddly shaded map showing the Americas—North, South, Central, and the adjacent islands and land masses. Two points marked with gold stars, one in Colorado and the other in Brazil, shocked the air from her lungs. Her hands gripped the edge of the table to steady herself. The Navajo and Brazilian Sources. Did he know about the others? Who *was* this guy?

"Over the past ten years, I've studied a type of energy attached to earth but not of its physical properties—the psychic energy I told you about. I call it delphic energy." With his attention riveted on the map, his voice assumed the cadence of a college lecturer. "It exists over all of the earth's surface but is stronger in some places than in others, and there are certain places where the energy is very intense. Founts of psychic power."

"The two stars on your map."

"Yes. I've identified five for sure and suspect there are two more. The delphic energy at each of these power points has its own characteristics—like a fingerprint—but becomes more neutral the farther from a power point you are." He glanced at her, she nodded and he went on. "The scientific community called the theory of delphic energy New Age crap and kicked my ass to the curb. Your brother offered me a grant and a *relationship* with Durand Tech to develop a scanner that senses and measures delphic energy."

"You work for DT?"

"No, I'm a researcher and work for myself. Where my interests and Mark's align, we share information. Durand Tech funded the development of the sensor and in turn provided me with specialized resources."

Lex knew well the kind of resources Mark could offer him, the location of the stars on his map—what the Durand called the primary Sources—for example. But her brother said Bodie knew nothing about the Durand family aside from their public image, so she needed to be careful what she revealed. "And I assume Durand Tech gained access to the technology in return."

"Yeah," he said. "That was the deal."

"So why are you here instead of in fancy digs on the beach in Malibu?" She glanced around the cabin. "Not that this set-up isn't sweet, but Fat Dog doesn't impress me as a hot spot for a guy like you."

"No shit."

"So why are you here?"

He scowled at her. "You really want to know?"

She nodded.

"Three years ago someone tipped off a government agency that my work could be useful to America's interests. Government agents broke into my condo and seized my computers for *national security* purposes. When I tried to stop them, things got rough."

For the first time since she'd met him, Bodie seemed truly dangerous. His outrage was palpable and she guessed the *roughness* was the reason he was now a revenant. "You're hiding out?"

"Fat Dog is my version of the witness protection plan."

Lex searched for a compassionate response that wouldn't sound condescending. "Guess it beats North Dakota, right?"

"You want to know why Durand sent you to me?"

"That *was* the point of all this."

"Just before I got to Fat Dog, I identified another form of metaphysical energy. Where delphic energy is neither positive nor negative, this other energy—what I call orphic energy—can be positive, negative, or neutral."

"How does it relate to the delphic?"

"Okay let's compare it to..." He thought for a moment. "To the internet. There's a worldwide web that creates a pathway or system for communication and connection which in itself is neither good nor bad. That would be like the way delphic provides a metaphysical connection between all consciousness in living beings."

"Okay."

"Then there's all the content on the internet which could be compared to orphic. Some of it is good."

"Like pictures of puppies and kittens?"

He cocked an eyebrow at her and she shrugged.

"Some of it is clearly bad—hate websites, violent porn, predator sites. There's neutral activity like nature webcams, and also a lot of noise—email, social media."

"But the web content is created by people."

"Yes, and people—specifically their emotions and actions—have an effect on whether the orphic is positive or negative. Let me show you something."

Fingers clicking on the keyboard, he zoomed the map in on a section on the Caribbean and Atlantic. "For the past two years, I've concentrated on this area." He reached for the mouse and highlighted a triangle from Bermuda to Jamaica to Barbados and back to Bermuda.

"The Bermuda Triangle?"

"Close enough." The colors shifted until they bore no relation to a typical map. "This is the energy grid of the Puerto Rico Trench from three months ago." He drew the cursor down the center of the Trench where the shading varied from pale blue to midnight.

The land masses, she noted, varied from blue to green to yellow with pockets of pale orange on Hispaniola.

"Normally land masses would be greens and browns, the darker blue would mean deeper water, lighter blue shallow," she said. "I know this part of the Caribbean and there's no correlation between topography and coloration."

"Right. The color indicates what we'll call for simplicity the temperature of the orphic energy. The shade indicates the intensity. The palest blue represents the coldest, least intense. The dark blue, the coldest, most intense."

"Let me guess. You classified the energy by moving around the color-wheel."

His grin, boyish and unexpected, tripped her pulse.

"Bingo. The green is warmer than the blue, yellow warmer than green and so forth. The orphic energy was more difficult to recognize and measure than the delphic because it can shift and morph in a particular location, unlike the delphic which is consistent and stable in any given location. The oceans are almost always blue with no change at all. The shifts happen on inhabited land masses."

"What makes the orphic change?"

"Lots of factors. Mass violence can do that. War. There's a lot of yellow and orange orphic in the Middle East right now."

"What does this have to do with my whales?"

"Look at this."

He called up an image on the left hand monitor which duplicated the coordinates of the original map of the Puerto Rico Trench.

"This was recorded five days ago," he said.

"The day the whales disappeared."

"Yeah."

Aside from subtle variations on the islands, the colors remained basically the same. The pointer landed on a blood red spot that hadn't been on the previous map.

"The spot of red corresponds to the coordinates where your whales disappeared."

The blanks filled themselves in. "Mark knew you'd discovered a hot spot of energy in the ocean so when I told him about the whales, he made the connection."

"Yeah." He leaned back from the console, rested his back against the mahogany cabinet and gazed at the screen. "Other red and orange spots have popped up now and then over the past year but this is the first time it seems connected to an incident."

Her hands trembled. "Temperature is a metaphor for the characteristic of the orphic energy, isn't it—cold temperature is good, hot temperature bad?"

"Yeah."

"So are you telling me my whales disappeared into a pocket of evil?"

He nodded. "That's what it looks like to me."

She shuddered, the horror of what might have happened to the whales wrenching her heart. Negative energy wasn't a new concept to her, but her experience had always involved human depravity or dark majik. "What is it? Where did it come from?"

He shrugged and shook his head. "I don't know. That's what I've been working on. You don't have a problem with this *theory*?"

"Why should I?"

He stared at her, the eerie gaze searching for something. Proof of her sincerity?

"Are you willing to help me?" she asked.

"The red spot only lasted for a few hours before it faded. Within two days, there was no trace it had existed at all."

Another dead end. "Isn't there anything we can do?"

His attention shifted back to the monitors. For several seconds he studied the maps. "You can give me access to your computer system and let me analyze your data. All of it." he said.

"Fine. You can fly back to Tortola with me. How long will it take you to get ready to go?"

"I'm not going anywhere. There's a covert government agency that thinks I'm dead and I plan to keep it that way."

"So you're going to spend the rest of your life in Fat Dog Harbor? If they think you're dead then they aren't looking for you, are they?"

"It's my head, not yours. I can download the data from here. Take it or leave it."

Neither. Her gut told her if he didn't come with her, he was going to blow her off even if he got critical data from the Foundation's system. No way was she giving up info without getting his full attention in finding Poseidon and the others. "So you're an expert on whale physiology, too?"

His eyes narrowed. "No. I'm an expert on the damned energy."

"Then how are you going to interpret Poseidon's physical response to whatever happened just before he vanished?" She stepped forward and locked eyes with him.

"A couple of whales aren't worth getting killed over. Sorry, princess, but if you want my help you'll have to come to me."

Okay, she shouldn't use her knowledge that he was a revenant against him, but he wasn't giving her any choice. "When was the last time you set foot on Fat Dog?"

"About an hour ago."

"Not the dock, I mean the island. The actual land. Do you go into the town for dinner? Have a girlfriend you visit? Meet up with buddies at the bar?"

"What's that got to do with anything?" he asked warily.

"Just curious." Bodie had clearly been wary of the

Obeah woman's power, and that could mean the old woman conjured spirits or jumbies that harassed him. She didn't know much about revenants, but she knew that without a psychic shield, a revenant like Bodie would be vulnerable. And who knew what other entities lurked on the shore waiting for him. Staying on the water was one way to avoid the problem.

He glanced away and stared at the monitor. "I've been to St. Vincent and Bequia. It's not as though I'm trapped here."

But his stance told a different story.

"Look, Bodie, if you come with me we can be in Tortola tonight and, who knows, maybe solve this mystery in a couple days. Then I'll bring you back here and you can go on with your peaceful life in paradise."

He didn't move but she sensed his resolve waiver.

"As long as you sit here, all you can do is watch the maps of your sensor. Come with me and do some field work for a change."

Seconds ticked by. It took all her willpower to remain silent and wait.

"Okay," he said finally. Only his eyes remained troubled. "I'm in but only if you agree to my conditions."

"What are they?"

"I sail the Talos to Tortola and live aboard. I don't mingle with your team unless I choose to."

"Fine. When can you be in Road Town?"

"That's not all," he said. "You don't have to pay me a salary or expenses, and since I won't be on your payroll, I can leave anytime I want without owing you an explanation."

"No problem."

"And I get unlimited access to all your equipment and data," he said. "And to your expertise."

"Do I get access to all of *your* equipment and data?"

"No."

"We'll try this partnership your way to start out," she said. "If I find out you're not being up front with me…"

"I won't lie to you."

With no choice but to agree, she nodded. "How quickly can you get to Road Town?"

"Two days if the wind and weather cooperate. How do we communicate?"

They exchanged ComDev codes. On her way out she retrieved her laptop, then paused at the foot of the companionway.

"How did you first discover delphic energy?" she asked, confident she already knew the answer.

Bodie planted his hands on his hips. "I felt it."

"Of course." She climbed the stairs with a knowing smile on her lips.

4

What kind of cold, heartless motherfucker used his own sister for bait? Mark Durand sipped his scotch. Today marked a new low, even for him.

The purple glow of the sun sinking into the Pacific Ocean reflected off the cream colored walls of his penthouse office, turning them lavender as night fell.

Mark sat in front of the window, gazing at the twinkling lights below. The odd energy activity in the Caribbean had been low on his list of priorities until Lex called him in panic over the disappearance of the whales. Since then he'd pored over the downloads from the last six months and tried to connect the red energy to other incidents, hoping to find a scientific explanation for the shifts and spikes. And he'd come up with zip.

The orphic energy on the islands from Cuba to Martinique was *heating up*, to use Bodie's terms, and too quickly for a natural explanation. The intel he'd gotten from Santo Domingo had been confirmed.

Among the Santeria and Voodoo practitioners, rumors of a great power rumbled in the islands, a specter with the ability to raise the dead, hold fire in his hand, and destroy his enemies with his mind. An eyewitness described him as seven feet tall, with black hair to his shoulders and yellow eyes that could turn a man to stone. The height was an exaggeration, otherwise Mark recognized his old enemy. Tolian—the Sentier who controlled the Brazilian Source.

If there was any other way to draw the master of the Dissemblers into the open, Mark would have gladly risked his own life to lure the bastard. But he'd blown his one and only chance to take the S.O.B. by surprise and so it was time to finally play his ace—Bodie Flynn.

The screen in front of him glowed with a chart of the Caribbean. Maybe Mark should feel guilty about using the guy, but he didn't. Flynn owed him his life. Mark had paid dearly for bringing him back from the dead and it was time to settle up on his debt.

The map on the screen showed the Talos sailing north. It also showed Lex had arrived in Mustique. The plan was in motion.

Tolian had tried to recruit Bodie himself once and had sent his minions on numerous other occasions. There was no doubt that Dissemblers had been behind the attack that had killed Bodie the first time, and once he resurfaced things would heat up quickly.

Until then there was nothing to do but wait. Unfortunately, Mark's few dubious virtues didn't include patience. He rose, stretching his long legs and flexing the stiff muscles in his back.

His cell phone buzzed and he checked the screen. Adrien. Adrien Durand, a.k.a the Durand Sentier, a.k.a Commander-in-Chief of the Protectors. And his cousin.

Mark answered. "Bodie's moving. Lex is in Mustique

before heading back to Road Town to join her team on the Ariel."

"I must have missed your call," Adrien said. "You briefed her, didn't you?"

"No."

"Damn it, Mark, you can't send her in blind. She's been trained to follow orders."

"Any slip-up that alerts the traitor in our ranks and Lex and Bodie are dead. Right now, she's focused on her whales and he's absorbed with the orphic energy shifts. I'm keeping an eye on them and can move in if I see trouble."

"I don't like keeping her in the dark."

"Me neither, but I see no other choice." Leaning on the wall, he gazed into the twilight sky. "I know both Lex and Bodie. Neither will give up until they figure out what's going on."

"And you're still convinced Dissemblers are behind the whales' disappearance?"

"All I know is someone's fucking with the orphic energy in the Caribbean big time. If not Tolian, who?"

The question hung in the air. The covert war between the Durand Protectors and the Dissemblers of the Brazilian Source had been going on for over two centuries. As long as the Dissemblers incited violence, chaos, and depravity to enslave *ordinaires*, the Protectors' mission would be to stop them.

"She deserves to know what she's up against. Bodie, too."

The muscles in Mark's back twitched, warning of worse things to come. "Objection noted, A. Got to run now."

"What about..."

He cut him off. "Later." His thumb hit the end button.

He'd waited too long and his body hummed with the

need for release. He punched a number in his cell and waited.

On the third ring a woman answered, her voice low and seductive. "May I help you?"

"I'm sending a car in half an hour," he said.

"Would you like anyone in particular, Mr. D?" Of course she recognized his voice. They'd never met in person but he paid her very well for the means to satisfy his proclivities. Her business thrived on personal service and discretion, after all, and he was a repeat customer.

"Someone new. Preferably tall." He didn't have to elaborate. The woman she sent would be professional, willing, and expensive. Still, he hated the curse that could only be appeased with his brand of sex. And when he was finished, the woman would remember nothing of him or what happened behind closed doors. Unfortunately he would not be so lucky.

5

The sun beat down on the deck of the Marine Mammal Research Foundation's boat, the Ariel, as it sat tied up to the commercial pier in Road Town Harbor, Tortola. A cruise ship loomed behind, dwarfing the one-hundred-sixty-five–foot vessel Lex had called home for the past two years.

"Tell me again why we're waiting for this guy?" David Latham muttered, his tanned forearms resting on the boat's railing as he gazed out of the harbor toward Salt Island.

As usual, every strand of his sun-streaked blond hair lay neatly in place. They were exactly the same height—six feet, no change—which put his broad shoulders at the same level as hers and reminded her she was much taller than most women.

"Dr. Flynn has detected energy activity in the Trench that could account for Poseidon's signal going dead." This was her story and close enough to the truth, although David had seen the whale vanish in real time. "Mark also thinks we can use Dr. Flynn's sensors to measure changes in water temperature and pollution levels from up to a thousand miles away." That was bullshit to divert his attention to his favorite subject—the effect of water temperature and pollution on the health and survival of bottlenose dolphins.

The furrow in David's brow did little to mar his aristocratic good looks. "Seeing is believing," he said. "Have you thought any more about the conference? If we're going, we need to book the flights and hotel." His fingers brushed her arm and she eased away.

"You go. I should stay here with the team. You're the one they want to hear, not me." The comment was true but the bitterness in her delivery surprised her. Was she still humiliated by the debacle of her one and only presentation to the International Society of Marine Science?

The theme of that conference had been *How Do Animals Think?* A subject right up her alley. Armed with thousands of hours of observation and data collected over five years, she'd arrived in Miami prepared to enlighten and inspire her audience. The laughing was bad enough. The contempt, liberally expressed during the Q&A, had devastated her credibility.

David didn't argue or try to talk her into going. She was grateful for that.

"Hungry?" he asked. "I haven't been to Le Cabanon in a while and wouldn't mind the walk. My treat."

Normally she'd jump at a late lunch at the island's French bistro. Today, waiting for Bodie made her restless. "Thanks. I ate at noon. You go on."

He patted her arm. "See you later then."

"Bon appétit." She watched him cross the deck and step onto the dock. Her eyes told her he was handsome and fit, with all the class of old New England money. Life might be simpler if she could fall in love with David. But he was *ordinaire*—a person with no extrasensory abilities—and knew nothing of her other world.

A sailboat rounded the point at the mouth of the harbor, its snowy sails filled. Although it looked like a dozen other boats docked in the marina, her stomach did a little flip.

Bodie.

The Talos was under full sail, the wind at her stern. Lex wondered how long he'd wait before he dropped his sails and started his engines. The charter boats usually motored most of the way, local sailors were bolder. The only person onboard, he didn't have the luxury of ordering the sails lowered while he steered. She watched in fascination.

As the sailboat drew closer, she spotted him at the helm —tall, tanned, and focused. "You can do it. Bring her all the way in," she whispered into the wind. She held her breath feeling almost giddy.

Along the dock, people stopped to watch the graceful sloop approach. The jib began to furl on itself, slowly winding until it was a thin blue line stretched between the bow and the top of the mast. As the Talos came parallel to the Ariel, Bodie looked up. Across a hundred meters of calm blue water their eyes met as though he'd known she'd be there.

Her heart slammed against her chest. Something was about to happen. Something important. Something she and Bodie had to do together.

He smiled and waved. She raised her hand in return.

A moment later he manned the winches and cranked the mainsail into the mast. Without hurrying, he returned to the helm and turned on the engine to maneuver the vessel into the crowded marina.

She had a lot of questions about Bodie, none of which were answered by Googling him. Aside from a mention in an article about a faculty function at M.I.T., a two paragraph entry in Wikipedia on his basketball career, and a review of a physics book on Amazon.com, there was nothing. Anyone could plant such flimsy background so she assumed Bodie Flynn wasn't his real name. Who was he?

The Talos glided into the marina and maneuvered smoothly into a slip. She wanted to play it cool with Bodie, make him come to her on the Ariel. Which wasn't going to happen. She pushed herself away from the railing and headed for the marina, reminding herself that Bodie didn't have to like her to be useful. The only logical thing to do was go say hello and get started looking for her whales.

"Yo, Talos." She waited on the dock, peering into the open hatch. "Bodie, you down there?"

His head appeared in the companionway and she drew in a quick breath. With a couple days of stubble he looked more like a pirate than a scientist—dangerous and sexy.

"You the welcoming committee?"

"How was the sailing? Did you miss the storm off Guadeloupe?"

"Yeah, but a series of squalls hit early this morning in the open water between here and Saba. Made things interesting for a few hours. I was about to get in the shower and clean off the salt spray."

"Right. Any change in the energy in the Trench?"

"No new hot spots in the area. Any news about your whales?"

Lex shook her head. "Get your laptop and we can go to the Ariel and start downloading Poseidon's physical data. I think I've filtered out most of the non-relevant readings and—"

He lifted a hand to cut her off. "Whoa, princess. I've been sailing twenty-four seven. I'm not going anywhere until I get cleaned up and eat."

"Sure. Sorry. I'm anxious to get started." Waiting for him

had already pushed her patience to its limits, but she certainly wasn't going to let him know that. "The team's meeting up for dinner at seven at a restaurant in town. We'd like for you to join us."

"Sorry."

"Sorry? What's that supposed to mean?"

The corner of his mouth quirked in a half smile. "It's a polite way of saying no."

"No?" Was he kidding? Planting her hands on her hips, she fixed him with her do-not-mess-with-me glare. "Wrong answer. Let me rephrase it. The team is meeting for dinner and you *will* be there. We'll get to work first thing in the morning so tonight is the best time for everyone to get acquainted."

"Do you get a lot of results with that hands-on-your-hips thing?"

"Usually."

"Our deal was I only mix when I want to and I'm not a part of your team."

A quick glance around confirmed they were drawing attention from the nearby boats. An older man with wiry gray hair on the catamaran in the next slip had the nerve to raise his beer can to her.

"Bodie, be reasonable. You'll need to work with these people, and this is just eating and chatting a little. Surely that isn't beyond you."

He crossed his arms over his chest, which stretched the cotton over his massive shoulders, and flexed an imposing pair of biceps. "How about a compromise? You have dinner with me at eight at the restaurant here at the marina. You can brief me on your team and we can discuss how we're going to investigate the situation in the Trench."

She knew when she'd met an immoveable object. On

the other hand, his compromise might be construed as a date by the others. "Do you object to David Latham joining us? He's the captain of the Ariel."

A brow cocked. "Do you need a chaperone, Ms. Durand?"

"Of course not. I just thought..."

"No Dave. You and me. Eight o'clock, unless you'd like to come by earlier for a drink." His deep voice held a challenge.

"Eight at the restaurant," she said and turned on her heels, ignoring his triumphant chuckle.

BODIE WATCHED Lex stride away down the dock. The white shirt and khaki shorts she wore looked like they'd been made for her, which, given she was rumored to be a shareholder in Durand Tech, they probably were. En route from Fat Dog, he'd done an internet search on Lex Durand. The woman certainly wasn't low profile. After wading through photos from animal charity functions, he'd discovered features in Vanity Fair, Vogue, and a variety of European magazines with her driving race cars, skiing in the Alps, and mixing with royalty in haute couture. At least the media left the Foundation alone or he wouldn't be here. Still, he couldn't assume he was safe.

He rubbed the stiffness at the back of his neck. Even with autopilot, forty-eight hours of non-stop sailing had been grueling—long stretches of sitting in the sun and hours in the dark interrupted with surges of intense activity. A quick shower rinsed off the salt and he changed into running clothes, all the while psyching himself up to venture on land.

His sensor hadn't picked up any orphic hot spots on Tortola and the online history of the BVI hadn't mentioned any massacres. But as he'd learned on his first day with the hostile spirits in Fat Dog, websites designed to promote tourism tended to leave out unsavory historic details.

After closing the hatch and setting the security, he took a couple of minutes to stretch on deck, glancing up and down the dock to see if anyone was paying a little too much attention to him. Three middle-aged women with their cocktails stared at him from the deck of a sailboat two slips down, otherwise everyone seemed absorbed in their own business. Of course, any assassin worth shit would be invisible and Bodie would be dead before he knew he was in someone's crosshairs. Cheery thought. He stepped up on the gunwale and onto the dock.

His pulse quickened as he walked toward land. Beneath his running shoes the wooden planks sighed under his weight. All of his attention focused on the asphalt ahead, he breathed deeply. In, out. In, out. The land's energy shimmered, simultaneously familiar and strange. This part he loved—the clean untainted delphic energy caressing his skin, welcoming, embracing. His exhaustion melted as his feet pounded the pavement that wound past the waterfront shops toward the hills.

A shadow loomed to his right. Then another farther along. Luminescent globes hovered among the palm trees lining the road. *Outrun them. Don't look. They're spirits without mass or bodies. They can't hurt you.* But he knew that they could. The angry *espectros* on Fat Dog had attacked him and stolen his breath the first day he arrived. If he hadn't crawled into the water, they might have killed him. These on Tortola lacked the aggressive malevolence of the Obeah witch's jumbies, but ever since he died and returned to the land of the living, ghosts and spirits had been a problem.

He picked up his pace, veering up a path leading to the hilltop where he sensed benevolent orphic energy.

The shades hovered ominously in the sunshine before blinking out.

6

————

"Can I get you another?" the waiter asked.

Bodie jiggled the ice at the bottom of his glass, surprised he'd already downed his second rum and tonic. "Sure, why not? And a menu, please."

Eight twenty-seven and Lex still hadn't shown up. He hadn't pegged her for the fashionably late type. Went to show how well he read women.

From his table along the side wall he could look out on the harbor and protect his back. He reached for his water glass and drained it in one long swallow. He'd been watching the dock but she'd entered by the terrace entrance from the street.

"Sorry I'm late." Lex said.

He turned to make a snide remark about punctuality and froze. "What the hell is that?"

In spite of her expensive navy knit tank dress and strappy sandals, her arms held a filthy bag of bones covered in brown and black fur. At least he assumed it was fur. Both of the animal's ears were torn and something had eaten away the skin around its neck.

"He's a dog."

"And you're carrying him because...?"

"I stole him from the backyard of a shack on my way here. He was tied up with no water, no food, and barely enough rope to lie down in the dirt."

The dog turned his head to study Bodie with sad brown eyes, as if to say *Give me a break here.* From the shape of his head, he looked like a pit bull or pit bull mix.

"What are you going to do with him?"

She scowled. "I'm taking him back to the Ariel. We have some basic vet facilities." She adjusted the dog in her arms, revealing a greasy mud spot on the front of her dress. "Sorry about dinner. I'm getting the feeling the waiter won't be thrilled if my friend and I join you."

As the young man stalked in their direction, Bodie sighed. "Need help with the pooch?"

Her smile beamed so warmly it took his breath away. The woman was a stunner. No doubt about it.

Her fingers tenderly stroked the dog's head. "If you don't mind. He needs a bath and I may have to stitch up his ears. I promise he'll be sweet but he may get frightened."

Promise he'll be sweet? A pit bull? Was she kidding? From the way she cuddled the filthy creature, apparently not.

Bodie rose and threw some bills on the table. He glanced at the battered dog and then at her dress. "Do you want me to carry him?"

"Thanks. I've got him." Then she added, "We're still bonding."

"Right."

Pedestrians strolled the walkway along the waterfront— sailors, island youth, tourists soaking up local color. A whiff of marijuana smoke and laughter drifted to shore from a dive boat tied to a finger dock, and a pair of old men sat in lawn chairs fishing from the end of the concrete pier. It had been a long time since he'd seen this many people in one place.

Next to him Lex murmured endearments and reassurances to the dog as though the little guy understood all the *good boy*s and *I'll take care of you*s. Aside from the starvation and ripped ears, he was beginning to envy the poor animal.

They cut across the point toward the commercial pier where the Ariel was docked, leaving the lively tourist activity behind. He sensed trouble before it came into high definition. Six young guys, definitely locals, dressed rasta-gangsta hung outside a sleazy bar. Their loud voices carried.

Bodie crossed behind Lex to walk between her and the thugs. "Don't look, don't hurry," he said softly.

She drew the dog closer in her arms. "Roger that."

In his peripheral vision, he sized them up. He had at least seven inches and forty pounds on all of them except a fat guy sitting in a plastic chair eating potato chips from a king-sized bag. One on one, none would be a problem. All six at once—not great odds.

He kept walking, steady, confident, his hand on the small of Lex's back. They passed under a street light and through his fingertips he felt her back muscles stiffen.

"Hey, man. That bitch got my dog!"

Automatically Bodie stepped between Lex and the punk swaggering in their direction. He was like so many angry guys from Bodie's youth—looking for a fight just for something to do. With his sorry-ass compadres egging him on, he pulled a couple feet of knotted leather from a back pocket and flicked it in Bodie's direction.

"Nobody thiefs nothing from me, man," he growled.

Shit. Fighting over a woman was one thing. A mangy

goddamned dog... hell, this wasn't how he wanted to spend his evening. "Leave it alone," he said.

The punk sneered. "You think you can make me?"

Lex's hand clasped his arm, her fingers digging into his bicep. He turned to reassure her and froze.

"Back off, Bodie. He's mine."

As Bodie started to object, the punk's eyes widened, first in surprise then in terror. He clutched his gut and doubled over with a panicked cry of agony. His knees buckled and he went to the ground, writhing on the concrete.

"That's how starvation feels, motherfucker," she spat. "How do you like it?"

An instant later, the young man clawed at his throat, choking and fighting for air, his fingers frantically tearing at the invisible noose around his neck.

"You like being strangled, asshole?" she hissed.

Bodie watched in paralyzed fascination.

Abruptly the punk fell still and greedily gulped in air between stifled sobs. His friends had split, all but the fat guy whose plastic chair shook like a Barcalounger on high. He crossed himself when Bodie glanced his way.

Lex took two steps toward her victim, her face now a pale mask devoid of emotion. "If you ever hurt another animal, I'm coming back for you," she said. "We clear?"

The punk nodded.

She turned to Bodie and studied his face. There was fear in her eyes, mixed with defiance. The specter of a childhood memory chilled his mind and twisted his gut. No, this wasn't the same at all. Common sense told him to put distance between himself and this woman.

Lex strode away toward the docks and in three strides Bodie caught up with her. "You want to tell me what just happened?" he demanded.

"I'm sorry you saw that."

"Yeah? And *exactly* what the hell did I see?"

"Nothing. Just forget it, okay?" The dog whimpered and she stroked his head.

"You talk or I'm out of here," he said.

Her eyes turned hard and cold. "What about my whales?"

"Your decision."

"It's complicated," she said.

"Try me."

The dog whimpered in her arms.

"Hey, Lex!" a young woman called from behind them.

A group of two young women and three guys—all wearing white shirts and Khaki shorts—headed their way.

"What did you do to that guy?" he growled.

"We'll talk tomorrow," she said, then called out to the others. "Come meet my new friends."

She made quick introductions and the other two women fussed over the dog. Fuming, Bodie didn't bother to remember their names.

"Jen and Ash will help me with the little guy. Why don't you go back and have that dinner I dragged you away from," Lex said.

She wasn't getting off that easy. "Why don't you let your friends take the dog and you can catch up with them after we discuss that little *incident* you were about to explain."

Lex shook her head. "This little fella trusts me now. I can't just hand him off. We can talk tomorrow."

He started to insist when the expression in her eyes hardened.

"Good night, Bodie," she said and followed her team in the direction of the Ariel.

He stared after her. What the hell had Lex done to that

guy? Unbidden, visions ricocheted around his head—a collage of old memories returning with a vengeance. He shoved them back in their dark hole. One refused to go. The rhythm of tribal drums pounded, the thick hypnotic tang of incense and blood filled the air. Zamora, his Orixá mother, swayed in the torchlight as her worshippers danced themselves into a frenzy. From his hiding place he had watched it all—what he now knew was an orgy where not all participants had been volunteers.

In his memory he saw Zamora, her Brazilian beauty glowing with the power of possession, long black hair swirling around her shoulders, black eyes full of fire. She raised her hand—the blood red talons exactly the shade of her lips—and the drums went silent.

An instant later the undulating mass had fallen to its knees and stilled. João alone failed to bow. In a rage, his mother collected the fire from the air and shot it at her lover. It snaked around his neck until he screamed and then it poured into his mouth.

The seven-year-old Bodie had wanted to do something but he'd been unable to move. And then it was too late. The only father he'd ever known burst into flames before his eyes.

7

"You know, Earl, I think you've put on a couple of pounds already." Lex broke off a small piece of her blueberry muffin and fed it to the dog. They'd climbed aboard the Talos at six-thirty with a thermos of coffee and eight hot muffins. Half the coffee was gone. Earl had eaten three muffins to Lex's one and was eyeing the bag with the others.

"Think we should wake him up?" she asked.

Earl rested his head on her thigh.

"Fifteen more minutes, that's it." The news David broke to her at breakfast would have had her in the air already if it wasn't for Bodie. She needed to see his scanner and daylight was wasting. After what he witnessed last night, however, his cooperation wasn't a given.

She'd lost control and let her emotions rule her head. She knew better and yet when she plugged into Earl's fear and memories her rage had taken over. The projections had never been so intense or painful before.

And Bodie had witnessed the entire ugly scene. Last night she'd been too shaken to come up with a reasonable story. Lying made the most sense although her pesky conscience kept badgering her to give him enough truth to respect his intelligence. He'd trusted her with his delphic energy explanation, maybe he'd take the leap to animal telepathy.

The hatchway rattled as it was unlocked from within. Earl watched the door, wary of the danger that might lurk there. She stroked his head to reassure them both.

Bodie's head emerged followed by a mostly naked and very impressive torso. He saw her sitting on the stern. "Shit."

"Good morning to you, too." She lifted the thermos. "I brought peace offerings. Java and muffins."

"Go away."

She poured coffee into a mug and got up. "I can't. We need to talk. You'll feel better when you've had caffeine."

Ignoring his scowl, she handed him the coffee. Up close the tattoo banding his right bicep was intricate and colorful, a masterpiece even to her untrained eye. "That must have smarted," she said.

His right hand flew to his chest, and he coughed and swore in the same breath. Only then did she notice the scars of three bullet holes and twin deep grooves between his pecs that appeared surgical and definitely not ornamental. Tempting as it was to pry, she knew she was already in deep water with him.

"I meant the armband. I'm not usually a fan of..."

"I don't care." He downed the rest of the coffee and handed her back the cup. "I quit. I'm leaving this morning."

"You can't quit."

Glaring down at her, he took a step forward. "Any time. That was our deal. Are you going to call your brother and tell him to force me to stay?"

The thought had occurred to her. "No. I wouldn't do that."

"And you wouldn't *make me* yourself?"

A shiver shot up her spine. After the data the team received this morning, she couldn't let him walk away, not if there was the slightest chance he could help.

"I'll never *make you* do anything you don't want to. I promise."

An eyebrow cocked over those shrewd silver eyes. "Not good enough. Come clean with everything or I'm out of here."

Oddly, part of her wanted to tell him everything, to bare her soul and ask for understanding. The rest wanted to tell him to stick it.

"Okay, everything," she said. "You'll want to sit down. Trust me."

———

She cleared her throat before speaking. "I'm an animal telepath."

"A what?"

"Animal telepath. It means I can communicate with animals telepathically. Read their thoughts and send them mine. Some species like dogs are fairly sophisticated communicators, especially if they have a lot of interaction with people."

He snapped to attention. "Wait, you read minds?" Great. He tried to focus on the larger implications. Had he imagined her naked? Of course he had.

Lex shook her head. "No. Not humans, only animals. People are a different..." She paused and thought for a moment. "People have a different mental wavelength that I don't pick up. Sometimes I pick up animals' emotions too, but their emotions are harder to understand than their formulated thoughts."

At least she couldn't read *his* thoughts. That was good.

"So why are you telling me this?"

Her gaze dropped to the dozing dog. "When that S.O.B. shouted at us last night, Earl panicked. I saw and felt what he did to Earl—the starvation, thirst, choking on his own collar, and being torn up by other dogs in the ring. I lost it. The terror Earl felt was so vivid and real inside me, I lost control and projected the whole horror show on that piece of shit. He deserved it and worse. I'm not sorry, Bodie. Not for what I did. I *am* sorry you saw it."

His mind reeled, trying to tune in to a channel he recognized. Was she kidding? Projecting the *dog's* memories on the punk? He shook his head. "You know how crazy that sounds, right?"

"Yeah."

"You read the dog's mind? What makes you think I'll buy this?"

"I believe you sense the earth's delphic energy and feel the good and evil in what you call orphic energy. That's a sophisticated psychic talent. I can't do that. Why wouldn't you believe I have the ability to sense energy you've never experienced? Isn't that rather narrow-minded?"

"I can't channel the energy," he said.

"Really? You're sure about that?"

The stadium lights went on in his head, and she took her point in for a touchdown. "You've never even tried, have you?"

Until that instant, the idea of controlling the energy with his mind had never occurred to him. Scientifically, yes, and, of course, electronically. Never being the conduit himself.

Was it possible? The physicist in him said no. The engineer said hell no. But what if it was possible?

"Intriguing thought, isn't it?" she asked.

"Fine. You transmit emotions. The guy was a nasty piece of shit and deserved to have his ass kicked. I'm fine with that." He noted her obvious relief. "So we're cool."

"Good, because something came up last night."

Another ploy. There was no way she knew about the new red spot and he needed to get going to investigate it. "Yeah, well, I'm taking off."

"I need to look at your sensor."

"Why?"

"Last night we lost tracking signals on two pods of dolphins, for sixty-seven minutes on the first and sixty-three minutes on the second. Only two males have a GPS tracker in the first pod and only one in the second pod. Both signals were lost in the same area about 800 meters apart."

The hair on the back of his neck prickled. "What time did you lose them?"

"The first pod at one-thirty-seven."

He pushed himself to his feet. The sensor had first detected the red spot around then.

"Come below." He descended down the hatchway and headed for control central. He typed in his password and the electronics came alive, flashing colorful maps on the three wall monitors.

"Here are the coordinates," she said and slapped a piece of paper on the work surface next to the keyboard.

Even before he input them, he was pretty sure he knew where they'd take him. Sure enough, the image on the center screen zoomed in on a scarlet patch of energy. The same spot in open water over the Anegada Ridge that his hand sensor had picked up last night. "And they started broadcasting again where?" he asked.

"A kilometer apart." She recited the second set of coordinates.

His fingers danced across the keys and a target appeared on a yellow energy spot just east of Virgin Gorda. "Are you sure these are right?" he asked.

"Yep. I checked them myself."

He used his finger on the monitor to drag the view and zoom out. "How fast do these guys swim?"

"Tops, twenty-five miles per hour. In a group like this, twenty is booking it."

He swore and ran his hand over his head. "You picked up the signal forty-four miles from where you lost it."

"So I noticed. And I did the math. They'd have to travel forty miles an hour to cover the distance." She stared at the map. "What's going on, Bodie?"

The scientific education which trained him to look for the simplest explanation for any event kicked in. "What about a strong current?" he asked. "Is it possible they could have gotten caught up and carried at a high rate of speed? That would also account for both groups experiencing the same phenomenon."

She shrugged. "It's possible. We looked at our data and existing charts and found nothing conclusive one way or the other. The team is leaning toward the current theory. I'm not."

"Because of the lost signal?"

"Yes. That and the red orphic in the exact spot their transmitters quit working. I don't believe in coincidences."

He didn't either, but he also didn't have a reasonable explanation. "The orphic could have affected the signal," he offered without conviction. "And we can't rule out a strong current without investigation. I'll sail out this morning and let you know what I find."

She shook her head. "No, we'll take Silverbelle. We can check out the yellow and red orphic areas and test the current, then track the dolphins."

His gut instinct insisted he put as much water as possible between himself and this woman, but the faster they got to the red spot, the more likely they were to discover something useful. "Okay, we investigate the energy and the current then you can drop me off here and go check on your critters."

Her eyes narrowed and her lips tightened. "Critters? Really, Bodie? Are you that dense or being intentionally insulting?"

"Neither, but I'm not flying around chasing a herd of dolphins when I could be analyzing data here."

"Tell me, did you believe anything I told you about what happened last night?" she asked.

He studied her, not sure what exactly she was asking him. "Yeah..."

"The part where I explained I'm an animal telepath?"

Understanding dawned on him. "You're going to debrief the dolphins?" he asked, unable to hide the incredulity in his voice.

"Forget it," she snapped. "I don't need your attitude. You sail away and do whatever it is you do, and I'll take one of the crew to help me."

"Wait a second," he said. "You're telling me you can ask the dolphins what happened and they'll answer you?"

"Bingo, Dr. Flynn. These bottlenoses have surprisingly sophisticated reasoning skills and minds that accept telepathy as a form of communication. I expect to get a clear, detailed account of what happened to them."

"Okay," he said. "I'm willing to suspend my skepticism and go with your plan."

"How generous."

"After my sensor picked up the orphic activity last night, I ran an analysis on it. You might be interested in what I learned."

"What?"

"I'll tell you on the way."

She hesitated then turned for a long look at the map on the monitor. "Pack to be gone overnight. Bring a wet suit if you have one."

He resisted the urge to argue with her. He'd negotiate his return later, after she gave him the intel he needed. "When do we leave?"

Her attention remained riveted on the monitor. "In forty-five minutes from the end of the cruise ship pier." And still she made no move to leave. Finally she spoke. "What will happen to you when we get to the red orphic? Since you can feel it, will it hurt you?"

Her question startled him. "I haven't a clue. I've never encountered it. Yellow gives me a headache and turns my stomach."

She nodded thoughtfully. "We'll circle in slowly, then, so I can veer off if you need me to."

He had no idea what to say. "Thanks."

"Better get a move on, Flynn. Daylight's wasting."

"Yes, ma'am."

"I DON'T UNDERSTAND why you're taking him and not one of the team," David said.

Lex shoved a large canvas duffle containing an inflatable

boat into the rear section of Silverbelle. The seaplane bobbed off the end of the commercial dock next to the Ariel, waiting for Bodie to show. "He *is* one of the team."

"Someone who knows dolphins." His words were infused with impatience, the kind parents suffered with stubborn adolescents.

The tone grated on her. "*I* know dolphins. Better than anyone. He's got the size and muscle to help me switch out the GPS transmitters so we can check them."

David's mouth thinned to a hard line. "A high priced assistant, don't you think?"

"Nope. We're not paying him." From the land end of the pier a hundred yards away, she felt Bodie's eyes on her back. Her pulse quickened. *Don't look. Pretend you don't know he's there.*

David frowned. "What do you mean, we're not paying him? Why not? What's going on, Lex? I'm still head of the team which means I have some say in what goes on around here."

None of his blah-blah-blah broke through her aware-ness of Bodie's approach. "Don't tell me that's Flynn," David said, staring over her shoulder. "He looks more like a hit man on holiday than a physicist."

She turned around and smiled. "That's him."

David shifted his feet on the rough concrete. "He may be a friend of Mark's, but I'd rather you take Mac."

"Mark and Bodie aren't friends. I'm pretty sure Bodie hates his guts."

David grimaced and grumbled something about common sense and safety under his breath.

She ignored him and called out to Bodie. "Hey, man, haul it, will you?"

As expected, Bodie didn't pick up his pace. When he

reached them his hard-ass expression cracked into a crooked smile.

"Bodie Flynn," he said extending his hand to David.

Holding her breath, she watched David shake Bodie's hand and tentatively return his smile. "David Latham. Welcome to the team." Awkward pause. "Lex says you know Mark Durand."

"We're acquainted."

Great. They're sizing each other up. "Enough chatter. Let's get this show in the air," she said.

"More orders." Bodie swung the leather bag into the space behind the pilot's seat. It landed with the dull thump of metal, heavy and solid.

"Anything in that bag explosive?" she asked.

"Only metaphorically."

His sensing equipment. "Bullshit," she whispered, loud enough for him to hear but not David. "You blow us up and I'll let your ass drown."

"Threat noted."

Five minutes later, Silverbelle's pontoons skimmed across the bay, gaining speed until the seaplane left the water in a steep climb. Lex banked sharply to the east. When she switched from fuel to electrical power the noise level in the cockpit dropped to a whisper allowing her to replace her headphones with an earbud and attached microphone.

"Well, well. Impressive little plane you have here," Bodie said.

"It's a Durand Tech prototype. Aviation fuel isn't readily available most places so I only use it for take-off and landing. Silverbelle flies on quiet, efficient electricity. The K-3 batteries are light, durable, and have solar and wind recharge options."

"And when money's no object, anything's possible."

"Only if you have the brainpower to make it happen. You've proved that, haven't you?"

He made a grunting sound of dismissal. "Where's Earl?"

"On the Ariel. Probably curled up on somebody's bunk sleeping."

"Lucky little dude."

"Yeah, but you get a plane ride and an adventure."

He shifted in his seat and studied her. "Latham wasn't happy about me coming, was he?"

"Not my problem."

"Is he your boyfriend?" Nothing in his voice betrayed more than casual interest.

"No."

"Does he know that?"

Lex wasn't sure of the answer. "Of course. Not that it's any of your business."

"Nope, it's not." He reached behind her seat, unzipped his bag and rummaged around until he found what he wanted—a hand sensor about the size of an iPad. "When the red orphic concentration appeared this morning, I ran a comparison of the orphic activity on nearby islands between midnight and two in the morning to see if anything unusual showed up."

"And?"

"Nothing." The sensor booted up as he continued. "The concentration showed up on the one-forty-five scan. The area was solid dark blue at one-thirty."

"So it scans every fifteen minutes, not continuously?"

He turned to peer at her over his Oakleys. "Do you have any idea how complicated that would be, not to mention the amount of memory it would take to record and store the information?"

"Apparently very and a lot," she replied, glancing down at the sailboats gliding the calm turquoise strait then at the rocky Fallen Jerusalem Island ahead. "Guess we're lucky to have the exact time from the GPS."

"Yeah, but it doesn't tell us where or how the energy transmuted. Last night I started work on reprogramming the sensor on the Talos to scan every twenty seconds and send the data to Durand Tech for storage."

"You can access that data with your ComDev, right?"

He shifted in his seat. "I didn't get that far before I had to get some sleep."

"So the answer is no?"

"Look princess," he grumbled. "I sailed for two days without sleep to get here. Then you showed up this morning and coerced me into coming with you."

"Persuaded you."

He snorted. "Coerced. I wanted to sail the Talos." His fingertips tapped and dragged on the screen which responded with shifting shapes and colors. Lex glanced at the device every couple of minutes, curious about what he was doing.

Finally he fitted his ComDev into a port on one end of the sensor. "That should work until I get back to the Talos."

"What did you do?"

"I set this hand sensor to scan the Caribbean and transmit the data through the ComDev to secure storage at Durand Tech. The encrypt and transfer takes about six seconds so we can get scans at ten second intervals to start."

Lex's own ComDev chirped, and she grabbed it and hit the answer icon. "What's up."

"Where are you?" David asked.

She was too conscious of Bodie's attention focused on

her. "On course headed toward the coordinates where we lost the GPS signals to drop the dye and check the current."

"We have a situation. You need to turn around and go to Jost Van Dyke."

"How about I put you on speaker so we can both hear?" Without waiting for him to agree, she tapped the speaker icon and set the ComDev on the console. "Go ahead."

"We had a call from some locals on Jost Van Dyke that the dolphin pods are causing trouble in Little Harbour. A dinghy was bumped and the passengers are pretty shaken up. When a local fisherman took his skiff to help them, the dolphins rammed it."

She frowned. "That makes no sense. Dolphins don't ram unless they're attacked first, and then only sharks."

"We located their GPS trackers. All three males were in Little Harbour when the attacks took place. You need to get over there before someone gets hurt."

She glanced at Bodie who was shaking his head and pointing to the red orphic spot on his sensor. "The red spot first," he mouthed.

"I'm going to drop the dye first," she said. "We're only ten minutes out."

"That's not important now. You need to get to Jost Van Dyke," David said, his tone carrying the weight of command.

The temptation to point out he had no authority over her made her clench her teeth. As much as she wanted to help the dolphins, her gut told her their behavior was linked to the orphic energy ahead. "I can't, David. We'll be there as soon as we can." She ended the call.

"We're turning back?" Bodie asked.

"No."

"Good." He studied her. "Want to fill me in on the chain of command?"

She fixed her gaze on the open water ahead. "I'm head of the Foundation. David's Captain of the Ariel and technically commands its crew including the research teams." The structure sounded simple. She wished the dynamics were. "I function independently most of the time."

"Your money, your rules?"

A protest rose to her lips and died. "Pretty much."

His chuckle startled her.

"Poor Latham. He doesn't have a chance, does he?"

"No." On so many levels. And yet she felt disloyal admitting it to Bodie. "He's a good captain and an excellent marine biologist. And a good friend. But he's also *ordinaire*."

"*Ordinaire*?"

"Non-psychic. Surely you've heard the term before."

"No. Why would I?"

She glanced at him to see if he was kidding. "Because you're psychic and..." She started to say a *revenant* and caught herself. "And apparently know my brother fairly well."

"What makes you think I'm psychic?"

She peered at him over her glasses and again determined he was dead serious. "You sense orphic and delphic energy." Then, testing bits of revenant myth she added, "And you see ghosts and spirits."

"How do you know that?"

"A guess. You do, don't you?"

Ignoring her question, he looked down at his sensor. "We're about a mile away."

Sensing his trepidation, she let the subject drop. "Are you feeling anything?"

"Not yet."

She consciously reinforced the psychic shield that was second nature to her. If Bodie was affected, it was one thing. If the orphic disoriented her, they could crash and die. The thought sobered her and yet her need to know why the dolphins' tracker quit transmitting outweighed her fear.

She glanced at Bodie. "What do you feel when you sense the energy?"

"A tingling in my gut that has both a smell and a taste. Delphic is neutral and pleasant, orphic can be delicious or noxious depending on its nature."

"Are you sure you want to do this? I'd rather bank on the periphery and test your reaction before ramming it."

Sweat beaded on his forehead. "Then you need to turn now."

She banked Silverbelle to the north but the plane was sluggish to respond. Within seconds the air in the cabin throbbed, heavy and nauseating. Bodie grabbed his stomach, groaning in pain. She veered more sharply, barely able to fight the overwhelming sense of doom that compelled her to crash the plane into the water and end their misery. It was like the world's worst case of seasickness capped with unbearable dread.

She fought to fly the seaplane away from the toxic area. Beside her Bodie clutched the door handle. The blood had drained from his face and sweat poured down his forehead into his eyes, off his chin. With eyes clenched tight, he grimaced in pain.

"Hold on," she urged. "We'll be free soon." Another half minute and the air cleared and the sense of doom drained away. She felt the pressure ease from her head and body and gulped in her first full breath.

"Jesus," Bodie gasped. "That about took me out."

"I don't have your abilities and I still wanted to kill us both."

"Would have been fine with me. Can you fly okay or do you need to put down and recover?"

"I think I'm okay now."

A bead of sweat ran down the side of his face and he wiped it away with the shoulder of his shirt. "What did you feel?"

She described the physical and emotional sensations, leaving out the disturbing detail that the energy had breached her psychic shield. "What about you?"

"That wasn't close to anything else I've experienced," he said thoughtfully. "The malice of the energy almost seemed alive. It was like a scaled monster kicked and scratched in my gut, trying to rip me to shreds from the inside."

Was the fiend real, was he hemorrhaging and dying right there beside her? "We need to get you to a hospital," she said.

He shook his head. "The monster wasn't physical."

"Are you sure?"

"No. But I'm feeling better. From past experience I expected the aura of the energy to have a despairing effect and the nausea was bad, but the clawing of my innards was what surprised me."

"I don't like this," she said.

"Thrills me."

She ignored the sarcasm. After what she and Bodie had experienced, the thought of what the dolphins might have been through chilled her to the bone. "We need to get to Jost Van Dyke."

"First let's dump the dye and prove what we already know—no current carried those dolphins in record time." He tapped the screen of his sensor. "I'll calculate a direct route between where they disappeared and reappeared. Come around and head directly west so I can eject the dye when we cross that line."

Her rational mind wanted to believe they'd locate a strong current, to cling to the remote possibility that the bottlenose pods had escaped the horror of the red orphic. Reaching behind Bodie's seat, she located a flare-gun type hand launcher and two cartridges of orange dye. "You'll have to open the door to aim."

"No problem." After wedging the sensor on the console where he could track their position, he took the launcher from her and loaded the two cylinders into it, one after the other.

The blue dot on the sensor screen moved steadily toward the white line. Lex's pulse ramped and her hands grew clammy on the controls. *Please let there be a current.*

Bodie jerked the door handle with his left hand and braced the door open with his right shoulder far enough to aim the launcher at the sea below. "Just a little farther."

Two loud pops echoed in the cabin followed a second later by a dull explosion as the canisters hit the water. He leaned out the door and peered down at the water. "Done. If the current is swift enough to carrier those pods at thirty-five knots per hour, we should see some movement in a few minutes."

"I'll circle around," she said, "The dye might not penetrate a deep water current where the dolphins can swim."

He pulled the door closed and locked the latch. Retrieving the sensor, he rested it on his knees and gazed down at the screen. She glanced at his sensor and corrected her course. "I'll take us down a little."

"The dye should be visible dead ahead." He reached for

the binoculars sitting at his feet and brought them to his eyes. "It's spreading."

As they approached their target, Lex checked the sensor screen to gauge their position. A mile away her pulse spiked. *Let the dye show a strong current. Please.*

"Shit," Bodie said. "Do you see this?"

Her heart sank. Instead of the orange river flowing northwest, the dye fanned out to the south-southeast toward the red orphic. "The dye is flowing in the opposite direction. They didn't get caught in a current."

8

Nothing on the scanner screen surprised Bodie, and the pale blue and green orphic suited him just fine. It didn't mean there weren't any ghosts or spirits on Jost Van Dyke, it just reduced the likelihood that any spirits there were really pissed off.

"You might want to stash your toys for landing," Lex said as Silverbelle dropped over the chop outside Little Harbour. "We'll anchor out here until I find out what's going on with the dolphins. I'd hate to land on somebody's head in there."

With a click the sensor went dark and locked. He slipped it into his bag, pocketed the ComDev and braced for his first rough-water landing.

Two skips and a bump and the pontoons settled with a rocking glide. Lex flipped a lever, releasing the anchor with a splash and quiet whirl of line before steering with the current to set the hook.

The bay in front of them sparkled in the afternoon sun. A half dozen sailboats and two small fishing boats spotted the pale turquoise water edged with rocky shore and short stretches of snowy white beach. Rock and scrub hills rose from the shoreline and three open-air beach bars offered cold drinks and hot food. At least their colorful signs did.

"Okay, here's the plan. I'll try to debrief the dolphins while you work on the sensor. When I signal, bring Silverbelle into the dock over there at Sidney's Peace and Love." She showed him how to raise the anchor and start the water jets to drive the seaplane in. "So at least try to pay attention to me while I'm out there doing the hard duty."

"Got it. Pay attention and take the plane to the bar."

With a pat on his knee, she opened the pilot's door. "Goddamn, Bodie, I can see why you were the pride of M.I.T."

Princeton, but whatever. She worked quickly pulling a pair of cords that instantly inflated the craft. A twist and pop of an aluminum frame and presto, a boat. With one hand she lifted a small outboard motor from the bag and clicked it on the stern. The Foundation certainly didn't scrimp on equipment.

"What if your homies don't show the love?" he asked.

She stepped into the boat. "Your attempt at humor is so lame."

The snap of her comeback was off. For the first time, he saw a glimmer of uncertainty in her bravado. "Maybe this isn't a good idea," he said.

"*This* is what I do. I'll find out what happened and maybe the intel will strike a chord in that brilliant brain of yours." And with that the boat took off toward the harbor at a brisk clip.

He figured she knew what she was doing. If anything went down with those dolphins, he should be able to get to her quickly.

He retrieved the sensor from his bag and took his ComDev from his pocket. While waiting for the sensor to boot up, he ran his thumb down the inside of his forearm where the mysterious symbols now marked his skin—ink put there by Durand while Bodie had been unconscious. He'd be damned if he was going to give the S.O.B. the satisfaction of asking what they were. Durand Tech QR codes, probably. And then there was the added bonus of the government agents who had shot him. One thing he and Mark agreed on was that those suckers would kill him if given half a chance—which is exactly what he was doing.

9

So Lex and Bodie had made it to Jost Van Dyke. Mark
zoomed in on their signals on the screen as he lounged in
the plush leather armchair of the Gulfstream V.

He'd logged into the Ariel's tracking system and after
listening to Lex's voicemail this morning he'd downloaded
the data on the dolphins' disappearance. One benefit of
providing all the Foundation's equipment was being able to
tap into the system at will. When the GPS data was
processed against Bodie's sensor data, he'd seen the red spot
and immediately wiped the data from the Durand Tech
monitoring system.

Flexing the tight muscles of his back, he rolled his
shoulders to ease the stiffness of two hours piloting the jet
through bad weather. When the skies cleared, he had
turned the controls over to his co-pilot and come back to
work. His long legs, clad in ancient jeans, ached for a
punishing run.

A notification popped up on the screen. Bodie had
attempted to log into the network. As Mark had ordered,
this time access was denied.

"Sorry, buddy, we can't let the mole find out what you're doing. You and Lex need to fall off the DT radar for a while."

Three denied attempts triggered a lockout. Invalid login. His cell phone buzzed. Caller I.D. read *Flynn*. He let him go into voicemail.

A text came through. *Access denied? WTF?*

Succinct and to the point. Mark liked that about Bodie. He tapped in a reply. *System down. Security breach. You're on your own.*

How long?

"Patience, man. It's for your own good."

HOW FUCKING LONG?

"As long as it takes." Mark said to himself. He then placed a call and heard two rings before the pick-up. "I'm on my way to Mexico. Bodie's locked out of Durand Tech until further notice. Don't be surprised if you get a call from Lex in the next twenty-four."

"She calls, I'm telling her the truth," Adrien replied.

Although technically he reported to Adrien, Mark needed the Sentier to do as he asked this time. "The truth is there's a security breach and it's dangerous for Bodie to upload his data. The guy's going to figure out what's causing the orphic disturbances and when he does, no one on our end except you or me can get that intel."

"You're sure Tolian's involved?"

"No, but whatever's going on is ugly and he's my prime suspect, just like he is in Mexico." They'd already argued about Mark's decision to look for the two Protectors who had gone missing on assignment on the border. They both knew that before becoming Sentier Adrien would have insisted on going himself, so he didn't have a convincing argument against Mark taking the mission.

"Don't let this get personal," Adrien said.

"A little late for that." Ten years give or take a few months. "I'll check in when we're headed home."

"Be careful."

Mark ended the call and glanced down at his ComDev. Two more texts from Bodie. Persistent dude. And royally pissed off. So what was new? Since that night three years ago in Boston they were forever linked by the bond of Bodie's resurrection. If he had a conscience, Mark might feel guilty about leaving the fledgling revenant to his own devices in a hostile environment. But educating him would have exposed him to too much of the psychic world and posed its own set of problems. So instead Mark had marked Bodie with the most powerful protection he could provide and stuck him in the relative safety of Fat Dog to face his new reality alone.

Need more memory for continuous scan. Critical!!

Sorry.

The message came back almost instantly. *Wrong answer!*

No doubt, but he'd figure something out. Just in case the big guy needed a little extra motivation to stay in the game, Mark tapped in a final message. *Work with it. Anything happens to Lex—I'm coming for you.* His thumb hit send.

Clicking the ComDev to vibrate, he slipped it into his jeans pocket. As long as there was a traitor within the Protectors, Lex and Bodie were safer on their own. Together they could be the perfect no-tech weapon—more powerful against the evil invading the Caribbean than any computers or sensors. Either they bonded and utilized their joint abilities or... the alternative could be worse than fatal.

———

THREE DORSAL FINS GLIDED toward the Zodiac. Lex slowed

the boat and waited, focusing on greeting the approaching dolphins telepathically. Her senses opened to their psychic energy.

A second later she jerked backward, her head reeling with a hard kick of aggression, fear and madness. Their emotions. What had happened to these gentle creatures? Reinforcing her shield to detach and steady herself, she collected her energy.

Further in the cove, a dozen agitated bottlenoses churned the azure water into a froth. The reality of the situation gripped her. They were out of control and she had no idea how to help them. Her own brief contact with red orphic had been horrifying. How much worse had it been for them?

At the mouth of Little Harbor the three gray bodies of the sentries arched and dove.

Concentrating, she projected well-being. *Friend. Help. Safe.* When in a cooperative mood, these mammals were capable of complex communication. Not speech thought, exactly, but narrative of a sort. All crazy jacked up, she'd be lucky if the telepathy and empathy combo blast penetrated at all. Why did the insanity remain this far from the red orphic spot?

A thump on the bottom of the Zodiac threw her off the flimsy fiberglass bench onto the heavy fabric floor. Another snout rammed the buoyant hull, pushing the boat away from the cove.

Her focus wavered and sweat ran into her eyes and burned. Another gray shape torpedoed toward her, this time with the speed to capsize the Zodiac and toss her into the clear blue. In their element, she was toast. Death by ramming—not how she'd planned to spend her day.

Clutching the frame of the Zodiac, she braced herself for

the hit and projected *friend calm safety peace* at the dolphin as best she could through her own anxiety. *Friend calm safety peace* over and over like a mantra. The dolphin veered away at the last instant, grazing the bow hard enough to shove the inflatable backward. Her lungs expelled the breath she'd been holding.

Her mind reached out to the two males cruising in front of the Zodiac, testing their thoughts and projecting calm. Their aggression had ramped down a little, but not the terror or confusion. *Friend. Safe. Friend. Safe.* Normally these beings didn't hold onto fear once the danger passed. Their minds didn't work that way.

A dark shadow came at her like a torpedo, hitting the canvas bottom of the boat so hard she was propelled into the air, pain shooting through her feet and legs. Time went slow-mo. *Friend. Friend. Friend.* Splash. Water was her element. Warm, familiar. She projected calm to the dolphins as best she could.

They backed off. The two she could see swam sentry between her and the cove while the flipped Zodiac drifted away toward Tortola. Treading water, she tried one more time to focus on a single dolphin and recognized the one the team called Chuy.

"Okay, big guy," she murmured. "How can I help you?"

Through the riot of impressions, an odd pattern emerged. A burst of light, the sensation of being whirled out of control. Pressure. Darkness. Despair.

The blow to her hip shocked her back to herself and she gasped in a mouth of water. Coughing, she kicked to keep her head above water, fighting the pain shooting up her side.

A dolphin had rammed her! Off to her right the fin surfaced heading away. Not comforting. Standard procedure. Get up to top speed and head-butt the target. Great way to kill sharks.

She watched the fin rise, the sleek gray body arch out of the turquoise sea and disappear. The Zodiac merrily escaped, bouncing on the waves in the channel a hundred yards away now. Lex gritted her teeth against the throbbing in her hip and swam for the boat.

Concentrate on distracting him. Unfortunately the pain and I-don't-want-to-die combo wasn't conducive to focusing. With every stroke she attempted to project *Turn back* and *All is well*, but dark and deadly came barreling at her from behind and her senses reeled.

She shoveled the water frantically. A wave crashed over her head from behind. Limbs flailing, she fought to break the surface. This was it.

A huge hand caught her wrist and yanked her straight up into the air. Her arm felt like it was being wrenched from her shoulder, then a heavy weight caught her around the waist and slammed her against a wall of muscle, knocking out the little breath left in her lungs.

Holding tight to the massive arm, she struggled for air and tried to find footing.

"Easy, princess," Bodie said close to her ear. "I've got you."

She sagged against him, her back pressed to his chest. He'd saved her life.

"Thanks," she managed, "I think I can stand on my own now."

He released her slowly, making sure she had a firm grip on the strut of Silverbelle and was steady on her feet before letting her go.

"Get in the back and hook the boat as we pass it," he said, climbing into the pilot's seat.

She started to argue then collapsed in the back exhausted. The Helio started to move, bumping her injured hip. Pain spiked up her side and tears filled her eyes. Her teeth clenched over a profanity.

"You okay?"

"I'm fine. Just shaken up a little."

Through the open door she saw the dolphins swimming alongside the plane for a full minute before turning back to the cove, but she couldn't bring herself to try to communicate with them. Her mission was a dismal failure. Whatever happened to those creatures had changed their very natures and no psychic suggestions or frolicking in the bay would heal them.

ONCE THEY'D PICKED up the Zodiac, Bodie assured himself Lex was okay before relinquishing the controls. He was relieved when she climbed back into the pilot's seat. Pulling out a knob near her foot, she glanced over at him. "We're just going to the next cove so we'll stay on the surface. You'll want your seat belt."

He clicked it in place just as the seaplane lurched into high speed. Jets on the pontoons shot them across the water at breakneck speed. They pounded into the waves heading west. Shit, the last time he'd gone this fast and hard in the surf he'd had a waverunner wailing under him, but these jets were disconcertingly quiet.

His legs braced to cushion the impact of the chop. "I'm guessing the debriefing didn't go well."

"Their mental patterns didn't even resemble dolphin thought. Hand me my ComDev, will you?"

Her device was exactly like his—Durand Tech's latest

model. Even so, his confidence in her multitasking abilities had its limits and he didn't hand it over. "I'll hold, you talk."

A beat of *you're-kidding,* and she ordered the phone, "Call David."

Latham picked up on the second ring. "How's it going?"

"Interesting." She glanced at Bodie and shrugged. "I need Ash and Olivia to dig up everything they can find on dolphin attacks and send it to me."

"Attacks on what?"

"Humans."

"Humans? They didn't come after you, did they?"

"I'm fine."

"Geez, Lex. I told you to take someone else with you. That Flynn guy..."

"You're on speaker, David."

Bodie couldn't resist. "Hey, Latham."

Silence stretched across the connection.

"Just have them run a search," Lex said. "We'll stay in Jost Van Dyke and keep an eye on them from the beach this afternoon."

"The Ariel will be there by tomorrow," David replied.

Lex's mouth tightened. "Not necessary."

"Not your call. See you in the morning." He disconnected.

"Shit." Lex muttered. "Remind me to fire him."

"Give the guy a break. He's besotted."

"Jesus, what kind of word is that?"

"It means..."

"I know what it means. I just can't believe *you* used it in conversation."

"So what's the plan? Assuming you have one."

"Get some lunch while you reprogram the DT scanners.

Then we try to figure out what happened to my buddies out there."

Reprogram the scanners, huh? "There's been a security breach at DT—I texted Mark and he said I'm locked out for the time being. By the time we finish lunch my access should be up and running again."

Her sidelong glance was full of suspicion. "Security breach? Does this happen a lot?"

"Never. Don't worry, I'm on it." Or he hoped he was.

Silverbelle rounded the point and headed toward a clear blue cove filled with an assortment of boats, mostly moored and anchored. Scrub-covered hills rose around the bay's rocky shoreline, which was broken at the center by a stretch of white sand beach. Lex slowed to a civilized speed that wouldn't create a wake and he gave her points for good boating manners.

The twenty or so vessels in Great Harbor ranged from small, beat-to-shit motorboats to an impressive sailing yacht and everything in between. As they passed a gleaming wooden ketch, a young, buxom blond in nothing but a miniscule white g-string emerged from a hatchway and waved. All over tan and breasts that stood up and saluted.

"Lively place," he said, tearing his attention from Naked Barbie.

"With the trouble in Little Harbour, they have to go somewhere to drink."

"Right." He'd been in the Caribbean long enough to know she wasn't joking.

A gaggle of dinghies cluttered the patch of white beach in front of a colorful establishment nestled in the palms. The open-air bar and restaurant sported blue awnings and roof, and tables extended from the shady interior out onto the white sand. As the seaplane glided to a stop at the end of the plank dock, he heard beach party music—*Cheeseburger in Paradise* to be specific—and cringed. Why did every beach bar in the Caribbean have to play goddamn Jimmy Buffet?

Lex had hopped out and secured the plane to the dock by the time he got his seatbelt off and climbed to the land side of the cockpit.

"Would you handle our bags? I need to hose the salt off." With that she trotted down the dock.

So she intended to stay here. Overnight. No hotels or resorts dotted the shoreline. How far would they have to go for accommodations? A wave of dread rolled over him. His sensor didn't show any pockets of yellow or orange orphic but that didn't guarantee unfriendly entities couldn't pop up en route.

10

The world famous Foxy's buzzed, crowded for mid-afternoon with locals, tourists and the boat crowd all talking about the dolphins. The bar itself was little more than a concrete slab, some wooden decking and a corrugated metal roof. Bodie had to duck under the assorted tee shirts hanging from the ceiling to follow Lex to one of the heavy wooden tables where three leathery older men greeted her by name.

"Wondered how long it would take you to get here," a lanky Brit in a faded Hawaiian shirt said. "A jolly bit of excitement we've had."

Lex stashed her backpack and duffel under one end of the long table. "Boys will be boys," she muttered and he wondered if she meant the dolphins or present company. "This is Bodie."

All three men eyed him curiously over half-eaten sandwiches and fries.

Climbing over the long bench, Lex plopped herself next to the Brit and gestured to each in turn starting with the guy next to her. "Colin, Briggs, and Hank."

Nobody bothered to offer a handshake, making do with a nod before turning their attention back to her. He was tempted to find a quiet spot in the back to retry the upload connection, but a loud roar of rebellion from his stomach convinced him to park his butt on the bench.

Half listening to the local gossip, he surveyed the bar-restaurant. The three dozen or so patrons were as varied as the boats in the harbor. Two scruffy young men eyed a pair of bikinied young women in the company of a white-haired gentleman. A four-top of middle-aged tourists were burnt pink and drunk. Farther to the front, a West Indian couple ate heaping plates of fried fish without talking.

Bodie's senses confirmed what he'd seen on the screen of his sensor—low delphic energy, orphic pale blue. All in all about as good as it got. Too bad he hadn't invented the orphic energy sensor before he picked Fat Dog as his refuge. Sure, the island offered seclusion. Unfortunately the eighteenth-century massacre of escaped slaves whose lost souls haunted the place hadn't come up in the scouting report.

A dark hand thumped a pint of deep gold beer in front of him and another in front of Lex. "Come to tame the naughty dolphins, have you?"

Lex laughed. "So far they've gotten the better of me, Cat. Bodie had to pull me out of the drink earlier."

The young West Indian woman turned to him, flashing white teeth in a broad grin. She extended her hand. "I'm Catalina."

He stuck out his hand to shake back. Her attention zeroed in on the inside of his arm and her eyes widened at his ink. When their palms connected an electrical charge sizzled under his skin and he quickly drew back.

She took a quick step away and murmured something in

patois he didn't understand. Surely the woman didn't recognize him and even if she did, that didn't explain the buzz.

"What's your special today?" Lex said, apparently unaware of Cat's reaction to Bodie.

Catalina recovered her poise and rattled off a list of local dishes he only vaguely recognized.

Lex ordered her usual, whatever that was, and he ordered two cheeseburgers, coleslaw and onion rings from the blackboard, then added a coke. As Catalina hurried to the kitchen, he would have sworn she crossed herself.

"The beer's local," Lex said, bringing his attention back to the conversation at the table. "Foxy runs the only microbrewery in the Caribbean."

Local and cold. Condensation ran down the side of the glass to soak the square cardboard coaster. He took a long draft. "Not bad."

"Damned good," Hank said. "Better than the local rum, for sure. Where you from?"

Fat Dog wasn't a good answer. Neither were Miami, Houston, Boston, or New Jersey. "Been sailing the islands for a couple years. You live here?"

"'Bout half the time. Rest of the time I spend at my ranch in Texas just west of Bandera."

"You're a big man. Ever play ball?" Hank asked.

"No."

Briggs elbowed his friend. "Who does he remind you of?"

Hank studied him. Bodie shrugged, pretending to be clueless.

"Come on," Briggs said. "Celtics, ponytail."

Bingo. Bodie's blood turned to ice. What were the chances?

"Damn. You're right. Joaquim Wilson." Hank cocked his

head. "Not as big as Wilson. That boy was what, six-ten, six-eleven? I saw the game that ended his career."

"I remember that," Bodie said and went in for the slam dunk. "Whatever happened to him?"

"Got himself killed," Briggs said. "Shot up in a drug war in Boston. It was all over the news."

Yes. Dead made an excellent cover. Bodie glanced at Lex. Her face remained expressionless.

Cat delivered their food and they ate while the two basketball fans traded recollections of other sports tragedies with Colin injecting international flavor.

Pulling some bills from his pocket, Bodie threw them on the table next to his empty plate. "I've got work to do." He reached for his bag. "Nice to meet you guys."

"I'll find us a place to stay tonight." Lex's voice lacked its usual sass. "Then we can review the data before I go back to the cove."

Not before he and she had a little talk about keeping under the radar and staying alive.

Lex followed Bodie in her peripheral vision until he settled on a quiet table at the back of the bar away from the other patrons. Her first impulse was to pull out her cell and run a search on Joaquim Wilson. Not subtle and she'd only confirm what she already knew. "Is anyone in your house at Little Harbor, Colin?" she asked.

"Nope."

"Could I rent it for a few days?"

"Nope, but it's yours until my sister gets here in three weeks. Take the jeep. It's out back." He winked. "No one's about so you'll have plenty of privacy."

She rose and kissed Colin on his weathered cheek. "Thanks. You're the best."

He chuckled. "If I was the best, you'd be going home with me instead of the young, brawny bloke."

Hefting her bags, she clenched her teeth as a pain shot up her hip. She carefully adjusted the weight and headed toward the rear of the bar where the 'young, brawny bloke' scowled at the screen of his sensor. Testy was a good look on him.

"Let's go," she said. "Colin's lent us his guest house. We can work there more comfortably."

He rose, nearly toppling the chair, and shoved his electronics into his bag. "How far is this place?"

"The next cove. We'll take Colin's jeep."

Between the rutted dirt road and the dust, the five minute drive in the open vehicle left them both grimy and jostled when they finally turned into the tropical oasis surrounding Colin's pink stucco guesthouse. She pulled up to the side door and parked.

"Nice place. Where does he live?"

"In a house overlooking White Bay. This is where friends and family stay."

"Which are you?"

"Friend. Let's take our things inside and I'll show you around."

A long, deep porch extended across the front of the house and overlooked Little Harbor. Well-used rattan and bamboo furniture lent it the air of an earlier era.

She retrieved the key from a potted palm and unlocked the front door. Once inside it took a moment for her eyes to adjust to the dim light in the long open space. Nothing had changed since she and her cousin Chantal stayed there the year before.

A low whistle emitted from her new housemate. "Big enough for us and ten of our closest friends. Where should I drop the gear?"

"The bedrooms are in the back." Her gaze drifted the length of his huge body. No way he'd fit in a double bed in the smaller rooms. "Come on. You can have the one with twin beds and push them together."

"Lead the way."

Readjusting her grip on her own bags, she bee-lined for the hallway at the back of the house. Behind her the mahogany floorboards creaking under Bodie's tread were the only sounds in the house, emphasizing that they were alone and headed for his bedroom. Adolescent nervousness fluttered in her stomach. Could she be more ridiculous? What did she think might happen?

She opened a door on the left side of the hall and stepped inside. "This one's yours. Mine's across the hall. You have your own half-bath. The shower's out back in the garden. Towels are in the closet."

He set his bag on a battered trunk and opened the shutters covering French doors. Light streamed into the high-ceilinged room, revealing three twin beds.

The corners of his mouth twitched. "Three should do it. With the legs tied together they should stay put."

The bed would be enormous. Her mind took a traitorous leap—her, him, naked and sweaty. He'd been able to pull her straight out of the water with one hand.

"Is anything you've told me about yourself true?" she asked.

His expression hardened and he sat down on a sturdy writing desk between the French doors. "Everything but my personal history."

"I assume you were shot. The drug angle was a cover-up, wasn't it?"

"What makes you think that?"

"Mark wouldn't have helped you. My brother has a thing about drug dealers. If that's what you were into..."

"He'd have killed me himself?"

She didn't think about her brother's darker side. "So who tried to kill you?"

"Killed me." The silver gray eyes bored into hers, his voice was cold and bitter. "I flat-lined in the hospital and didn't wake up for two weeks."

Neither moved. The warm cheery room did nothing to dispel the prickle of alarm on the back of her neck. His gaze pinned her. She knew it took extraordinary psychic power to bring a person back from death, to create a revenant. Whatever happened to Bodie couldn't be attributed to medical science alone. She shuddered. Did her brother wield that kind of power? Did Adrien? He had still been in the field back then.

"You didn't sense orphic energy before you died, did you?" she asked.

"No."

"And you didn't see spirits either."

His arms folded over his chest. The lines of his face hardened. "This again? Who said anything about spirits?"

His fear and distrust pulsed at her in waves. Hadn't whoever saved him explained the natural laws of his new life? Did he even know what being a revenant meant?

She set down her bags and sat on the edge of the nearest bed. Educating Bodie wasn't her responsibility. Hell, she wasn't sure of the specifics of his current situation herself aside from bits and pieces she'd picked up from legend and psychic mythology.

"When people with psychic abilities have a temporary death experience their abilities usually ramp up a notch or two. If a psychic person dies and is brought back to life, they can attract spirits and ghosts afterwards, or can at least sense them."

"And you know this how?"

Within the Durand, the subject of revenants was off-limits, especially where Mark was concerned. Of course Bodie didn't know about Mark, had never seen her brother without his blue contact lenses. "A classical education?"

"Try again."

If he was ever going to trust her, she had to give him reason. The thought startled her. Did she care if he trusted her? Yeah, she did. "Over many generations my ancestors encountered psychic phenomenon and passed the knowledge to their direct descendants. I'm sorry I don't know more." She stood and picked up her bags. An ache in her hip reminded her of the reason they were on Jost Van Dyke. "I'm going to unpack then we can go down to Little Harbor. You have everything you need?"

"I'm good."

When she was halfway out the door his deep voice stopped her. "Lex."

She turned back. "Yes?"

"You see the *espectros* too, don't you?"

A lie came automatically to her lips but she bit it back and went for the truth. "Yeah, sometimes I do."

11

Bodie wasn't surprised that no one complained when Lex dumped her gear bag on the wooden pier that ran along the water in front of Sidney's Peace and Love. A pair of young men, offered their services and she politely declined. They went back to their table and watched with interest when she dropped her shorts and pulled her tee shirt over her head.

"What can I do?" Bodie asked.

"Crowd control for now."

Amidst helpful and not-so-helpful suggestions from her audience, she removed a sling and filled the pontoons from a small bottle of compressed air. Meanwhile he surveyed the bar like a bodyguard with a rock star. Eventually the men took the warning and refrained from calling out to her. Bodie couldn't stop the gawking.

She straightened, holding two small silver pistols and handed him one. "You may need this."

Too light and oddly shaped for a normal weapon. He glanced around at the bar crowd. "Who do you want me to shoot?"

"Very funny. It's a tranquillizer gun." Pointing hers at the water, she flipped a catch that released a chamber where bullets might have gone. Instead, two tiny canisters lay side by side.

"Seems a little unfriendly," he observed.

"One of the male dolphins tried to kill me. We'll go in from the beach and wade out. I'll call one of the females and hope she's not too agitated to work with. The tranq guns are a last resort in case of another attack."

"You sure this is a good idea?"

"No."

"Maybe you should wait for the Ariel."

"And tell them what?"

"None of them know about your little *talent*?" he asked.

"No."

"Not even Latham?"

"No."

"Why not?"

She peered at him over her glasses. "David's not *in the club*."

And now he was. Officially. The Doctor Doolittle I-See-Dead-People Club.

Without further explanation she dug another float from the bag and arranged it on the edge of the dock, inflation cartridges up. "If we need another sling, grab this one," she said. "Ready?"

His baggy swim trunks floated around his legs as he waded into the clear water. Lex had already retrieved the sling and stood chest deep, gazing over the bay. Minutes went by and no gray body appeared.

The smooth surface of the bay sparkled in the late afternoon sun. He squinted at what might be fins in the distance. The skeptic in him still found the concept of debriefing dolphins absurd, and yet he'd witnessed too many impossible phenomena in the past three years to dismiss it. If one of these creatures could tell her what happened, perhaps he could figure out what caused it.

The hot tropic sun beat on his scalp beneath the short bristle of hair. Filling his hand with water, he cupped it over his head. Twenty yards out, a gray fin broke the surface and glided toward them.

Lex pushed the sling behind her. "Take this. I won't need it," she said quietly. "You're a sweet girl, aren't you?"

The huge gray body slowed less than three feet from her outstretched hand, barely moving. Through the crystal clear water he could see the bottlenose's snout nudge Lex's palm like a dog looking to be petted. She obliged, running both hands over the gray head and down the sleek back. The dolphin swam away to circle back.

"She's curious about you," she said. "I vouched for you so be nice. Put out your hand and touch her."

Fascinated and wary, he tucked the tranquilizer gun into the waistband of his trunks. The female approached him, her eyes friendly enough. Not that he knew what unfriendly dolphin eyes would look like. And she was enormous—nine feet, five hundred pounds—much bigger than he was. Could he trust her? Hell, he didn't even totally trust Lex. "What do I do?"

"Come out a little deeper. When she gets close, stroke her like you would a horse."

No point explaining he'd never touched a horse. Wading deeper he reached toward the female as Lex had. Instead of swimming under his hands, she stopped directly in front of him and lifted her head from the water. A thrill shot up his spine.

"She senses you're male," Lex said with a laugh.

The dolphin's smooth head glided over his hand and she

rested her beak in his palm. Then he felt it, faint but distinctive. The residue of negative orphic energy. A wave of nausea hit his stomach and he fought it back.

The dolphin squeaked and twisted away. The water pressure from the powerful fins and tail threw him backwards. The sandy footing shifted and he grabbed for the pontoon of the sling and missed as he slipped under the surface.

"Are you okay? Did her tail hit you?"

"I'm fine."

"What happened?"

A sharp whistle from farther out in the cove pierced the air. An answering whistle followed.

Lex frowned and nudged him toward the shore. "Damn. The aggressive males are getting closer. Let's get out. I've got binoculars in my bag."

He followed her onto the sugar-white beach and stepped up onto the wooden planks of the deck. While she rummaged in her bag he slipped on his sunglasses and scanned the bay. "There's something going on out there. Will the males hurt that female?"

She focused the binoculars on the churning offshore. "Normally, I'd say no. Now? I don't know. She isn't afraid of them, though."

The glare of the sun reflecting off the water distorted the dolphin activity. Their whistles, squeaks and clicks carried across the cove to the dock.

"What about the female?" he asked. "Is she okay?"

"She's more emotionally stable than the males who attacked me. When she encountered the nasty orphic energy she felt a falling sensation and lost consciousness."

She lowered the field glasses and studied him over her

shades. "She doesn't remember anything except a *bad thing* then being herded here by the aggressive males out there. Your reaction startled her. That's why she flipped you on your ass."

"When I touched her, I felt residue from the orphic. It hit me in the gut and I jerked away." The queasiness had almost passed but that was the least of his concerns. "That was the first time I experienced orphic energy in an animal. Otherwise I thought she was pretty amazing."

"She liked you too."

He fought a grin then gave up. How cool was it that a dolphin liked him. Lex's relationship with the cetaceans was making a hell of a lot more sense.

She opened the big dive bag and began stuffing the unused sling back into it. "At least she's not showing signs of physiological damage resulting from the experience. Her emotions are skittish but there's nothing wrong with her cognitive abilities."

"So why did the males go crazy and not her?"

Lex shrugged. "I don't know. Because she passed out maybe? I'd like to get close to the other females but not with the males out there looking for trouble. When the team gets here, I'll try to connect with the other females and see what they know."

"So what do we do in the mean time?" he asked.

"Pack up. Can you carry the inflated sling to the jeep?"

As he lifted the float, a bottlenose whistled from offshore. He looked up as she rose out of the water and squeaked at him, almost dancing. An invitation to join her? A farewell?

"What's happening?" he asked.

"She wants you to come back in the water." Lex chuckled. "The little tart is trying to seduce you."

With a final whistle, the dolphin dove gracefully, flicking her tail in the air as she disappeared.

As soon as they got back to the house, they rinsed off the sling then themselves. Lex leaned on the long dining table, half sitting, half kneeling in the chair next to him, and squinted at the screen of his sensor. "So where are you sending your data?"

"The clouds. I have a secure account and my ComDev encrypts the data for transmission. The retrieval isn't as seamless as using the Durand system and my sensor can't scan continuously like the one at DT. Five-second intervals is the best it can do."

She rearranged herself on the chair to see better. "What exactly are we looking for?"

"The system is set up to monitor the entire Caribbean and alert me of odd orphic activity, especially anything that creates a red spot."

"So we're just going to sit here and stare at the screen?"

"I have an idea." With a tap of his finger, he focused in on Little Harbor and dragged the image so the bay filled the screen. By touching a tiny icon on the edge of the image, he filtered the picture to show orphic energy. The pin-points might not have been visible had he not already known what he was looking for. Zooming in, the three spots of orange grew and slowly moved on the blue-green background. "What do you know."

"Is that possible?" she asked. "You said you never sensed orphic energy in an animal before."

"I haven't."

"And orange is bad. This doesn't make sense. Dolphins

are one of the most gentle species on the planet. What's going on?"

"Assuming the orange spots are the guys who attacked you, what do they have in common that the others don't?"

She stared at the screen for several seconds and frowned. "Shit."

"Shit, what?"

The grimace on her face deepened. "Those three are wearing GPS trackers. Nobody else is."

"And the whale who disappeared had a tracking device, right?"

"Yeah."

Damn. Marine mammal disappearances, the sudden appearance of red orphic energy and GPS trackers—there had to be something targeting the tracking devices. But what? There had to be clues in his data somewhere. Without a link to Durand, there was no way to pull up the data for time and location of the whale's disappearance on his hand-held. He needed to access his computers on the Talos to run the analysis he wanted.

"I need to get back to Road Town," he said.

She shook her head. "Not tonight. It'll be dark soon. We can leave in the morning although I'd rather meet the Ariel and brief them on the situation."

"If we leave at sunrise, you can be back way before noon."

"What about you? Aren't you coming back?"

Of course he was coming back. For the first time in a long while he had a tangible problem to solve. "If you get me there by nine, I can sail the Talos back here by late afternoon."

She studied him. "I'm trusting you to keep your word."

The veiled threat irritated him. "If I say I'll be back, I

will." He angled the sensor screen toward himself. "I need to get back to work."

She rose and his gaze involuntarily skimmed down her body. "I have some research to do, too," she said, "If you need me, I'll be in my room."

What he needed was off limits and the last place he was going was her room. He nodded and when her door closed he let out a deep ragged breath.

An hour later Lex opened her bedroom door and paused to watch Bodie engrossed in the screen in front of him. He ran a hand over the stubble on his jaw and something in her chest fluttered.

"Hungry?" she asked.

Her question startled him out of his concentration and he blinked a couple times before his silver eyes focused on her.

"Yeah." He stretched his back and rolled his shoulders, then rubbed the back of his neck. "Is there anything to eat or do we have to go out?"

"Let's see." She surveyed the contents of the kitchen. "Could be worse. How does grilled cheese and tomato sound? Or fried egg sandwich? Colin left a six pack of beer."

The cheese turned out to be aged gouda and the bread was homemade. While she cooked, Bodie moved his electronics to one end of the dining table and set placemats and flatware at the other.

"Tell me about Joaquim Wilson," she said.

The good humor drained from his expression. "He's dead."

"Then there's no reason not to talk about him."

He set his beer down on the table with a thud. "Why are you doing this?"

"The people who killed you, are they likely to come after you again if they find out you're not dead?"

"Ask your brother," he snapped.

"I'm asking you. Why did they come after you?"

"They wanted my delphic energy research. One of the guys said it was a matter of national security or some such crap."

"Why do you believe they were government agents?"

He stared at her a moment. "That's what they said when they flashed their credentials."

Her Protector training made her suspicious of any volunteered information. The U.S. government had always harbored covert branches, some of which researched psychic abilities, noetics, remote viewing, extraterrestrials, and other off-the-record phenomenon, so she couldn't dismiss the possibility one of these agencies had zeroed in on his research. She also knew there were plenty of other entities interested in psychic power. "So you think we should expect company."

"Probably."

"Then tell me who Joaquim Wilson was."

The muscle of his jaw clenched. The guy clearly had serious issues with his past, but if their safety was in question, she needed to know about it.

"A Hispanic newscaster in Houston created the persona of Joaquim Wilson in Jack Wilson's sophomore year at UH —University of Houston. Jack was making a show on the basketball court and the guy dug up his birth certificate."

So Jack became Joaquim. Hearing Bodie talk about himself this way in the third person was kind of creepy. "How did you get named Joaquim?"

"My mother's Brazilian. My father was an American merchant marine. They met in Rio and he dumped her in Miami pregnant. She gave me my first name, he gave me my last."

"So you grew up in Miami?"

"No. In a shithole town south of Houston. My father's mother raised me."

"What about your mother?"

"Out of the picture." His eyes warned her not to push the subject. "I lived with my grandmother until she died. All her money went to the church and I was homeless."

"How old were you?"

"Sixteen. Basketball was my only hope for going to college and escaping redneck hell. The high school coach saw me as a ticket to a better job and took me in." He folded his arms over his broad chest. "The University of Houston offered me a scholarship to play ball and get a college degree. Celtics drafted me and I went to Boston for a glorious eight-game career. The rest you know."

"Laughed out of M.I.T. Right."

After several beats of silence he fixed her with an intense stare. "Princeton."

The grilled cheese sandwich suddenly felt like lead in her stomach. "Which is where you met my brother." And never had a chance. "How did you meet?"

He sighed and uncrossed his arms. "A reception for some hotshot alumnus. Someone mentioned Mark had just gotten back from three months in Tibet. For some time I'd wanted to see the Himalayas to test a theory about delphic energy in the region."

"You asked him about delphic?"

"No, just his travels. He surprised me by alluding to a high level of psychic energy at a monastery he'd visited and invited me to see some sacred objects in his flat in New York."

"The family flat." She could never tell him about the powerful telepathic abilities Mark had certainly used to discover Bodie's talent. No, family secrets must be kept at all costs. "Did you go?"

"I almost didn't. Who wouldn't be suspicious of a rich alumnus inviting a lowly grad student to his New York penthouse for dinner?"

"Why did you go?"

"Curiosity." A frown creased his brow. "Now I can see Durand set me up. He dropped all the right details to make it impossible to refuse. By the end of the visit I had a grant to measure and prove the nature of delphic energy."

"What did he get?"

"Besides my soul?" He laughed bitterly. "The commercial rights to any product of the research."

Truth with a twist. Clearly more had gone down than a business transaction.

"Did you get to see the artifacts?" she asked. The Durand penthouse covered the entire top floor of obscenely expensive real estate overlooking Central Park. A five bedroom residence and garden took up half the area, a private museum of objects having spiritual, magical, or psychic properties filled the rest. Whatever objects Bodie had seen, they'd been brought to him at the residence. Only family—and selected members of the family at that—entered the museum itself.

"Yes. They turned out to be very impressive."

"But disconcerting?"

He held her gaze. "Some were beautiful. Others were fucking sinister."

And he hadn't even been a revenant back then. Nor had he understood what he was seeing.

He stood abruptly. "If you're finished with the interrogation, princess, I'm going for a run."

"It's dark."

"I've got a flashlight and a key to the back gate. Don't wait up."

She watched him disappear into his room. Running wasn't her first choice of exercise or even her tenth. Besides, he hadn't invited her to go along. The more she learned about him, the less she blamed him for his hostility. Mark had used him. Probably still was.

She rose and cleared the table. While she washed the dishes, Bodie's story replayed in her head. Mark knew everything about him and he knew very little about the Durand aside from their tech empire. Something didn't make sense. Her brother was a master of strategy who never did anything without a plan. So why had he sent her to Bodie with no more than a "this guy can help you"?

BODIE HEARD music from the bars along Little Harbor below the house which set his route in the direction of Great Harbor. The road was packed gravel and visible under the bright moon. And best of all there were no *espectros* between the cottage and Foxy's, and no Lex.

His legs stretched and pounded on the narrow road in a familiar rhythm. He wasn't sure which he wanted to avoid more, angry spirits or the woman. Right now? The woman.

The uphill slope burned his calves and worked the stiffness from his thighs, but it did zip for the mess bouncing around in his head. At the top of the hill, he paused to enjoy the cool breeze on his sweaty skin. He lifted his arms to let the delphic flow around him. Reggae music drifted up from the cove and the lights at Foxy's glowed on the water. Putting rubber to the gravel he took off again, picking up his pace on flat terrain. He took a dirt track above Great Harbor. On a moonless night he would have run right past the narrow trail bisecting the main path at the crest of the hill, but moonlight glinted off something shiny in the dirt, bringing him to a sudden stop. He stared, refusing to process what he was seeing. Twenty-five years and he still knew a spell when he saw one.

At each corner of the intersection someone had placed an assortment of objects. He studied them and their placement.

His gut clenched when a familiar pattern emerged. "Shit."

One corner held seven coins placed in a circle about ten inches in diameter. In the center of the circle a red candle had partially burned and two pieces of red chalk had been carefully positioned like spokes on either side.

The next corner contained a white bowl of dark liquid—blood, he guessed—surrounded by seven cowrie shells and seven feathers. In the third, seven large nails weighed down a round white cloth on which a trident, sun, moon, and star had been carefully drawn. In the final corner stood a wooden figure of a horned man, naked with an exaggerated aroused phallus, surrounded by seven cowrie shells.

Bodie had no idea what kind of spell was being cast or undone but he recognized the wooden figure as Exu, one of the best known deities of Yorùbá religion. He resisted the urge to destroy the patterns, to kick the dirt until none of the spell remained intact, to hurl the wooden devil far into the night. Without knowing the magic's purpose, he might do more harm than good. The neutral *feel* of the place's orphic energy led him to assume the spell was not working evil, but what did he know?

A cloud passed across the moon and unease prickled on the back of his neck. He'd lingered here too long. The spell wasn't for him and the sooner he forgot what he'd seen, the less likely the spirit of Exu would follow him. It was a lesson his mother had taught him before he could talk.

He crossed himself although he'd never been a practicing Catholic, then added, "I am not interfering and wish to leave this place alone. Do not follow me. Do not remember my face."

Taking off in the direction of the harbor, he thought he heard a voice in the wind. "Proteja sua alma, irmão." *Protect your soul, brother.*

12

Oxley Cowan pushed open the heavy, camouflaged steel door and stepped out of the bunker into the night. The full moon illuminated the stark white landscape and the sea beyond. By day, the tropical sun baked the surface of Sombrero Island to temperatures well over a hundred degrees. The cavern below, however, stayed a constant seventy degrees to accommodate his delicate electronics.

He breathed the fresh night air, no longer noticing the metallic tang of guano. Every day his successes grew and with them his confidence. Six months ago he'd received an untraceable email containing a piece of information that had allowed him to finally crack the code Jack Wilson used to safeguard his notes. If the fools who killed Wilson had first tortured him into turning over all his data, the Disruptor wouldn't have taken three years to develop.

The hum of an outboard engine announced the arrival of his supplies. Three hundred yards offshore a small freighter lay anchored, lit by only a half dozen dim lights. The open provisioning boat approached without running lights, guided by the beacon of the unmanned lighthouse—

not a simple feat given the steep rock face edging the island and the coral reef in the surrounding sea.

Oxley took a remote control from his pocket, keyed in a six number code and watched the glowing landing platform rise above the surface of the water. The Boss thought of everything, or almost everything, and his organization had very deep pockets.

"Right on time." The voice so close by startled him.

He glanced at the island's only other inhabitant, a sturdy American-educated Haitian in his mid-twenties, assigned to him as bodyguard and assistant. Henri Sardou loathed him. The feeling was mutual.

"Do you have the garbage ready for them?" Oxley snapped. "It's beginning to stink."

"No problem. I'll get the supplies first." Henri sauntered toward the boat, halting at the rim where the rock dropped off fifteen feet to the sea. He hailed the sailors in Creole and they laughed at whatever he said. The jovial exchange continued as plastic supply boxes were passed up from the boat.

The sailors' easy camaraderie set Oxley's teeth on edge. He knew the difference between paranoia and perception. Without the Boss's protection, he'd be dead. As it was, the sailors sent here with supplies always crossed themselves whenever he looked their way. Almost funny, given most practiced Santeria, Voodoo, or even, like Henri, Candomblé. Henri had made it clear that superstition about Oxley's albinism ran deep in their African roots and his tall skinny frame added to the impression of a walking skeleton.

He turned from the Haitians and picked his way along the rocky surface toward a hatch camouflaged a hundred yards away at the edge of the drop-off. The mechanism that opened it had stuck just before dawn, delaying the next phase of testing. He didn't trust Henri with fixing it, and exposing his own ultra-sensitive skin to the tropical sun for more than a couple minutes wasn't an option.

Pulling a mag light from his pocket, he clicked it on to examine the hinge for corrosion. What he saw stopped him cold.

He glanced back at the others. He knew Henri wanted off the island ASAP and that wasn't going to happen until the Disruptor was fully operational. Besides, Henri's assignment was to gather the energy for the laser with dark majik and the Boss didn't tolerate insubordination. But if this wasn't Henri's work, then whose was it? The island's sophisticated surveillance system couldn't be circumvented.

He turned his flashlight back on the hatch. Only a forceful blow with hammer or a heavy rock could have mangled the metal so badly—a disturbing observation, but not what made him shudder. A white dove lay on the lens cover, its neck broken. He was certain white doves weren't native to this part of the Caribbean.

13

Lex woke in the living room chair with her book on her lap and glanced at her watch. Not quite midnight. The house was silent, the same lights were on as when she fell asleep. If Bodie was back, he was in his room and probably asleep. Part of her wanted to knock on his door but she had no idea what to do if he opened it. No, a hot shower and a good night's sleep were more sensible if she was going to wake early and fly him back to Road Town. With a little luck and good weather, she'd be back in Little Harbor checking on the dolphins before the Ariel arrived.

After turning out the lights and locking the front door, she headed for her room to get a towel and shampoo.

A cacophony of insect and gecko chirps greeted her when she opened the French door from her bedroom into the walled garden behind the cottage. Like many islands, Jost Van Dyke had no natural fresh water sources so residents collected rain from their roofs and stored it in cisterns and tanks. The sun-heated water was stored in a black tank on the roof of the house. Gravity then delivered it to the stone shower room in the garden.

With low, sparsely placed lights marking the edge of path, she wound her way through the dense foliage. The sweet fragrance of frangipani blossoms filled the warm breeze that caressed her skin in the moonlight. Only when she approached the wooden door did she spot a blue beach towel hanging from a hook on the outside wall and hear the quiet splash of water on stone.

Her pulse spiked. She should turn back to the house. Now. She took a couple of steps further. He'd left the damned door open. Her tongue ran over her lips which had suddenly dried out.

The full moon illuminated his profile as he stood under the rain-dome, his face angled to the sky. With one hand he pulled the chain that turned on the water. With the other, he splashed his body until he was drenched. Releasing the chain, he reached to a shelf in the wall, grabbed the bar of soap and rubbed it between his hands.

She forgot to breathe. Being here was a gross invasion of his privacy and yet her feet were rooted to the ground. In her world of boats and diving, nudity had never been a big deal. This man—wet and glorious—turned her reality upside down.

Transfixed, she watched him lather his neck, shoulders, arms, and chest. With each stroke of his hand over his skin, the heat pooled deeper within her. Muscles flexed and relaxed as he made his way down powerful thighs and calves. Pale suds gleamed on smooth tanned skin and slid sensuously down his body to the floor.

She should slip away back to the house, now before she was discovered. But she couldn't move. Steam filled the air and rose into the night carrying the scent of sandalwood soap. She inhaled deeply, mesmerized by the perfect sculpture of muscle and flesh.

He straightened, lathered briskly again and dropped one hand between his legs while the other slid down the length of his heavy cock.

She gulped for air.

A second stroke sent her pulse into warp speed. *Oh, yes.* Her faint moan escaped into the night.

"Go away," he growled without looking up.

Her stomach flipped and she fought the urge to slink further into the shadows. How long had he known she was there?

"I, ah... I'll just wait until you're finished," she croaked.

Cock still in his hand, he turned his head and shot her a stare so intense her heart backfired. "And watch?"

That would be her preference but her mouth stayed open and treacherously silent.

To her disappointment, he turned his back and yanked the chain. Water streamed over his glistening bronzed skin, creating rivulets that wound down broad shoulders, past his tapered waist before narrowing to rinse the two perfect dimples on the small of his back. She gazed unblinkingly as the last of the suds slid over the curve of tight buttocks and sculpted calves to swirl around the drain between his feet. All too soon the water stopped. He whipped a hand over his closely cropped hair and droplets of water pelted her.

"You missed some soap on your left leg," she offered, pleased at the nonchalance in her voice.

Those powerful shoulders rose and fell once as he breathed deep and then he swiveled slowly to face her. Instinct took over and her gaze dropped. Her mouth went dry.

Fully aroused and unsmiling, he crossed the twelve feet of stone tile that separated them. The top of her head barely reached his stubbled chin and she felt tiny and fragile—

another foreign sensation that shook her to her core and knocked everything off-kilter.

"What do you want?" His voice was low and husky.

Her gaze involuntarily flipped south and up again. Magnificently aroused. Her cheeks warmed. "A shower?"

Without breaking eye contact, he brushed his knuckle gently over her nipple. "Really?"

A gasp caught in her throat and her heart pounded. Her breasts ached for his touch.

"You know where this is going?" he asked.

Lust washed over her. Her head bobbed once. Nothing in her uninspired experience with

men gave her more than a generic idea, but she was dying to find out.

Their faces were inches apart and drops of water still rolled down his cheek, curving along that flexed jaw and dripping to the stone. She longed to lick the wet paths, feel the force of his mouth on hers but as a point of pride, making the first move was out of the question. She willed him to kiss her.

Instead, deft male fingers peeled the bathing suit straps from her shoulders and down her arms. With one swift pull her breasts burst free, the nipples hard and begging for his attention. His silver gaze devoured them, caressed them, but he didn't touch. Her shoulders drew back instinctively, thrusting her breasts up and forward. Offering.

"Beautiful," he murmured, his thumbs grazing her wrists before freeing her hands from the straps.

She stood rigid, need welling in her chest, between her legs. Only stubborn pride prevented her from pleading with him to kiss her, to use his mouth and teeth on her aching nipples, to put his hands all over her body. She bit her lip and waited.

Dropping to one knee, he tugged the pink tank to her ankles in a single slow unveiling. He lifted one foot and then the other, his mouth dipping so close she could feel his warm breath on her sex. It would be so easy to rest her hands on his shoulders and lean into him. To show him what she wanted him to do to her. Hands fisted, she remained perfectly still. She refused to let him know how desperately she wanted him.

He rose and nudged her to the spot directly below the rain dome. A firm grasp on her shoulders turned her away from him to face the stone wall of the shower.

She stiffened. What the hell was he doing? Had she misread his intentions? Waiting for his next move became seconds of sheer torture.

He reached around her and pulled the chain and water flowed deliciously over her flushed skin. She tilted her head back letting the warm water wash her face.

Seconds later it stopped and she heard movement behind her. The soap lathering briskly in his hands again, the sound itself filled her with anticipation.

The first firm slide of his slippery hands on her shoulders sent an electrical charge through her that almost knocked her off her feet. Wide palms stroked her neck, her shoulders, then joined together down the narrow of her back. They kneaded the tense muscles along her spine, his thumb massaging the knots from her back. With steady efficiency, he crouched and continued down her waist, her ass, her legs, never hesitating or lingering or fondling. She wanted to scream with frustration.

His knees creaked as he stood and she smiled, knowing he now had to turn her to face him. She couldn't stand this game much longer. If he didn't get down to business soon, she wasn't beyond a little encouragement.

The sound of soap between his palms again. She drew in a deep breath, quivering in need and anticipation. *Here we go...*

His powerful hands slipped around her waist and split in opposite directions, one slid under her breasts, the other to her crotch, and drew her gently back against his body. His erection, huge and rock-hard, pressed from the slit in her ass up the small of her back. Blood drained from her head and she gasped in surprise.

His lips grazed the side of her neck drawing a shiver from deep within. "You're making me crazy," he groaned.

Crazy wasn't cutting it. She wanted him to need her as much as she needed him. Wordlessly she ground against him but he immediately pinned her to his hips, stilling her as easily as he might restrain a small child. The heat of his hard body dizzied her.

Expert fingers went to work rolling her nipples and sent a charge of pleasure directly to her core. She clasped his biceps and arched into his hand savoring the delicious roughness of calloused fingertips caressing her flushed skin.

The hand between her thighs began to play her. His thumb circled her clit and his long fingers explored, stroking around and within her slowly and masterfully. Legs trembling, she clutched her hands over his, whether to stop them or urge them on, she had no idea. And in the end it made no difference. Bodie had complete control and she surrendered to him.

Her hips bucked against his hand wantonly, knowing only that she wanted what he alone could give her.

"Come for me," he rasped in her ear.

She did. Wave after wave of intense pleasure rolled through her. Her throaty cries echoed in the night as she gave herself up to him until her knees finally buckled. Heart racing and breathless, she collapsed against his chest, enfolded tightly in his massive arms.

He held her trembling body tenderly for a full minute then brushed his lips across her shoulder. "Open for me, princess."

Need surged through her core. Need to feel him inside her. She spread her legs and leaned forward slightly. Her breath caught when fingertips feathered down her ass and tested her slick heat.

"Come on, Bodie," she ground out.

A laugh rumbled in his chest. "Yes, darlin'."

He seized her hips and positioned himself at her opening. Impatiently, she pushed against him. That was all the enticement he needed.

In a slow powerful thrust he entered her, stretching and filling her until she didn't know where she ended and he started. Closing her eyes, she felt his pulse through his cock and flexed her inner muscles to grip him.

He groaned. His palm slipped to her breast and caressed it, his thumb circled her nipple. They seemed frozen in time in a place too intimate to bear.

He started to move. Slowly at first and when she caught his rhythm he moved faster, the sweet friction of him hard within her soft slickness set every cell in her body on fire. The hands on her hips tightened as his thrusts grew harder and deeper. She braced her hands against the stone wall and rode him. Every stroke drove her higher until she exploded with a rush that lit up her body, her mind, and the tropical night around her. Moments later his fingers dug into her hips and he bucked within her, groaning his release.

He drew her back against his body. Panting, blood pounding, she remained perfectly still. His ragged breathing rasped against her neck. His arms held her so firmly she felt his heart racing in time with hers. He still filled her and she didn't want to let him go. Resting her arms on his, she leaned into his damp chest. She wanted to say something but no words came.

A moment later, his hands dropped away and he slipped out of her. The wondrous spell broke.

"I'll rinse off and let you finish your shower." His voice was gentle, but distant.

She turned to him and searched his face. Surely he'd been as blown away by this as she was. In the glow of the moon his expression was shuttered and his silver eyes unreadable. He moved past her and pulled the chain, keeping his back to her as water splashed over him.

A vise squeezed her chest. Was that it? His tender washing and caressing had been so intimate, and nothing in her experience compared to the erotic thrill of him claiming her body with his.

The water stopped and he headed for the doorway to the garden. "All yours," he said, reaching for his towel.

"Bodie…" she began then stopped.

He flashed her a questioning glance as he wrapped the beach towel around his hips. "Yes?"

The realization struck her like a right hook to the jaw— she'd been in the throes of passion, had felt a raging desire for *him* she'd felt for no man before, and he'd just been horny. He'd never even kissed her, just washed her and fucked her. It had meant nothing to him. *Nothing*. A sudden chill made her shiver. Just like that he was going to walk away and leave her. Damn him.

Naked and wet, she cloaked herself in her last shred of dignity. "Be ready to go at seven. If you get up first, make coffee. The stronger the better."

He had the nerve to salute her. "No problem. Sleep tight, Lex."

And he was gone.

BODIE SHOVED the door of his room shut and sagged against it. Jesus Christ. He'd just fucked Mark Durand's sister. Had he lost his goddamned mind? Chills covered his body, the result of the overhead fan stirring the night air on his wet skin. Drying off quickly, he pulled on a pair of clean boxers and dropped his ass on one of the narrow twin beds.

It didn't take a genius to memorize Durand's last text message: *Anything happens to Lex—I'm coming for you.* Shit. And the S.O.B. always seemed to know *everything.*

Gee, so how would the conversation go? Hey, man, I was minding my own business jerking off in the shower when your sister showed up so I nailed her. Yeah, Durand would be cool with that. Christ. More likely he'd rip Bodie's heart out and feed it to him.

He heard Lex's bedroom door slam. She was probably pissed and he didn't really blame her. He hadn't exactly been his most chivalrous, but how was he supposed to act? He wasn't used to being with someone like her. "Thanks, baby. That was great" just didn't seem to cut it.

And it had been great. The blood rushed from his head directly to his cock. He looked down at the tented boxers and shook his head in resignation. She was Lex Durand and he was a junkyard dog with a price on his head and some serious baggage where women were concerned. He might get hard every time he got close to her, but his dick sure as hell wasn't getting an encore performance, not if he intended to stay alive.

STRETCHED out on the double bed, Lex stared at the patterns of shadows on the ceiling and listened to the scrape of a bed being dragged across a wood floor. She wondered if her door was locked. Not that it mattered. She wasn't opening it and not much chance he would either.

"Damn you, Bodie," she muttered softly. What had she expected, that he'd go down on his knees and pledge eternal devotion?

She smiled. The guy had very talented hands. And the way he'd thrust into her... Heat pooled between her thighs. Shit. Now she was getting turned on just thinking about the sex. She was so in trouble.

The heavy crash of metal on metal jerked her back to full consciousness. The entire house reverberated with the pounding of the massive front door knocker. Her thoughts flashed to Bodie and the people who tried to... no, they *had* killed him. Had they tracked him down already?

The door of her room flew open and Bodie burst in.

"Stay here," he ordered. "Do you know how to use a pistol?"

"Of course." Now wasn't the time to explain her Protector training.

He handed her a small Beretta and two clips, then yanked an evil looking weapon from the waistband of his cargo shorts. "It's loaded. If anyone comes in, shoot."

"I'm coming with you." She scrambled out of bed, glad she'd decided to pull on a tank top and yoga pants to sleep in.

He strode to the door leading into the living room and cracked it to check for intruders. "No, you're not."

She jammed a magazine in place. "You think they found you already?"

"No, but I don't want to have my head blown off if they have."

The knocker pounded again.

"Not very subtle for assassins," Lex observed, following him into the darkened front room.

"They weren't last time either." With weapon in hand, he approached the heavy mahogany door then glanced back at her and swore. "Listen to me. You need to take cover."

His tone, deadly serious and resigned, gripped her gut with alarm. He was prepared for a shootout that could leave them both dead.

"We do this together," she said and took a post behind the door, pistol braced in both hands.

He fixed her with his silver gaze and for an instant she thought she saw tenderness there before his eyes flashed ice.

"Shit," he said and reached for the doorknob.

14

Bodie's heart thumped loudly in his chest. It was unlikely he'd already been tracked down on Jost Van Dyke, which didn't mean he hadn't been spotted back in Road Town.

"Step back," he hissed at Lex.

"Open the damn door."

He raised his massive pistol, turned the knob and jerked the door open.

The scruffy young man standing on the porch jumped back in surprise.

"Who the hell are you?" Bodie demanded.

"Shit, Serge," Lex barked. "You almost got your head blown off."

"You know him?"

Serge shook where he stood—dirty hair, barefoot in grimy shorts and a ratty AC/DC t-shirt.

Lex lowered her weapon. "More or less. He's a regular at Stanley's." She spoke to their visitor in rapid French.

Bodie uncocked the Desert Eagle and shoved the barrel into the waistband of his cargoes, while the wide-eyed Frenchman stared at him.

Lex grabbed their visitor's arm to get his attention. "Come on, Serge, focus. Why are you banging on our door in the middle of the night?"

The guy finally recovered his wits. "Stanley said to come get you. One of the dolphins beached itself."

Whatever she muttered in French garnered a look of surprise from ole Serge. "Okay. Let me throw on a bathing suit and get some equipment and I'll be right there."

The Frenchman nodded then scurried down the steps to his transportation.

Bodie chuckled. "Sorry about that."

He turned to find Lex studying him. "You seriously thought we might die tonight, didn't you?" Her tone was curious rather than frightened.

"There was a possibility." Just as there had been every time he encountered a stranger since he'd opened the door to his condo in Boston that night. He waited for her to flinch or show some kind of alarm. He deserved a tongue-lashing for putting her in danger.

Instead she folded her arms across her chest, Beretta dangling from her right hand, and leaned against the wall. "Here's the deal," she said. "From now on, you're straight up and honest with me. If we're going to keep you alive, no more secrets that can get either of us killed."

"Agreed."

"Wherever we go, we'll be armed. Maybe that cannon of yours can stay home." She nodded at the handle sticking out of his waistband. "Got anything smaller, something more discreet?"

"Oh, yeah," he said. He had to hand it to her, the woman had guts.

"Good." She pushed away from the wall. "Now get

dressed and meet me at the jeep. We have a dolphin to check out and I may need your help."

Lex strode across the living room, all business now. His body remembered how she'd felt naked and wet and aroused. He shook himself and headed for his room.

———

THE HUGE GRAY body lay motionless in the sand. Bodie hadn't been able to judge how big the dolphins were from the plane and even his brief encounter with the female at the beach hadn't prepared him for the ten-foot marine mammal.

Lex reached the dolphin first. "Well, well. What are you doing here?"

"Is it my girlfriend?" he asked.

"No. One of the boys who attacked me this afternoon. Chuy. The one who rammed me."

"How do you know?"

"The piece missing from the top of his fin and the transmitter attached at the bottom." She crouched next to him to touch the gray skin and rested her hand on his head.

As the seconds passed, Bodie guessed she was doing her telepathy thing and waited. The animal's visible eye was closed and he didn't move at all when she ran her hand down the side of the huge body.

Touching the beast who had tried to kill her that afternoon didn't strike him as a brilliant move. Then again, he didn't know jack about sea mammals. "Is he alive?"

"Definitely but he's unconscious. If he was a land species I'd say he was asleep," she said thoughtfully.

"Funny place to nap."

"Dolphins only sleep with half their brains at any given time. The other half stays awake to keep them swimming and breathing. Otherwise they'd drown."

"Right. So what do we do now?"

"Get him into a sling and keep him wet until he wakes up or the Ariel arrives." She continued to stare at Chuy. "I can't tell if he's dreaming or his subconscious is remembering. Images are flashing in there like a rapid video collage. By the time I recognize something, his mind is two or three images ahead."

He squatted next to her and propped one knee in the sand. Without even touching the dolphin he felt the presence of intense negative energy. Nausea hit him square in the stomach and he had to force himself not to back away. "He's been contaminated—it's like he ingested red orphic."

"Is that possible?"

"No, I don't think so."

Gently, she stroked Chuy's head. "Something scrambled his mind."

"How do these guys usually think?" Not a question he'd have ever considered asking before this morning.

"A lot like we do. Perception, recognition, processing. They're surprisingly analytical about their world and self-aware." She frowned and chewed on her lower lip. "I'm getting the impression he believes the GPS he carries for us caused whatever happened to the pod."

Lex stood and brushed at the sand clinging to her knees. "You inflate the sling. I'll get the clippers to remove the tracking device."

They unloaded the gear without talking. Lex used both hands to work the clippers. The pin snapped and she carefully wriggled it out of the fibrous flesh of Chuy's fin, releasing the GPS device.

Maneuvering the huge gray body took both of them. Bodie inflated the pontoon to float at the edge of the water, avoiding touching the dolphin as much as possible. Pushing and tugging, his head pounding and stomach rebelling all the way, they managed to get the dolphin into the sling. They then used the buoyancy of the waves and brute strength to pull the sling into the water so the other pontoon could be inflated.

With his blowhole above the water, Chuy could breathe and his skin could be kept wet. With Bodie and Lex on either side, they walked the dolphin into the water until they were hip deep.

Lex stroked the bottlenose's head. "You go get some rest."

"I'll stay. This dolphin tried to kill you. What if he wakes up and is still pissed off?"

Her attention remained on Chuy. "I'm going to try to calm his mind while he's asleep. It'll be easier to concentrate if I don't have any distractions."

"You can do that? Go into his mind and alter his thoughts?"

Her fingers grazed the wound where the tracking device had been attached. "I don't know. I have to try." She looked up, her eyes filled with sadness. "Dolphins are highly intelligent and extremely intuitive beings. Chuy's visions or memories or dreams, whatever's going on in his head, tell me he believes the tracking device was responsible for hurting his pod. I can't ignore that possibility."

"Are you getting any information about what happened?"

"Bits and pieces. Chuy has no frame of reference for the experience."

Bodie understood that feeling. "Do you?"

She dropped her gaze back to the dolphin. "Maybe."

"We're a team here, Lex. I can't help you if I don't know what happened to your friend out there."

"I used my empath senses to probe beyond his visions to the sensations he felt." She drew a deep breath. "A vortex sucked the pod into what appeared to be another dimension or plane of reality."

The scientist in him wanted to demand details, back-up, proof. He shut that skeptic down. "Okay. That's pretty scary."

She shrugged. "Not in itself, it isn't. Remember these guys live in the sea and yet they're aware of our land-based world. They move constantly so their environment is always changing—the sounds, the light, the food, even the taste of the water. The other plane was so alien, its elements bore no resemblance to a dolphin's experience of earth. What's more important is how Chuy felt. The fear and despair of the other dimension were completely new to him as was the truth he instinctively knew, even if he had never encountered it."

"Like we felt at the red orphic?" A deep foreboding gripped Bodie's lungs. He tried to brush it off with annoyance. "Okay. So what exactly drove him crazy enough to want to kill you?"

"Pure evil and sixty-five minutes in hell."

Her words hit him like a shotgun blast to the chest—an all too familiar experience. "Impossible," he choked out.

"You don't believe me?" she snapped. "Or you don't believe him?"

The water lapping at his hips rocked the sling and he adjusted his stance to keep from being pushed over. Was it possible? He stared at Lex, who stared right back with a whole lot of attitude.

"I believe you both," he said.

She studied him. "You know what happened to Chuy and the others?"

Nothing about Lex was soft or submissive now. The no-nonsense set of her mouth, the intensity of those dark blue eyes made it clear she wouldn't accept a bullshit answer.

He took a deep breath. They were in this Twilight Zone together now. "Remember me telling you I got laughed out of Princeton?"

She nodded.

"My discovery of delphic energy was only part of the reason." He hesitated, but the proof lay unconscious under her hand. "I came to believe there were different planes of existence that were separated by properties of the delphic energy."

"Did you have any proof?" she asked.

"No, it was only a theory. Once I started perfecting the sensors, I concentrated on them." At Mark's insistence, come to think of it.

She nodded as though every word he'd said made perfect sense. "And after you died, you had a whole new set of problems to solve."

An odd warmth spread through his body. Nobody but Durand had ever accepted his wild-ass ideas before and here she was totally getting him. "Yeah, I began sensing orphic, too, and had to figure out how to measure its good and malevolent variations. You know how crazy we sound, right?"

"I'm going to throw something out," she said, "and I want you to listen before you say anything. Okay?"

"Sure."

"I think the red orphic he absorbed at the spot where

the pod disappeared is the reason Chuy isn't responding to my telepathic manipulations. We both felt what it did to us in the plane and it must be much worse having it inside him. As long as he's saturated, I don't think he can shake the horror."

"Makes sense."

Shifting her footing, she rested both hands on the pontoon and gazed down on the huge gray body that floated between them. "I also think you may be able to push the bad orphic out of him with your mind if you try."

"That's impossible. Nobody can push energy with their mind."

"I can," she said. "But only certain delphic and only in one specific place."

He tried to beat down the cynic in his brain that screamed she was putting him on. "How? And why only one place?"

Her teeth scraped over her bottom lip. "I can't explain how in words, only guide you the way I was directed the first few times. I'll have to project the *feeling* of controlling the energy into your mind."

Lex in his head? "No. You're not projecting anything into my mind."

"Why not? I can teach you to do things, things that might help you."

The vision of his mother shooting flames at her lover flashed in front of his eyes. "I have an active imagination and not much stomach for supernatural power."

"What I can teach you is no more supernatural than your ability to sense the energy. These dolphins need your help," she insisted.

"Sorry."

Her expression softened. "Why are you frightened, Bodie?"

He wasn't going to bare his soul on the Mommy Dearest horror show of his childhood. Better to ask his own questions. "Where is the place you can channel energy?"

"You're changing the subject."

"No shit. And you're avoiding answering."

"You could figure it out if you thought about it."

"You want me to let you into my mind but you won't tell me about your own ability? I'm not feeling much give and take here."

She shrugged. "I told you I'm an animal telepath. But I've never told anyone outside the Protectors what I can do and nobody's ever seen..." She hated to remind him of what went down in Road Town, but figured he wasn't forgetting that incident any time soon. "Nobody except Adrien has ever seen me project sensations on somebody else."

Adrien Durand—Mark's cousin—now controlled the Durand global business empire from Paris. Bodie had hypothesized a cloaked European delphic fount. Was it possible? "Is there a delphic energy concentration in Paris?"

"I'm not authorized to give you that information."

Authorized his ass. "Then we're at a stand-off. You don't trust me and I don't trust you."

"It's not that I don't trust you exactly. Telling you more than you need to know will put you in danger."

"Some government assassins killed me once, and the minute they figure out I'm alive they'll probably try to do it again. I'm willing to risk a little more danger."

"Then why won't you let me teach you to drive the evil out of Chuy?"

"Why can't you do it yourself?"

"Because I don't sense orphic the way you do. I was affected by the red spot, but I only experienced the symptoms not the energy itself. I can only show you what I feel when I channel the delphic. Won't you at least try?"

Before he could answer, headlights appeared on the road above the cove and slowed. Two open-topped jeeps bounced down the dirt drive headed toward them.

"Damn it," she muttered. "Why does he always show up with a posse?"

Latham descended the steep path to the beach followed by three young men. "We got a call that one of the dolphins beached itself. Who is it?"

"Crap timing," Lex muttered under her breath, then addressed Latham. "What are you doing here? We weren't expecting you until tomorrow."

"We're early." David waded knee deep into the water and stopped. "Chuy, isn't it? I want to do an exam and get a blood sample."

"Yeah, and he's the one who came after me this afternoon," she said.

"So you tranquillized him?" David's tone held disapproval and Bodie wasn't at all surprised when Lex got indignant.

"Give me some credit," she snapped. "He's unconscious, just as I found him. All I did was check for injuries and remove his tracking device. As far as I can tell, his vital signs are okay."

David gestured to the guys on the beach and one approached with what looked like a plastic tool kit. "Without any medical equipment, that's just a guess. I brought a full kit so Mac and I can take over from here."

Lex didn't move but Bodie saw her hands tremble on the

inflated pontoon. If her assessment of Chuy's mental state was accurate, no amount of veterinary care was going to fix him. And after his own experience with red orphic, he agreed that the energy in the animal was probably causing his violent behavior. Not a diagnosis they could share with Latham.

David approached the slinged dolphin and ran a hand down its back. "Good night, Lex." He threw Bodie a dismissive glare before directing his attention back to Lex. "You've done what you can, so go get some sleep."

Lex's eyes flashed fury. "No."

"No?" Latham asked indignantly. "You're tired and there's nothing more you can do for him tonight. Let us relieve you."

"All right. We all want what's best for Chuy so I'm conceding his care to you for now. Tomorrow we talk when I get back from flying Bodie to Road Town."

David nodded. "We'll have a full report by then."

She glanced down at the unconscious dolphin and ran her hand softly down the side of his head and rested it there. All of her concentration focused on the bottlenose and her body visibly tensed.

Watching her, Bodie wondered what she was seeing in Chuy's orphic-tainted mind. How could she delve into the evil so fearlessly? Her jaw muscle tightened as though she was resisting pain and she shivered. He closed his warm hand over her cold one.

"Let's go," he said gently.

"Not yet."

His hand tightened over hers and followed her gaze down to the dolphin. His pulse ricocheted when he saw the open eye watching them.

In one powerful motion the massive gray body flipped

out of the sling. The force of the pontoon shoved her off her feet and under the water.

"Lex!" he gasped and dove for her. One of Chuy's fins caught the side of his head propelling him backward.

The world went dark.

15

The sun had been up for over an hour when Lex knocked on Bodie's bedroom door.

He was fully dressed in a wrinkled blue cotton button-down shirt, khaki shorts and boat shoes. "Ready to go."

"How about some coffee first?" she asked.

"Sounds good." He moved past her and into the kitchen. "Can I pour you some too?"

"Mine's on the table."

He seemed deep in thought or annoyed. From the scowl on his face, she suspected the latter. "The Ariel has a great cook. We can eat breakfast there if you want."

"No." He peered inside the refrigerator. "Where'd the OJ come from?"

"The guys dropped it off this morning. Milk and fresh bread, too." He poured some juice into a large glass from the drain rack on the counter, downed it, and set the glass in the sink.

"Are you still pissed off about last night?" She understood the indignity of being hauled onto the dolphin sling and given mouth-to-mouth.

"I was surprised, that's all." His stance appeared relaxed but a resentment that made little sense to her simmered under the surface.

She joined him at the kitchen counter and poured herself some more java. "What's going on?"

"I'm drinking coffee."

"Is this about me asking you to push the orphic out of Chuy?"

When he turned and met her eyes, the silver gaze was even more haunted than usual. "No." His hand tightened around the coffee mug. "I was up most of last night trying to make sense of what the dolphins experienced. I keep coming back to the same suspicion and it pisses the hell out of me."

"Okay. I'm listening."

"Has anyone ever taken your work, work you believed was good and worthy, and subverted it?"

"Someone hurt my dolphins, probably killed Poseidon and his mate and offspring. Maybe because of our tracking devices. So yeah, they have."

"Well, I think we're talking about the same person or people."

"Who?"

"Someone who knows about my early work with delphic."

"Are you sure?" she asked.

With a shrug, he set his mug on the counter. "No. I spent the last few hours trying to piece the facts together but there are big holes. It's clear the red orphic had something to do with the dolphins' disappearance and reappearance. The question is did the orphic cause the time-space leap or is it a side effect of something else."

"Okay, so what does that have to do with you?" she

asked.

"I told you I was working on a theory that multiple planes of reality coexist in the same space separated by a dense form of delphic energy. I was playing with the idea that by focusing delphic into a laser-like beam, a passage could be created between realities."

"You pierced the barrier between planes?"

"Hell, no! That would be insanely dangerous. Do you really think I'm that irresponsible?"

"There are psychics who would do anything to gain personal power. Our enemies' mission is to destroy civilization with violence and chaos."

He glared at her. "Do you think *I'm* that irresponsible?"

"No. But how could you attempt..."

"I didn't. My theory was concept and mathematics, not practical application. Aside from a few late night discussions with other grad students—usually fueled by large quantities of alcohol—I never discussed my hypothesis. Everyone threw out drunken bullshit."

"What about Mark? What did you tell him?"

He shifted uncomfortably. "During my recovery..." He patted his chest. "We explored the possible motives for the hit team sent to kill me. All the possible motives. The parallel reality angle was discarded early as too esoteric."

"Was this before or after you discovered you could sense orphic energy?"

"About the same time. It didn't seem relevant to my theory."

"So if the dolphins really dipped in and out of an evil parallel reality, you think it's possible someone else figured out how to break through the delphic barrier."

"Yes. The red orphic could have leaked through the hole."

She shuddered. "A universe of red orphic? That *would* be hell."

"I struggled all night with the likelihood that someone could have come up with a similar concept independently. My gut tells me my theory was stolen."

"By who?"

"I have no idea. Everyone at Princeton thought I was crazy when I discovered delphic. To accept it, understand it, and discover a way to use it? That's a hell of a stretch."

"Unless your theory fell into the hands of someone who already knew about delphic."

"And had the resources to build a device that could gather and focus the energy into a powerful beam. Someone like Mark."

"No. It's not my brother. You don't like him but he's one of the good guys." She ignored his smirk. "Can your sensor detect a laser-like ray of delphic?"

"I don't know. It would depend on how strong it was and how long it lasted. The sensor on the Talos is more sensitive and powerful than my handheld, and I can program it for continuous scan without the time delay to encrypt and transmit to the clouds. Unfortunately, the sensors are useless without laser activity to detect." He studied her, his expression grim.

"So the only way you'll find him is for him to use this weapon of his again?"

He nodded.

"Maybe on humans?"

"We don't know that, but yes. It's possible."

A chill rolled over her. The whales and dolphins who had been attacked were very dear to her. The prospect of the laser claiming more victims nauseated her. "We have to stop him."

"Now that I know what I'm looking for, I may have useful data from your whale's disappearance on the Talos. The sooner I get to my sensors, the quicker we'll have answers."

"Then we'd better get going. You packed?"

"Packed and ready to go as ordered."

They loaded their gear into the jeep and set off on the gravel road for Great Harbor. The bouncing and noise didn't facilitate discussion, so they rode in silence.

Bodie grabbed her arm. "Pull over."

She'd barely stopped the jeep when he hopped out and darted up a narrow dirt path flanked by scrub. His head and shoulders rose well above the thick, low bush as he wound up the steep hill then suddenly vanished as though he'd stepped into a hole.

A hot breeze lifted the hair on the back of her neck giving her the sense someone was watching.

"Bodie," she called out. "What the hell are you doing?" Something just felt wrong. In spite of the bright morning sun, the lonely stretch of road felt sinister. She leaned on the jeep's horn in a couple short bursts.

His head popped up above the foliage and even from a hundred yards away, his face looked grim.

"What was that about?" she asked as he climbed into the passenger seat and slammed the door.

"Know anything about Santeria?"

A shudder rippled through her body. Her Protector training had covered all types of practices, especially those that leaned toward dark magic. "Yeah. Why?"

He told her about his night time run and finding the spell at the point where the paths crossed. "Why did you go back?" she asked.

"To see if the offerings were still there."

"Were they?"

"No." He opened his hand to her revealing a gold heart charm—not the Valentine variety. "Nothing except this."

"*El corazón.*"

"*O coração,*" he said in Portuguese.

A shiver shot up her spine. Hearts—usually those of small animals—figured in many powerful spells, few of them benevolent. A golden heart charm could probably go either way. "Why did you pick it up?"

"It wasn't at the intersection where the spell was. The gold caught my eye on the path." He dropped the charm into his shirt pocket. "Once I touched it, I couldn't leave it behind."

As limited as her understanding of the details of the rituals and sacred objects was, that much she understood. Once an object used in majik was touched, it absorbed life energy of whoever touched it and a spell could be cast on him from afar. "How do you know so much about Santeria?"

The jeep bounced from the gravel road onto the blacktop surface of the main thoroughfare into Great Harbour. Bodie stared out over the bay below. He let out a deep breath. "My mother was an Orixá, a Yorùbá priestess of Santeria."

"*Merde,*" she whispered, the implications too dire to comprehend all at once. "Did she teach you?"

He laughed bitterly. "Hell, no. Not intentionally. Once I was born, she forgot I existed. Her devotees took turns looking after me more or less. I was like the furniture—there and invisible."

Under the bitterness she sensed a deep-seated fear and revulsion. No love, not even a little affection.

"And being a bright, curious child, you learned things."

"Yeah."

"What about your father?"

"Merchant seaman gone back to sea. He'd met Zamora at a carnival in Rio and married her." The jeep hit a bump and the sun flashed off his Oakleys. "He claimed she bewitched him to get to Miami."

"How'd you end up in Texas?"

"What is this, twenty questions? I told you how I learned about Santeria. I'd rather not discuss the rest."

A Brazilian Orixá mother, the ability to sense delphic and orphic energy, a revenant, and a gold heart charm in his pocket. No way could she let this go. She pulled over onto the shoulder of the road and turned off the engine.

"What are you doing?" he demanded.

"Sorry, Bodie. I need some answers starting with: how involved were you in your mother's rituals? Did you cast spells, summon spirits, practice magic?"

Even through his sunglasses, she felt his glare.

"I was a kid, damn it. I wish to God I'd never seen any of it."

"Like what?"

His lips thinned. "You don't want to go there."

"Yeah, I do," she said. "And we're not going anywhere until I get some answers."

"Okay. I saw it all. Possession. Orgies. Zamora murdering her lover. João was the closest thing I ever had to a father."

Her stomach lurched. "Murdered how?"

He looked away.

"Bodie, murdered how?"

A sheen of sweat glittered on his forehead and his hand went to his neck. "With a snake of fire that strangled him then slid down his throat and burned him from the inside."

"Jesus. And you saw this?"

He nodded. "That night I ran away and never saw Zamora again."

"How old were you?"

"Seven."

"So young." She reached out to lay her fingers on him and he pulled away.

"Okay, Dr. Phil, can we get a move on here?" he snapped.

"Did you tell the authorities?"

"What don't you get about Santeria? The *authorities* couldn't touch her and pissing her off would've landed me just as dead as João. My only chance was to disappear."

Not an easy feat for a seven-year-old in a city like Miami. The tropical sun beat down on her head and a bead of sweat ran down the back of her shirt. She started the car and pulled back onto the road. They began their descent to the village.

"Ever told anyone else?" she asked.

"No, princess, you're the first."

THE GOLD CHARM weighed heavily in Bodie's pocket, almost as much as his confession weighed on his mind. What had he been thinking telling a complete stranger about Zamora? Knowledge was power and the last thing he needed was another Durand with information that could be used against him.

When they reached the village, Lex swerved into the space between two palm trees twenty yards down the beach from the dock.

While he began to unload the bags from the back of the jeep, Lex called David to find out if the team had any update on the dolphins.

He hoisted the bags and set out across the sand to the seaplane tied up to the far end of the dock. Silverbelle bobbed gently against its bumpers. He dropped the bags, unlocked the rear door and hesitated. The hair on the back of his neck stood on end. Turning, he scanned the beach.

Aside from the group around the patio bar table, the only person on the shoreline was Lex. Still, he felt watched. A flash of movement behind the jeep caught his eye and he squinted. In the shadows stood the waitress from the restaurant—Catalina—the one who had noticed his tattoos, staring at him. He felt disquiet, but not fear. Her attention lacked the malice of the Obeah woman on Fat Dog. This was different. Then Catalina vanished, disappeared into thin air. He shuddered. The sooner he got back to his boat, the happier he'd be.

Lex hopped into the cockpit and started up the engines with a quiet hum. Silverbelle lifted off across Great Harbour and flew west over the five mile strait between Jost Van Dyke and Tortola.

Her hand eased back on the throttle and the plane began to climb. "That first day on Fat Dog I asked Mark if I could trust you."

"What did he say?"

"He told me to decide for myself."

"Have you?"

"Can I trust you?"

"I can keep a secret," he said. "Who would I tell?"

"And if I ask you to vow you'll never reveal anything I tell you, will you?"

"Could this information get me killed?" he asked warily.

Her ponytail bobbed when her head nodded. "We'd be even."

Hell, with someone already out to snuff his ass, why not

make the situation worse? "I promise never to tell anyone anything you tell me in confidence."

"To the world, the Durands appear to be a family of wealthy French aristocrats with global business and philanthropic interests. We're also a covert organization of Protectors with a long history of fighting an enemy who would enslave the *ordinaire* world with mind control and violence. Evil exists and has the advantage of not playing by any rules. You've felt the red orphic energy. Watched a man killed with your mother's dark majik."

He winced. "You said *we*. Who exactly are these Protectors?"

"I'm one. I've been highly trained for combat—one-on-one, weapons, covert ops. I'm a soldier and when the time comes to face whoever's behind what was done to my whales and dolphins, I'm going to be there."

If anything happens to Lex, I'm coming for you. Durand's message was clear. And yet her plane and training could be very valuable if he found the laser or whatever it was. No way was he making her any promises he'd regret later. "Let's not get ahead of ourselves."

She must have taken that as a *yes* since she didn't push the subject.

Silverbelle crested the last hill and Road Town stretched out below.

"Looks like there's been some excitement in the yacht basin while we were gone," Lex said nodding toward the marina on the eastern side of the bay.

Sure enough several official looking vessels loomed near the slip where he'd left the Talos. Coincidence? The security on his boat was impenetrable, the equipment protected by blast-proof, fireproof walls, and the data encryption could not be broken. And the last line of defense, if all else failed...

"There are binoculars in the chart box," Lex said. "I'll circle around so you can check it out."

He swallowed hard and fumbled with the latch. Rooting through charts and manuals, his fingers finally landed on the binoculars. His hands trembled as they adjusted the knob that brought the image into focus. An icy vise squeezed his lungs as he stared at the chaos below.

The last line of defense, if all else failed, was that the Talos and everything onboard would self-destruct.

His boat was gone.

The blood drained from his brain leaving him stunned and numb. His entire life was on the Talos. All lost.

"What's happening down there?" Lex asked.

"The Talos blew itself up."

"Are you sure?"

He scanned the harbor hoping to find the sailboat had merely been moved. "Yeah."

"Why?"

He turned to study her profile as she took the seaplane down for a landing on the opposite side of the harbor from the commotion. One night, that's all they'd been gone. Had Lex intentionally lured him to Jost Van Dyke so someone could board his boat? Why would she do that when Mark Durand had provided all the equipment and security? No. The dolphin crisis was real. Someone else had discovered he was in Road Town.

The seaplane glided to a stop next to an empty pier at the end of the charter docks.

Lex removed her sunglasses and her dark blue eyes studied him. "Could it have been an accident?"

He stared past her to the chaos in the marina. "Abso-fucking-lutely not."

16

Lex expected Bodie to be furious about losing his boat. His cold resignation worried her.

She rested a hand on his forearm. "I'm going to go find out what I can from the cops."

He reached for the door handle. "I'm coming, too."

"Bad idea. You're not exactly inconspicuous."

"You are?"

"The Ariel and Aurora have done plenty of search and rescue missions for the local authorities over the years. I have connections who will talk to me. You need to lay low until we know what happened." She opened the pilot's door and hesitated. "Or maybe we should get the hell out of here now."

"No, go check it out. I'll try to reach your brother and find out if DT picked up an intruder on the security system."

The midday sun beat down on her head as she walked along the road that edged the bay. She pulled her ComDev from her shorts pocket and sent her brother a text: *Talos blown up in Road Town. Call me.*

The closer she got to the excitement, the more wary she

became. Two large white boats with *Royal BVI Police* in black letters idled just offshore to block boat traffic from entering or leaving the marina. Yellow tape cordoned off the street adjacent to the docks where it seemed every police officer and harbor employee milled around, waiting for orders. A half dozen divers in wetsuits sat dripping on two benches. A long-haired, bearded blond waved to her. He rose and headed her way.

"Hey, Damon, what happened here?" she asked.

"Sailboat blew up in the middle of the night. Damnedest thing. Sucker sunk before anyone knew what happened."

"Been down on it?"

He grinned. "First one as soon as it was light. Don't know who the son-of-a-bitch was, but he had some radical shit on that boat."

"Oh?" Radical shit could be almost anything in Damon's world.

"Man, he must've been a smuggler or something. Grenades, knives, assault rifles, even a bazooka. Nobody else sails armed like that." He lowered his voice. "And the electronics. Never seen so much high-tech equipment on a boat before, not even the Ariel."

"Is it salvageable?"

"Nope. Just a twisted mass of fried metal. Must have been one hell of an explosion." He glanced behind him at his buddies then returned his attention to Lex. "Weird thing, nothing around the boat was damaged except a little scorching on the dock. No fire, no flying debris, no shrapnel, nothing."

"So no one was injured?"

Damon winced and for the first time lost his bravado. "We pulled a body out. It was pinned under a ceiling beam and pretty messed up."

A pressure in her chest eased. One of the intruders. A body might cover for Bodie's disappearance, not with whoever broke onto the Talos, but with the authorities. "The owner was killed?" she asked.

"Hard to tell. The coroner just got here to examine the body." He ran his hands down the sides of his wetsuit as though unconsciously groping for pockets. "Witnesses claim the guy who sailed the boat in was real big with a buzz cut. The dead guy had thick dark hair and can't be more than five-ten."

So Bodie wasn't off the hook. The sooner they got back to Jost Van Dyke, the better.

A murmur of voices and the rattle of wheels on the pier alerted her to the approaching stretcher. The coroner, a lean man in his late thirties, nodded to her as he neared. They'd met twice before when her team recovered the bodies of drowned tourists who had fallen off chartered sailboats after too much partying. Today his usual crisp white shirt showed patches of sweat under the arms and moisture shimmered on his ebony skin.

He paused in front of her and the procession with the body halted behind him. "Miss Durand," he said. "You didn't leave on the Ariel yesterday?"

The question surprised her. Why would the coroner track the comings and goings of the research vessel? "I flew to Jost Van Dyke yesterday morning, stayed the night and just returned a half hour ago. Is there anything I can help out with here?"

The wind shifted and the familiar stench of Dissembler majik nearly gagged her. Her gaze shot over the nearby faces. Bodie's enemy could be among them, she smelled the majik in the air—and yet the malice that usually accompanied it was missing. Still, even if a Dissembler was shielding his mind, he couldn't hide the echo of evil he carried. Not from a trained Protector.

Quickly she surveyed the crowd on the dock. Surely no one would dare attack her in front of all these *ordinaires*. Deep breaths regulated her apprehension. As the body in its black plastic bag passed, her head filled again with the stink —not of decomposition or decay. Even in death, her adversary still reeked of his depraved past.

Head reeling, she staggered backward into Damon.

"Whoa," he said, catching her before she went to ground. "You okay?"

"Sorry." She steadied herself and smiled at him. "That's what I get for skipping breakfast."

"Let's get you out of the sun," he grasped her arm.

"Thanks, but I've got to run." She wove through the mass of gawkers. Open space and fresh sea breezes did little to alleviate the lead in her stomach or the weight of guilt in her chest. The dead guy was a Dissembler. That meant Dissemblers had broken into the Talos, and not to steal a TV or the silverware.

All Protectors assumed they were under surveillance most of the time, and the Sentier's first cousins—the First Order Durand like Lex—were the highest profile of them all. Up until now, no one had ever messed with the Marine Mammal Research Foundation, its facilities or personnel, as far as she knew. There'd been no reason to suspect Bodie would blip the enemy's radar. If there had been, Mark never would have recommended she enlist his help. Hell, she never would have even known about Bodie if not for Mark.

She really needed to talk to her brother.

She turned right on Waterfront Drive and glanced behind her to see if anyone was following. A young woman with a baby in a stroller waited to cross the street at the corner in front of the market, otherwise the pedestrian traffic flowed in the opposite direction. Lex picked up her pace and dug in her bag for her ComDev.

Mark's voicemail picked up on the second ring and she swore before leaving a message. "Call me immediately. BIG trouble."

Fifteen minutes later, feeling sweaty, dusty, and irritable, she climbed into the cool cockpit of Silverbelle. "The police are looking for you. We need to get out of here."

17

David didn't look happy when they appeared at Foxy's an hour later. The restaurant was half full of customers—pretty much the same crowd as the day before—including the three ex-pats playing cards. David and two crew members sat at a table on the patio drinking cokes and bottled water. He scowled at her. "You said you were taking him to Road Town."

She pulled out a chair and sat down across from him. "Change of plans."

Bodie dropped into the seat next to her. "We need to borrow a couple laptops from the Ariel," he said.

David cocked an eyebrow. "Why?"

"Classified," Lex interjected. "Bodie has an assignment for Durand Tech. You know how my brother is."

David paled under his tan at the invocation of Mark Durand and Durand Tech. "Fine. Sam can take you out when you're ready."

"Thanks. So what's going on in Little Harbor?" she asked. "Any luck examining Elvis and Moondog?"

David's mouth tightened and a furrow appeared

between his two blond brows. "One of them rammed our Zodiac when we entered the bay and came at us again a little farther in. He tried to flip the boat."

"Was anyone hurt?" she asked.

All three of the team shook their heads in unison.

"We're fine," Mac said, "but they could have been hurt had we been in a hard hull instead of an inflatable. There didn't seem to be any choice but to tranquilize them at that point."

David straightened in his chair and squared his shoulders. "I ordered them slinged and towed into shallow water on the eastern beach of the bay away from the bar crowd. It'll be easier to monitor them and perform some tests without an inebriated audience."

Lex nodded. "I'd like to see the test results then examine them myself."

Colin came up to her from behind and rested a hand on her shoulder. "Did you find everything you needed at the house?"

She turned and smiled. "Yes. Thanks. Do you mind if we stay on another day or two?"

"You're welcome to use it as long as you want."

"Thanks. It'll give us a place to work close to Little Harbor."

David's disapproving glare darted from her to Bodie. Not that she blamed him. Bodie had a way of filling a space. Without even speaking, his presence dominated the table.

"I only packed for overnight," Bodie said. "Is there somewhere I can buy some shorts and a shirt?"

Colin gave him the once-over and grinned. "Foxy sells t-shirts and the dive shop probably has some baggies that would fit you. Great Harbour doesn't have much in Big and Tall."

"Mark left a few shirts and shorts on the Ariel last time he was here. They might do," Lex offered. Her brother wasn't quite as big as Bodie but his loose-fitting tropical wear was their best bet. "We'll pick them up while we're aboard."

She rose and Bodie followed her lead. "Ready, Sam?"

The young marine biologist scrambled to his feet. David shoved back his chair at the same time.

"Can we talk for a minute?" David asked her. "In private?"

She nodded for the others to wait and followed David to the deserted back of the patio.

"What's going on?" he demanded. "And don't give me a crock of shit because I know his boat sunk."

Her pulse spiked and she found herself unable to meet his eyes. "How do you know that?"

"The radio. A sailboat blowing up in Road Town makes the news."

"Did they say it was the Talos?"

"No. It wasn't hard to guess when he showed back up here." The lines in his face deepened as he frowned at her. "What are you doing with that man?"

"Someone broke into his boat and tried to breach his security—Durand Tech security. Whoever it was knew he was working for Mark and wanted the information onboard."

"Go on."

"The system self-destructed and the Talos sank. Nobody was hurt except the intruder."

David's eyes narrowed. "And the intruder?"

"Killed."

"Shit. How did you find all this out?"

"I went ashore while Bodie stayed with the plane.

Nobody saw him in Tortola and plenty of people know he was here last night—all night." She took a deep breath. "He has an alibi for the explosion and the man's death."

"But?"

David knew her too well not to know she was leaving info out. Telling him, however, was worse than pissing him off. "That's it."

"So why is he hiding out instead of going to the police?"

"It's complicated."

"It always is."

Not this complicated. David was a good man and she wouldn't force him to choose between his conscience and Bodie's welfare. "I need to talk to my brother before I explain further. I'm trusting you to give me the chance to assess the situation before you do anything."

"Twenty-four hours, Lex. I'll give you one day from right now then I'm calling the authorities."

"I can't let you do that. We need more time."

"You don't want to cross me on this," he warned. "Flynn's in big trouble and I won't let him drag the Foundation down with him."

"It isn't your Foundation."

His eyes hardened. "Twenty-four hours."

18

Lex stared at the screen of her ComDev, willing a message from Mark to appear. Two of their twenty-four hours were up and she knew David was unlikely to budge from his deadline. Earl snored at her feet, sleeping contently after gobbling down a bowl of dry dog food, while Bodie worked on his scanner and the laptops he'd borrowed from the Ariel. She sighed and set the ComDev down on Colin's dining table.

"Mark's still MIA." She glanced at her watch. "It's only nine o'clock in Paris. We need to call Adrien."

"So he can do what?" His fingers didn't even pause as they flew across the keys of his laptop.

Good question. She couldn't explain the implications of a dead Dissembler on the Talos to Bodie without revealing a hell of a lot about the Durand Protectors and the covert war. And if the authorities arrested Bodie, they might never find whatever was causing the red orphic. As commander-in-chief of the Protectors, Adrien needed to be briefed on their present situation before it got any worse. "He can keep you from going to prison for the rest of your life if the authorities catch up with you."

He stopped what he was doing and looked up at her. "That could take deep pockets."

"Guess you're in luck. Adrien's pockets are very deep."

"Call away, princess." He went back to his work.

She picked up her ComDev and headed for the privacy of her bedroom. At best the head of the Durand family would be ticked off at what she was about to tell him. At worst? She wasn't even going there.

"You did what?" Adrien boomed on the other end of the phone.

Lex cringed. "You heard me." She dropped onto the bed. "After losing it with the creep who tortured Earl, I had no choice. If I hadn't explained about my animal telepathy Bodie would have bolted."

"You should have let him. By telling him about your abilities, you exposed us all. I told Mark this was a bad idea."

Interesting that Mark had discussed sending her to Bodie with Adrien. They were closer as cousins than most brothers were. Still, in addition to commanding the Protectors, Adrien was trying to get a handle on the multi-billion euro international empire he'd recently inherited and Mark had Durand Tech. They both must have more pressing crises than her missing whales. "It wasn't a bad idea. He was already in deep. You know about his sensors, right?"

"I monitor them through DT"

"Somebody must have told him about the Sources."

"Maybe you better tell me what's going on there."

She gave him the abridged version of their visit to Road Town and finding the Talos had sunk.

"What possessed you to land?" he demanded. "If someone saw you with Bodie, you could end up in custody yourself."

"He stayed in the plane. I walked to the dock and hung out in the crowd until one of the divers gave me the scoop. Nobody connected me with Bodie or his boat."

"You can't be sure."

"I'm not going to hang him out for the authorities. I don't know what Mark's game is, but he outfitted that boat, not Bodie. We owe him protection. That's who we are, or it was last time I heard."

"Lex, I'm not saying we won't get him out of there. My point is you screwed up telling him about your abilities. We keep our talents secret for a reason—to keep us alive. Have you forgotten Gala and Bertrand?"

She lay back against the pillows and closed her eyes. "I asked Mark if I could trust Bodie and he told me I should decide. So I did."

"Why didn't you call me first?"

Because it was easier to apologize than get permission. "I made an executive decision based on my brother's message. I've been trying to reach him but he hasn't bothered to call back or answer my texts. It didn't occur to me I needed your permission."

Adrien's response was one of his favorite profanities in some obscure language. The sentiment was clear even if she didn't understand the exact translation. "Mark's on a rescue mission, not avoiding you."

She knew better than to ask about the mission. "What about Bodie's access to DT's data system?"

"The security breach is legit," he replied.

"Someone hacked into the system?"

An ominous silence hung on the line for a little too long. "No. There's an internal problem. Someone inside Durand Tech is leaking highly confidential information. Bodie's data is too critical to risk it getting into the wrong hands."

"*Merde*." Given that most of the company's employees were Protectors, or at least of Durand blood, the implications of a traitor within DT were staggering. "How long have you known?"

"Mark's suspected for a while." Adrien's voice sounded weary. "But let's get back to your situation. What does Bodie think happened to his boat?"

"Someone boarded it and tried to breach the security. It self-destructed on them, sunk itself and took the guy out. Bodie has an alibi for the explosion, but it's the explosives and guns Mark provided that will nail his ass with the local gendarmes."

"I'll get the lawyers on this as soon as we hang up," he said. "What worries me is that a Dissembler was on his boat so quickly."

A chill shot through her veins as a light went on in her head. Of course. The enemy kept track of her whereabouts, always had. "They found him through me, didn't they?"

Only dead air at his end.

"Adrien?"

"Lex, be careful and keep Bodie out of the hands of the authorities."

The gravity of his tone worried her. Her cousin had sent Protectors on countless dangerous missions and had been a fearless field agent himself until he became Sentier. "What aren't you telling me?" she asked.

"It's time we include Bodie in this conversation."

Although she agreed, Bodie was still an unpredictable

ally. She rose and headed for the dining room. "He's setting up a continuous scan of the Caribbean and uploading his data to one of his secure storage sites in the clouds. He'll explain."

Bodie still sat where she'd left him. "Adrien wants you in on our discussion." She set the ComDev in speaker mode on the table between them.

Bodie frowned at the device. "Sure. Why not?"

"Good evening, Bodie. Sounds like you've had some action down there," Adrien said.

Bodie mouthed *What did you tell him?*

"I already briefed him on the Talos sinking," she said, and smiled when he visibly relaxed.

"Have any ideas about the connection between the orphic and the whales?" Adrien asked.

Bodie leaned back in his chair and rested his elbows on the table. "And the dolphins. It's a wild-ass connection and, if valid, opens up a much bigger problem."

"Okay, you two. Start at the beginning and give me the details. And don't censor anything to cover your ass, Lex."

She shot Bodie a sheepish grin. "The night before last, two pods of dolphins vanished and reappeared sixty-six minutes later, forty-three miles away," she began. "Bodie's sensor picked up a red orphic spot where they disappeared so we went to investigate." She explained her and Bodie's physical and emotional reactions to the evil energy and the result of the water flow test.

"So you believe the orphic caused the dolphins to jump time and space?" Adrien asked. "How?"

"We'll get to that." Bodie nodded for her to continue.

She brought Adrien up to speed on arriving to find the males out of control and what she'd learned telepathically from Chuy when he beached himself in Little Harbor.

Mercifully the Sentier didn't chide her further for revealing her animal telepathy. He seemed to accept that the information she'd gleaned and shared with Bodie was mission critical.

Bodie took over and explained his delphic laser theory and the possibility that a parallel plane of existence had been breached.

"You think the dolphins dipped into an alternative reality and back?" Adrien asked, then added almost to himself, "Who would have the knowledge and resources to build that kind of laser?"

Lex exchanged a grim glance with Bodie, then said to Adrien, "I thought you might have some ideas."

"Don't push your luck," her cousin warned. "You're not doing him or yourself any favors by opening doors you won't be able to close again."

In other words, telling Bodie too much about the Durand was dangerous to everyone's well-being.

Bodie leaned in toward the ComDev. "If I'm right and someone's figured out how to send matter through the planes, continuously scanning the Caribbean and recording all delphic and orphic activity is the way to pinpoint the location of the laser."

"Can you do that from Jost Van Dyke with the equipment you have?" Adrien asked.

"Absolutely, assuming these people use that sucker again."

"Which they will," Adrien replied. "What were you planning to do then?"

Lex hadn't thought that far ahead. Her training for military operations aside, a direct assault on an unknown enemy powerful enough to build the laser was likely to get them killed.

Bodie had no such reservations. "We'll find the weapon, figure out how it works, then destroy it."

When Adrien didn't ask for details or offer to plan their strategy, Lex's heart sank. As much as she respected Bodie's intelligence, the Sentier's genius for planning complex missions was legendary.

"You're going to need back-up to handle the authorities," Adrien said. "Victor can be there by tomorrow afternoon. I'll brief Mark when he gets back."

"Thanks," Lex said.

"Good luck and be careful." Adrien ended the call.

BODIE RUBBED his hand over the top of his head and considered his options. Clearly he'd be arrested on his own and his sensor research seemed to be a high priority to the Durands. The question was why?

The only time he'd met Adrien in person had been years ago at the Durand family penthouse in New York. Mark had been called away at the last minute and Adrien had shown up in his place. Over dinner Adrien turned the topic to the sensor Bodie was working on and surprised him with his detailed knowledge of the project. Adrien had not only accepted delphic as fact, he'd posed questions that broadened the focus of Bodie's thinking. By the end of that evening, the missing piece of the puzzle that had stumped him for months fell into place. He wasn't sure how or why, but the truth became crystal clear... the key to measuring the delphic was to aim the sensor at the primary energy concentrations and record their wavelengths and differences. Everything else evolved from there.

Now, Adrien Durand was back in the picture. Bodie wasn't sure if he was glad or worried.

"So who's this Victor?" he asked.

Lex picked up the ComDev and wiped the screen on her sleeve. "My cousin."

"What can he do?"

She fidgeted with her device and didn't meet his eyes. "Hire a good lawyer."

"You know what I mean. What are his psychic abilities?"

She looked up and her expression hardened. "Look, I just got my ass chewed on for telling you about my own abilities. There's no way I'm discussing anyone else's. Clear?"

"If we're going to find this laser and destroy it, you can't hold out on me. When you asked Adrien who he thought could channel delphic and orphic energy, he shut you down and I'm guessing not because he couldn't produce names. Did you ask me to try to push the orphic out of the dolphins because you know people who can do that?"

"Not orphic, no. Only delphic from their specific Source, and for the most part on a very limited basis."

Humans controlling energy with their minds? The physicist in him had a hard time believing that was possible. "What do you mean by *Source*?"

"Mark never mentioned the Sources?"

"No."

She shook her head. "Unbelievable. How did you come up with the starred points on your master map then?"

He started to answer then stopped. How exactly had he discovered those points? Had it been Mark or Adrien who'd given him the coordinates? One of them had pushed him in the right direction. "I discovered them with my sensor." Or thought he had. "Adrien told me to look for concentrations of delphic to use as a baseline. Why are you calling those points Sources?"

Lex swore and grimaced. "Because that's what we call them. There are seven primary Sources of what you call delphic energy on the Earth's surface. You've identified them, even if you don't know their names and know that each has its own psychic fingerprint. Someone who has strong abilities and a bond with a specific Source can, in some cases, channel his own Source's energy."

"How do you get a bond with a Source?"

"Usually you're born to it. Please don't ask me to go into detail because I can't."

"So you can channel delphic energy at a Source?" he asked.

"Yes, I can channel delphic at my Source. If you promise to attempt to help the dolphins, I'll teach you how it feels so you can try it."

"Teach me how?" he asked warily. *How it feels* sounded like more hands-on instruction than he was up for.

"I'll project the feeling of channeling into your mind."

"No. You're not getting into my mind."

She fell back into her chair. "Come on, Bodie. Projecting will only share my perceptions with you. I'm making myself vulnerable to you, not the other way around."

"Okay, say I can learn to channel the energy, I still have that little problem with my physical reaction to the negative orphic. I can't push it if I'm incapacitated."

"Which is why I'm also going to teach you to build a psychic shield." When he opened his mouth to ask what that was, she raised her hand to silence him. "Same process as the energy channeling tutorial only this skill will change your life. The shield will protect you from any psychic attack or invasion. No more problems with spirits, and you won't have to worry about anyone reading your emotions or casting spells on you."

His jaw dropped. "You're kidding, right?"

"No. My gift to you for helping me." Nothing about her posture said *happy*. "You in or not?"

Was he really considering letting her project shit into his mind? "Maybe. If I help you, will you return the favor?"

"So what are we negotiating?" she asked.

He turned his attention to the screen of the sensor he'd linked to the laptop. "I programmed the sensor to scan continuously and dump the data on this machine. It's linked to your laptop which will encrypt and dump everything to the remote server. I've set up a signal to notify my ComDev if there's any sudden delphic or orphic activity anywhere in the Caribbean. Now all we can do is wait."

"So what do want from me?"

"To fly me wherever I need to go to get the laser."

"That simple?"

He shrugged. "We'll need your plane, some weapons, and a lot of luck. You can use some of that bad-ass covert operations training of yours and I'll play James Bond."

She smiled. "It's a terrible plan."

"Got a better one?"

"Let's see how you do on your energy training and I'll think about it."

He leaned back in his chair and clasped his hands behind his neck. "I haven't agreed yet."

"You will. I saw it in your eyes," she said. "You want to know what kind of power you can command."

"You're right. I do."

"So we have a deal." Her gaze followed the bulge of his biceps stretching the sleeves of Mark's golf shirt then slid to the hieroglyphics on the inside of his forearm. "What do those symbols mean?" she asked.

He studied her for a moment, wondering if she was testing him or genuinely didn't know. "They're none of your business," he said and lowered his arm to cover the ink.

"That geeky, huh? We all make mistakes," she said with a half smile. "But for the record they look very cool."

"How does this projection thing work? Do I just sit while you invade my mind or what?"

"There's too much interference here for you to practice manipulating the energy. You up for a walk?"

"No. If we lose the sensor and laptops we're fucked."

"I can buy us a couple of hours."

A quick dip into a hidden compartment inside her duffle produced a tiny remote control and a titanium cylinder about the size of a shotgun shell. High-tech security, with Durand Tech written all over it. She placed the cylinder on the table next to her laptop where it looked harmless enough.

He leaned in to examine it. "What does it do?"

"Emits sound waves kind of like a sonar. If anyone approaches within thirty feet of the table, a potent blast of knock-out gas will drop them for three to six hours. I'll arm it with the remote when we get outside."

His eyes widened. "You always carry this thing?"

"Not always. I picked it up from my cabin on the Ariel. After last night, I figured we'd sleep a little better with a silent sentry at the door."

Not a point he'd argue. Hell, the more security the better as far as he was concerned.

She carried Earl to her bedroom and deposited him on her bed. Aside from a soft whimper, he didn't even seem to notice his new environs. On her way out she closed the door behind her. "Ready to go?"

He reached for a faded blue Ariel baseball cap Sam had given him.

They started up the hill away from the shoreline. Only the trade winds carrying sea-cooled breezes from the east kept temperatures bearable. Beside him, Lex climbed easily up the steep path from the house to a gravel road. He tried not to notice the sleek tan muscles of her legs or imagine what those legs would feel like wrapped around his waist.

She glanced over her shoulder at him and smiled. "Are you checking me out?"

"Sorry."

"We can have an affair, you know. Just sex, no strings."

He nearly choked. "No, we can't."

"Why not? We're attracted to each other. Two consenting adults, blah, blah, blah." Something in her voice was off, less confident than usual.

"It's a bad idea."

"I don't think so."

"You're just bored and I'm here. You don't want to get involved with somebody like me."

Lex smiled up at him seductively. "What about last night?"

"A momentary lapse of sanity that won't happen again."

"Bullshit." She turned away.

All he could do was stare at her back as she ascended the dusty road. They continued up the hill in silence until the road forked and they took the steeper road to the right. The terrain was rocky here with scrub and twisted bushes dotting the landscape.

He asked the question weighing on his mind. "You asked me if you could trust me and I said *yes*. Can I trust *you*?"

The question seemed to startle her. Then she straightened indignantly. "Of course. I'm the most trustworthy person you'll ever meet."

"How many years have you been lying to David?" he asked.

Her mouth tightened. "That's different. He's *ordinaire* and wouldn't understand what I do."

"And yet you told me a couple days after we met."

"You told me about delphic and orphic energy minutes after we met. I knew you were one of us so..." She caught herself and hesitated. "I've been as open and honest as I can be with you, Bodie. I promise you can trust me."

He wanted to believe her. And wasn't that a shocker.

They were almost to the peak of the road and a small shelter. She looked down at the ocean below. Following her gaze, he took in the sea pounding the rocky coast at the foot of the steep cliffs.

"Quite a drop," he said.

A cloud passed over the sun and she shuddered. "Can we move on?"

At the top of the ridge they entered the hut. Its waist-high stone walls and palm frond roof offered partial refuge from the sun and a view in all directions. He followed her inside. A wide wooden bench about eight feet long stood in the center of the floor.

A quick survey of the surrounding hillside confirmed they were indeed alone. The only things on the stark terrain were scrub and a couple of goats down the hillside.

"What now?"

"Sit. We should be facing each other so straddle the bench."

He lifted his leg over the wooden plank and dropped his ass on the hard surface. With considerably more grace, she mirrored his movements, sliding toward him until their bare knees touched. His heartbeat thudded in his chest and the muscles in his thighs twitched under his cold fingertips.

"Okay," she said. "Take my hands and close your eyes."

He forced himself to extend both hands palms up on his thighs and enfolded her hands in them. A tingle of electricity surged between them, and he fought the impulse to pull back.

"Clear your mind and let it drift if you can," she said quietly. "Concentrate on breathing deeply through your nose. Relax your muscles. I'm going to remember how it felt to channel the delphic and project that feeling to you. Ready?"

He swallowed past the dryness in the back of this throat. "As I'll ever be."

He focused on the sea air flowing into his lungs and out again. Awareness of the pressure of her warm hands in his swam somewhere in the periphery of his mind anchoring him to her. A new sensation seeped into his consciousness. A gentle warmth caressed his consciousness like a tender embrace, calming his anxiety.

Then he felt it, the sensation of willing the delphic molecules from the air to form an invisible wave and pushing that wave out to sea. The sensation was real and vivid.

Abruptly the sensation stopped while the warmth remained.

"Now you try it," she said. "Feel the delphic around you and recreate the process I showed you."

He let his body sense the energy around him and concentrated on reproducing the mental magnetism he'd felt through her. At first nothing happened. He tried harder with no more luck.

"Have faith in your abilities," she urged softly. "Let go of doubt. Seduce the energy until it's ready to do your bidding."

Her voice stroked away his frustration and he breathed in deeply, seeking the delphic and tasting its nature. He pictured it as minute snowflakes swirling together gaining momentum and mass. Around him the energy intensified until he almost believed he could reach out and hold it in his hand. It was there. He'd collected delphic to him.

"Now propel it out to sea," Lex said.

With only an instant of mental prodding from her, he blasted the mass and launched it into the atmosphere.

He'd done it! The realization stunned him. He opened his eyes and gazed into hers. She grinned at him and squeezed his hands.

"I knew you could do it," she said, dropping his hands and snapping the connection between them.

The loss of her presence shot an unexpected pang of loneliness through him.

"With a little practice, you'll be able to draw as much energy as you want," she said, "and direct it with exact precision."

He knew she was right and he couldn't wait to hone his new skill. "But the dolphins weren't infected with delphic and there's still the problem of the violent effect the red orphic has on me."

Her expression sobered. "I can't help you manipulate the orphic but couldn't it work the same way as the delphic? Since you can sense them both, why don't you try directing your will to attract the orphic and see what happens."

Easy for her to say. Still, this place of clear blue orphic—benevolent orphic—offered ideal conditions for experimentation. When he was running, the benign energy slid over his skin, flowed into his mouth and nose and lungs, seeped into his pores. His body recognized it and welcomed the positive energy as a tree welcomes a soft spring rain. Drawing orphic into him came naturally. Manipulating it externally? How the hell did that work?

"I've only ever absorbed orphic and not through a conscious effort," he said. "That's why the red orphic makes me so sick. My body acts like a sponge whether I want it to or not."

"Will you show me? I may be able to help."

He held out his hands and she took them. Once again warm exhilaration washed over him. This time it was tinted with an unfamiliar emotion that lifted his spirits even though he didn't understand it. These were her emotions—clean, clear, optimistic, devoid of the anger permanently etched into his soul. For an instant the intellectual realization overwhelmed him before he collected himself.

"Close your eyes and clear your mind of everything but the orphic," she said. "Open yourself to the energy and use your will like a magnet."

While she spoke, he felt her soothing presence in his mind and concentrated on smelling and tasting the energy he wanted to attract. He breathed in deeply, willing the orphic to flow into his nose and mouth and lungs. Energy poured into him, surging through his bloodstream, charging through his nerves and muscles until every cell vibrated with positive power.

As if from a distance he heard her gasp and opened his eyes to find her staring at him. The intensity of her gaze heightened his awareness of the connection between them, the pounding of her heart in the pulse of her hands in time with his and the oneness of their joined perception. He wanted more, though he had no idea what that meant.

"Push the orphic out of your body, Bodie." Her voice came out strangely breathy. "Project it toward that tall bush in the distance in a strong beam of energy."

As she spoke, her presence within him strengthened his ability to focus and expel the power. Once the purging was set in motion, his body took over and he needed only to think what he wanted to do for it to happen. The orphic streamed out toward the scrub until it was all expelled, leaving him both stunned and rejuvenated.

Across from him Lex's shoulders rose and fell with each deep breath. Her skin glowed in the late afternoon sun giving it a surreal vitality. It took him several seconds to realize her hands trembled in his.

"Are you all right?" he asked, stroking the backs of her hands with his thumbs. He wasn't ready to let her go.

She nodded. "I'm just a little overwhelmed."

"Did you feel everything I did?"

"Yes. Do you mind?"

Oddly, he didn't. He liked the idea of sharing the experience with her. "No. I couldn't have done it without you."

Her smile twisted something in his chest. He slid his hand behind her neck and eased her face toward him as he lowered his mouth gently on hers. Her lips were warm and soft. The scent of the sea filled his head and she tasted faintly of honey and lemon. A flick of his tongue opened her lips to him. Reverently he explored her mouth, intoxicated by the caressing response of her lips and tongue.

Christ! He jerked away from her. "You're still in my head." Except the connection had snapped closed. "You did that."

"Did what?" Her eyes flashed with indignation. "*You* kissed *me!*"

And seeing her so flushed, he wanted to do it again.

"Only because you..." She what? Manipulated him to kiss her? That egotistical accusation would get his face slapped or worse. The truth was he'd felt—what had he felt? He had no frame of reference for his feelings.

"Yeah, because what?"

He ran a hand over the top of his head. "Hell. I don't know."

He expected a smart-ass comeback. Instead, she slid away from him and lifted her leg over the bench.

"Why don't you practice with the orphic on your own for a while," she said and rose. "Then if you still want me to, I'll try to teach you to build a psychic shield."

He nodded. "Where are you going?"

"Just for a stroll on the path. That way." She pointed east. "There's something I want to check out."

"You okay?"

Slipping on her dark glasses, she flashed a half-hearted smile. "Fine."

She was lying, and he wished he didn't care.

19

Lex marched up the path swearing under her breath. How could she have left herself so open to him? Had her subconscious wanted him to know how she felt? Christ, how *did* she feel?

The sun was no longer directly overhead, but there was still plenty of time for him to work with the dolphins, assuming he didn't change his mind now that he'd acquired his new powers. No, he wouldn't go back on their deal and she still hadn't fulfilled all of hers.

The problem was she hadn't expected to learn so much about him when he let her into his head. She'd used a relaxing technique Adrien had taught her to make him open to the projections of her memories and in doing that had stripped away the armor he'd built over a lifetime to cover his deepest emotions. That shell was a lot like the shield she was going to teach him to build. Sure, she'd figured the guy was suppressing hurt from his past, just not how much or how ingrained those feelings were.

Maybe it was sensing her own loneliness and isolation reflected back from him that had touched her. Maybe it was sharing the victory of him using his power. Either way, the revelation was the same. She was falling in love with him.

She stopped and gazed out over the sea to the north. The angry dark clouds over the open ocean indicated a squall in the distance. Could the weather front be affected by a blast of delphic or orphic energy? She made a mental note to ask Bodie. The possibility he could change the weather thrilled her.

The only fair thing to do was to teach him to use a psychic shield. It should protect him from the worst of the negative effects of the red orphic in the dolphins. It would certainly also block Mark's telepathy and her brother would be pissed as hell about that. So would Adrien. She cringed. Too bad. Bodie deserved protection and privacy, even from her family. She'd made him a promise and she'd keep it, no matter the price.

Stiffening her spine, she began walking again. The skin on the back of her neck prickled and her muscles tensed. The unmistakable scent of magic drifted on the breeze. Magic, not majik. Someone had been here recently. With slow, deliberate steps she approached a crossroad, carefully inspecting the scraggly foliage along the way for signs of a spell. Someone had crushed a stick on the path, and near the cross the residue of the magic grew stronger.

From childhood the Durand were taught to smell and taste sorcery—not unlike how Bodie smelled and tasted delphic and orphic energy—so they could detect the majik of their Dissembler enemies. Years of Protector training had honed her innate ability to identify the degree of malice and malignancy in a spell. Her senses told her the magic performed here had positive intent, so she walked on.

Something still remained where the two paths crossed. With each careful step, she scoured the trail and brush for clues to be sure she didn't inadvertently tread on a piece of the spell. Twenty feet farther and the carefully arranged objects lay at her feet. A chill slithered over her skin. Powerful magic was at work here, although she had no idea what practice it was. Vodoun? Santeria? Obeah? Whatever it was, the sorcerer had been here recently. She knelt on one knee and studied the objects on the ground.

A square of white linen, perhaps a napkin, occupied the center of the intersection with its corners pointing at each corner of the path. Three cowrie shells anchored each corner. A symbol had been drawn in the middle with a thick red liquid—not blood—ketchup or hot sauce maybe, and a thick line of white granules which was likely salt formed a circle around the symbol. The only object that seemed wrong was a cheap stainless fork lying on its side inside the salt circle where a priestess might put a piece of hair or finger nails or a personal object to direct the spell.

Whatever this was, it wasn't her area of expertise. She pulled out her ComDev and snapped a close up picture then stood up for a larger view. Normally she'd post the photos on the Protector board and mark them urgent, and someone would identify the ward in no time. That would be normal procedure had Adrien not warned her of the traitor. Now she'd have to try something off the radar.

The clock on the ComDev said 4:38 p.m., so it would be 6:38 a.m. at Chantal Durand's campsite in Australia. Her anthropologist cousin was an expert in symbols and much better than Lex with spells. She was also First Order Durand and above any suspicion. Texting the photos to her was the safest way to get a read on them. *Found this on JVD. No stink. What can you tell me?* She hit send and slipped the ComDev back into her shorts pocket. Chantal's reply could take five minutes or several hours and she still had a promise to Bodie to fulfill.

WHEN SHE ENTERED the shelter he was sitting in lotus position on the bench, eyes closed and facing north. The late afternoon sun cast a golden glow on his skin. She cleared her throat.

"How was your walk?"

"Good." She wasn't ready to tell him about the spell she'd found and complicate what she needed to do now. "Have you perfected your energy controlling technique?"

His face took on an expression of boyish wonder. "You were right. Within a couple of tries, the entire process felt second nature. Maybe it's because I've lived with the energy for so long, but it seems to want to do whatever I *think*. Does that make any sense? Orphic cooperating with me, following my mental orders?"

"Yeah, I understand. That's the way I've always felt about animal telepathy. I just do it and the animals respond. This is your talent. Now how about I teach you to build a shield?"

"What's that going to entail?"

She didn't blame him for being reluctant and wasn't all that keen to reestablish the intimacy either. But the sooner this thing was done, the better for both of them. "Same as before. You let me show you how forming a shield feels and then do it yourself with me on the sidelines."

"And once I form this shield I'll have some kind of psychic protection against anyone who tries to get in my head?"

"There are people and entities who wield all kinds of powers to invade and control unprotected minds," she explained. "Our enemies are masters at subverting *ordinaires* to do their evil work—serial killers, mass murderers, leaders committing genocide, and terrorists are some of the more overt examples. Your shield will prevent anyone from exerting any kind of mind control through majik. Spirits and ghosts won't be able to plague your dreams or subconscious. If I'm right, the shield will also keep delphic or orphic from entering your body when you manipulate it unless you allow it in. I don't have much experience with energy, just feeling it through you, but in theory you should be able to control the red orphic externally with your will without getting sick."

"And if that doesn't work?"

"If that doesn't work and you try to help the dolphins, you'll probably throw up and we'll have to find another way to help them."

He nodded. "Fair enough. So we sit again?"

"Yes."

They took the same positions as they had before and he extended his hands on his knees, palms up. This time the warmth of his skin on hers felt more intimate and she forced her response to him to the back of her mind. *Concentrate on the task. Show him how to build the shield.* Physical awareness shimmered between them, quickening her pulse. "Breathe in through your nose and out through your mouth," she said quietly. "Relax and allow yourself to sense what I'm going to make you feel."

His even breathing fell into rhythm with hers and she reached inside herself for the sensation of forming a psychic shell around her mind without actually creating it.

"Imagine a hood of glass forming around your head from the molecules of light floating in the air. The glass is thinner than paper, lighter than air and tougher than any material you've ever known." As she spoke she mentally led him through the process, feeling the barrier form, waver, solidify, and waver again. She'd experienced the psychic power he could command and nudged his confidence. "Don your armor, Bodie. You can do it."

His attention waivered for a moment, refocused, and she felt a psychic shell begin to form before it crumbled.

"I can't hold it," he said. "It'll never stay in place."

"Yes, it will. It isn't a mental or intellectual function but a psychic skill. Once it's in place, your shield will hold itself."

"How is that possible?"

"It is."

"But how?"

"I have no idea," she said.

"Then how do you know…"

"Goddamn it, will you quit being a physicist and start being a psychic? Relax and let's go back to breathing." She slipped into his mind and repeated the process of showing him how it felt to build a shield. When the sensation was almost solidified, she pulled out. "Now finish it yourself."

His shield snapped in place, locking her out. She smiled.

The pressure of his hands gently squeezing hers forced her to open her eyes and face him.

"I did it, didn't I?" he said. "Amazing. I never imagined doing anything with my mind except think."

Pandora's box came to mind. "Will you promise never to use your abilities against *ordinaires,* except in self defense?"

He grip stiffened. "I promise."

"Or the Durand?"

His gaze hardened. "Only in self-defense."

A protest rose to her tongue and she bit it back. "The Protectors are the good guys."

"Nothing's ever that simple." He let go of her hands and

pushed back on the bench so he could swing his leg over it. "If you want me to work with the dolphins, we'd better get going. I need to check on the scanner first and it's getting late."

She got to her feet and their eyes locked. A puzzling new emotion swirled deeply in his.

They were equals now and there was no going back.

20

Oxley Cowan gulped for air and sputtered into the cell phone. "You're sure it's Jack Wilson? *The* Jack Wilson." He dropped into the desk chair in front of his computer screen. How could the son-of-a-bitch have survived? He'd seen the surveillance video of the bloodbath himself.

"Of course, we're sure," the heavy voice replied. "How close are you to testing on a human target?"

The cold air in the bunker seemed to drop another ten degrees. Oxley had known the question was coming and wished he had the answer the Boss wanted. Unfortunately when Sardou tried to open the bent hatch last night, the lens had cracked, and Oxley didn't trust him to replace it with their only spare. At sundown he would perform the task himself.

"Tonight?" he said and immediately regretted the question in his tone. The Boss preyed on weakness.

"You will report when you are ready."

"No problem." He hoped. He couldn't help himself asking, "What are you going to do about Wilson?"

The silence on the other end of the line was like a blast

of liquid nitrogen. "You do your job and don't worry about Wilson. We'll get what we need from him this time." The line went dead.

In other words, none of your business.

Oxley's head throbbed. He rubbed his temples with his cold fingertips to curb the pain. Three years of busting his ass to reconstruct Jack Wilson's work and the motherfucker had been alive the whole time. What had he been doing? The knowledge that Jack was out there made him shake with rage.

How many nights had Oxley sat at the edge of the drunken collection of wannabe scientists listening and absorbing, while Jack threw out all kinds of crazy speculations. The others had laughed at his outlandish theories, but not Oxley. And when the head of the organization he only knew as Unit XE approached him, he'd been ready.

He took a deep breath. Wherever Wilson was, he couldn't have had access to the kind of resources Unit XE provided. The Boss knew his business. Scary, powerful business that gave the laser the energy it needed. Oxley had even begun to feed it a little himself and one of these days he'd be rid of Sardou. Wilson had never even imagined the existence of the kind of majik these people wielded or how to affect the perfect marriage of majik and science.

But Oxley had done it and now that he had more power than Jack ever dreamed of at his disposal, the payback for dismissing Oxley Cowan was going to be a bitch.

21

Leaning back in her chair, Lex shook her head. "The team has run every test they could think of on Elvis and Moondog and there's not a single piece of data I can use to explain a miraculous recovery for our cover story. No chemical imbalances, nutrient deficiencies, nothing, and David's not going to buy a laying-on-of-hands healing."

"Especially if I'm doing it. What about a simulated electromagnetic shock treatment?"

Rolled blue eyes told him what she thought of that idea. "He'd never believe I'd torture the dolphins like that. Besides, electricity and water are a bad idea."

"Invoke Durand Tech like you always do."

"No, I don't."

Now it was his turn to roll his eyes. "Yeah, well, it works. We can make up some DT device that does some ultrasonic electromagnetic crap that shocks the dolphins back into sanity."

"Nobody'll believe that."

He shrugged. "The proof's in the results, princess."

The workings of her brain played out on her face and he wondered why he'd never noticed how transparent she was.

"Okay," she said. "You got anything in your bag of tricks that looks like an ultrasonic whatever?"

"It won't pass close examination, but, yeah, I think I can dig something up."

"David isn't stupid. He'll want details."

"Well we'll just have to come up with some if you want me to try to rid them of the orphic."

He didn't wait for her answer but headed for his room. He checked to be sure the exterior doors and windows were locked then rooted through his shaving kit for a prototype hair clipper DT had produced from his specs. It was water-proof and odd shaped with a flat plastic cover over the blade mechanism. Best of all, it vibrated. Audibly. No way would it pass scrutiny up close, but hopefully it would look impressive from twenty feet away. Slipping it into his pocket, he grabbed the Desert Eagle, wrapped it in a beach towel and closed the bedroom door behind him.

FROM THE PASSENGER seat of the jeep, Bodie looked out over the calm water of Little Harbor as Lex drove along the shoreline. "You have a plan or do we just wing it?"

"Both," she replied. "We'll take over monitoring the dolphins and let you do your thing. If it works, we'll give them the antidote for the tranquillizer and let them go."

"Hope I can remember all those details."

She grinned at him. "Want me to write them down?"

"Just coach me as we go."

The jeep bounced over the sorry excuse for a road toward

a long dock and a beach on the far side of the bay. One of the Ariel's Zodiacs was tied to the dock and two crew members tended one of the floating dolphins. Farther out, Mac and Sam attempted to get the other gray body into a larger inflatable.

Lex pushed the car door open. "Great, Mac's taken charge. All we can do is bluff through some obscure research observations and hope he doesn't call me on them." She got out and reached for the canvas equipment bag but he beat her to it.

"Bullshit and a prayer," he said. "Glad you've thought this through."

"Well enough. You have your DT 'electromagnetic' device?"

He patted his shorts pocket with the clippers in it. "Yup."

"Then tuck the tranq gun in your other pocket in case we need it."

"For the dolphins or your crew?" he asked.

She slung a neoprene cross-body pouch over her head. "We'll leave our options open."

Adrenaline rushed through him at the reality of what he was about to attempt. What if it didn't work? What if it did?

The two techs with the dolphin greeted Lex and eyed him curiously. She introduced them as Ashley and Carlos. Deeply tanned, the team members all wore matching yellow Ariel shorty wetsuits and no one except Mac appeared to be older than their early twenties. At thirty-three, Bodie felt ancient.

"How are our boys doing?" Lex asked.

"Mac took the blood samples back to the Ariel and ran every test he could think of," Carlos said. "He couldn't find any physiological reason for them to freak out or attack."

"Any ideas?" Ashley asked.

"A few," Lex replied with a sidelong glance at Bodie. "Why don't you guys take a break and I'll examine them."

"You might need our help," Ashley said. "We used the most mild dose of tranquillizer we could. They might revive enough to make trouble."

"I think Bodie and I can handle them," Lex assured her. "And you'll be close enough to step in if we need you."

Ten yards away, Carlos and Mac were arguing about who had screwed up the harness as they struggled to re-sling Moondog.

"Unless you want to spend the night out here," Mac growled, "Follow my damned directions."

"Before you guys get your asses kicked again, I have an idea," Lex called to them.

"Do you?" Mac snapped.

Bodie automatically stepped forward and she grabbed his arm. "Yeah. I found an article about a bottlenose pod in Australia a few years back. A couple of the bulls were extremely agitated and beached themselves in a sandy cove after ramming a dinghy. A local animal rescue group formed a party to drag them back to deep water. The local vet was a diver and interested in marine mammals so he documented the rescue."

"These guys didn't beach themselves," Mac said impatiently, and Bodie would have happily bounced his ass across the bay like a stone.

"Before the dolphins were towed to open water, he did tests on them and discovered an abnormality in their ability to distinguish certain frequencies of sound which he attributed to high levels of underwater noise pollution."

Carlos and Ashley floated Elvis and his sling closer, listening with interest.

"So noise pollution made them crazy?"

Bodie piped in. "Aside from all the ship traffic that didn't exist a few years ago in this part of the Caribbean, technology has put sonar and high level ultrasound equipment in the hands of everyone from various countries' Navy to fishermen to cruise ships, not to mention most private yachts and sailboats. A direct hit with a high concentration of sound could stun or even kill an animal that relies on echolocation for its survival."

Mac fixed him with a skeptical look. "I'm aware of that."

"Can it, Mac," Lex snapped. "I know you're frustrated. Dr. Flynn's on loan from Durand Tech to help us find out what happened to Poseidon and now these dolphins. He has an experimental device DT is testing with humans that uses electromagnetic vibrations and ultrasound on people with epilepsy and chronic pain. Dr. Flynn believes it might reset the dolphins' sonar."

Mac snorted and shook his head. "Electric shock treatments?"

It sounded farfetched to Bodie too, but he had red orphic to exorcize and time was wasting. "Got a better idea?"

Sam, who had been listening silently while holding Moondog's sling stable, spoke up. "And what about losing their GPS signals just before they arrived here? That couldn't be a coincidence."

"Bodie's got the techs at DT on that," Lex said. "We can stand here speculating or Bodie and I can get to work."

Mac started to protest but Sam interrupted him. "What do you need from us?"

"We'll start with Moondog."

Mutiny filled Mac's eyes. Bodie moved forward to take charge of the sling and dragged it across the surface of the water to float between him and Lex.

"What are you planning to do?" Sam asked.

The guy's tone wasn't disrespectful but Bodie wished he'd go away. Apparently so did Lex and she had the authority to get rid of him. "You can read my report. Right now I want you and Mac to head back to the Ariel and research any unusually intense sonar or ultrasonic activity in the area over the last thirty-six hours."

"This is a waste of time," Mac grumbled as he launched himself over the side of the inflatable boat. "Come on, Sam. Let's get some dinner."

With a last glance at Lex, Sam climbed into the boat and started the outboard. Bodie exhaled in a long breath as the Zodiac took out over the bay.

Lex turned to Carlos and Ashley who had backed away with the sedated Elvis. "Okay, you'll need to take Elvis farther up the bay in case we have a problem with Moon-dog. We're going to try to reset his brain." She explained a simple procedure and asked Bodie to produce the "ultra-sonic electromagnetic brain stimulator." A couple mentions of Durand Tech and her audience was hooked. They retreated another twenty yards down the shore with their charge to watch the action from a safe distance.

"Gullible Mouseketeers you've got there," Bodie said softly.

She scowled at him. "Marine biologists. They all have Master's degrees and are on their way to getting doctorates."

"Smart little Mouseketeers. Did you use your magic powers to snow them?"

"Of course not," she huffed. "For your information, I'm a very plausible liar when it's important."

He studied the huge gray body floating between them. "So what now?"

"Show time. I'll run the brain reset machine over his head while you do your thing." Her expression sobered.

"His thought patterns are like Chuy's, full of fear and despair. How are you doing? Are you feeling any discomfort from the orphic?"

"So far, no." Although his body sensed the corrupt energy, to his surprise his shield prevented it from entering and sickening him. His pulse quickened and a bead of sweat rolled down his neck. Could he control the orphic inside these animals?

Bracing himself, he stepped closer to Moondog.

"Here goes," he said and focused directly on the red orphic. He willed the energy to detach from the flesh, blood and bone and to condense into a mass hovering over the dolphin. It pulsed and churned, but his mind held it tight. He drew a deep breath and mentally hurled the orphic into the sky, imagining it breaking out of the earth's atmosphere and into space. For an instant his being seemed to follow the energy then he returned to his body with a gasp as his empty lungs sucked in air.

His eyes focused on Lex's wide-eyed face. "Are you okay?" she asked.

He could only nod. His body confirmed no red orphic remained in the unconscious dolphin. "He's clean."

"You did it." Awe filled her voice.

Running a hand down the huge gray body, he grinned at her. "Just like you taught me, princess. How's the patient?"

"His thought patterns have settled and the fear and despair are almost gone. He's a little worse for wear but should be fine. Let's give him the antidote and wake him up."

She retrieved a syringe from her pouch and placed the barrel between her teeth. She then opened a packet containing a betadine and alcohol swab and prepped a spot on the dorsal muscle of Moondog's back at the mid-point of the dorsal fin. She took the cap off the syringe, held it needle up and pressed the plunger to expel any air. Without hesitation she pushed the needle through the dolphin's skin, deep into muscle and administered the antidote.

Her hand lovingly stroked down the length of the dolphin's side. "I'm so sorry, Moondog. Forgive us."

While the antidote took effect, Bodie clipped off the tracker and tucked it into his back pocket. Long seconds passed.

"Come on, buddy. Wake up," she coaxed.

Moondog's eyes opened and she gasped. Bodie watched Lex's face. "What's he saying?" Bodie whispered.

She shook her head but responded to Moondog in a soft voice. "You passed through bad energy and it got inside of you. This man sent it away."

Pause.

"No, he doesn't *connect* but he knows we're connecting now."

Another pause and she laughed. "No. Just a friend. Like you. Are you well enough to return to the pod?"

A longer pause and she stroked the gray head affectionately. "Yes. My...ah, friend will heal your brother now. He will join you soon."

She glanced up. "Deflate your pontoon. He's ready to go."

When Bodie popped the tab on the pontoon, air rushed out, quickly collapsing the buoyant bladder. Lex held her breath as the dolphin floated on his own.

"I'll tell him. Farewell, friend," she murmured as Moondog glided away.

Bodie watched the dolphin leap and fall back into the water with a flip of his tail. Something warm and fuzzy lodged in his chest. "Incredible."

"He told me to thank you for helping him."

A grin spread across his face. "Bullshit."

"Not bullshit. You made a friend."

He tried to quit grinning with no success. "That brings the total to one."

It took five minutes and a direct order before Ashley and Carlos reluctantly headed for the beach. They successfully repeated the exorcism and revived Elvis who slipped off into the bay only to return a few seconds later.

"What does he want?" Bodie asked. "For us to swim with them."

"Sounds dangerous."

"Why don't you swim across the bay to Stanley's. I'll take the jeep and meet you there."

"I could use the exercise if I'm going to sit up all night with the sensors."

"Go." The dolphin nudged her with his snout. "Take care of him Elvis."

Bodie braced himself and started swimming, all too aware of the huge gray bodies gliding through the water around him.

By the time she pulled the jeep up to Stanley's, a cheering section of the bar regulars had spotted Bodie and the dolphins cavorting in the water. Based on recent events, they'd concluded Bodie was being attacked and maybe eaten by one of the belligerent males—a conclusion that didn't spur anyone to attempt to rescue him.

She looked at her dive watch. They'd been away from the scanner for over an hour with no alert on Bodie's ComDev. "Where's Flynn?"

She jumped, startled by David's voice directly behind her. "Geez. You nearly gave me a heart attack."

He sat down on the dock next to her. "So where is he?"

"Out there." The water of the bay glittered with the light of the full moon.

"Please tell me Elvis and Moondog drowned him." His attempt at humor had an edge.

"They responded to the electromagnetic stimulation and seem to be okay now. He'll be in soon."

A shape broke the surface of the water a couple hundred yards from shore, a fin and a man clearly visible heading to shore.

"Lex." David said.

She didn't want to look at him but the command in his tone warned her not to push him.

"What?"

He rested his forearms on his tanned thighs and clasped his hands. "What's going on?"

She stared out over the bay, unwilling to meet his eyes. "Pertaining to...?"

"Damn it, Lex, you know exactly what I mean. You didn't use some bullshit DT device to reset any brainwaves. If you had any useful technology, you'd have shared it with the team. What did Flynn pull out of his ass and call a medical gadget?"

She'd expected David to call her on their story, but he'd overlooked so many of her evasions and idiosyncrasies over the years, she'd hoped he'd go along with the miraculous healing. Pressing her eyes shut, she tried to come up with a believable explanation that didn't involve the truth and failed.

Finally she turned to David. "I can't tell you and you wouldn't believe me if I did."

A frown creased his handsome face. "Why not?"

She shook her head. Years of lies and secrets lay between them and she was tired of hiding what she was.

"You can trust me," he said. "With anything. I've never been anything but open and honest with you, even when you wished I'd kept my feelings to myself."

"You've been a good friend, David, but..."

His pained expression cut her.

"But now you have Flynn and don't need me. Got it. I still want to know what you did to those dolphins though, and I'm not leaving without an answer."

"Have you ever wondered how I establish a rapport with the dolphins and whales so quickly?"

"Well, yes."

"I have abilities, psychic abilities that allow me to communicate with them."

He laughed until he realized she wasn't joking. "You expect me to believe that?"

"Yes and I expect you to trust me when I tell you the dolphins have been healed and let it go."

"Jesus, Lex," David grumbled. "I don't know what to say."

"God, that was amazing!" Bodie said as he approached. "But I'm sure you both know that."

David glared at Bodie. "I had a visit from the Royal VI Police this evening. They're looking for you and Lex in connection with your boat. People on the dock in Road Town saw her and Earl aboard the Talos yesterday morning."

"What did you tell them?" Bodie asked.

"That you were both here all of last night and that I didn't know where you were—which was technically true while I was talking to them."

"Thanks." Bodie looked David in the eye. "I didn't do anything."

"Except bring an arsenal into the BVI." David held up his hand. "And I don't want to know what or why. You're trouble, Flynn, and I'm not going to jeopardize the Foundation's welcome in the islands to cover your ass. Clear?"

"Nobody's asking you to."

David stood. "Lex told me you work for Durand Tech. That's the only reason I'm giving you until tomorrow night to fix whatever shit you're in. In the meantime, stay away from my team and the Ariel."

"David, there's too much at stake here for Bodie to be arrested. I wouldn't ask you to cover for us if it wasn't important."

"I've chosen to overlook your eccentricities over the years," he seethed. "I figured you'd open up to me when the time was right. I was wrong and now I have to decide whether protecting Bodie is worth risking everything we've all worked for. Either you give me a good reason why I should believe you, or my deadline stands."

"We can do that," Bodie said quietly.

Panic welled in her stomach. What was he thinking? David was an *ordinaire* and there was no room in his black and white thinking for the psychic world.

"No, we can't," she said.

Bodie gave her shoulder a squeeze. "Yes, we can. I'm working with Mark Durand on exploring an alternative energy source. Someone stole our research and used it to destroy the whales and injure the dolphins. They tracked your research subjects with the GPS signals. I'm pretty sure they've only been testing their technology so far and never expected anyone to notice some missing whales and crazy dolphins. Mark sent for me to stop them before they hit humans."

David folded his arms across his chest. "So what are you doing here?"

"Waiting for the signal which will tell us where to find

the bad guys." Nothing in Bodie's voice betrayed anger, just dispassionate recitation of fact.

"Satisfied?" she asked.

David dropped his arms to his side and nodded. "For now."

"So you'll back off?" she asked.

"Until tomorrow night. It's the best I can promise." David turned and climbed the steep path toward an ancient Land Rover.

"We're screwed," she mumbled.

"Latham's the least of our problems. I have a bad feeling the delphic laser is going to take out a bigger target soon."

"Let's hope your sensor will point the way to its origin before that happens."

THEY PICKED UP TAKE-AWAY from Stanley's and headed back to Colin's house. While Lex set out dinner, Bodie checked the scanner, confirming there had been no delphic laser activity while they were gone. Just as well. She didn't relish telling him they'd have to wait until daylight to leave the island. He worked while he ate and she checked her messages, neither wanting to discuss the stalemate they were in. The laser could hit in minutes, hours, even days and all they could do was wait.

Earl whimpered and nuzzled Lex's hand. "Earl needs to go out. I'll take him."

"No," Bodie replied a little too sharply. "I'm coming with you."

"That's not necessary. We'll only be out in the front garden."

The stubborn set of his jaw told her he wasn't budging.

"Not without me. Someone on this island is practicing Santeria, voodoo, or some other shit which makes night a dangerous time."

She remembered the spell on the hilltop. No point in telling him about it until she heard from Chantal. "Fine. Earl and I don't mind having a bodyguard. Do we, little guy?"

Earl wagged his tail and she scooped him up in her arms. His skin still clung too closely to his bones but he'd put on a little flesh in the past two days.

Bodie stared at his computer. "Damn it. I don't want them to use the laser, but just sitting here waiting is nerve-wracking."

"Maybe some fresh air will help."

"The alarm's set to alert me on my ComDev if there's any activity out of the ordinary. Guess that's all I can do." He slipped his feet into his boat shoes, stood up and tucked the Beretta unto the waistband of his shorts.

Once they made it to the front walkway, Earl wiggled to be let go. No sooner had she bent down than he twisted free, trotted toward a clump of hibiscus bushes and lifted his leg. *Stay in the clearing where I can see you*, she projected to him.

Bodie sat down on the top step of the porch and pointed to the sky behind her. "Look at the moon. It doesn't look real."

It didn't. The huge amber disk looked more like a prop from a science fiction movie than the moon. A shudder rippled through her. "Eerie, isn't it?"

He patted the floor next to him. "Come sit down."

For a woman who didn't take orders well, she found herself quite happy to do as he asked. They sat silently side-by-side while Earl sniffed and marked his new territory. She sensed alert tautness in Bodie's body, tension that would allow him to spring into action instantly.

"We're safe," she said.

"Are we? Something's off here. Can't you feel it?"

What she felt had nothing to do with lasers or voodoo and everything to do with the male body inches away. "So what haven't you told me about this spell you found last night?"

"I felt someone watching me." He glanced at her. "Yeah, I know that sounds paranoid."

"No, when you sense someone's there, they usually are. Any idea who it might be?"

"The woman from Foxy's, Catarina, reacted oddly when she saw the tats on my arm. Like she recognized them."

Lex had known Cat for several years, although they never crossed paths outside Foxy's. "Interesting. What are they?"

"I don't know. I didn't put them there."

"Who did?"

He laid a heavy hand on her arm. "Shhhh."

She glanced up at his face. He seemed to be listening for something.

"What is it?" she whispered.

"I felt a shift in the orphic density somewhere ahead. It felt like a ripple of yellow over the blue."

"How far ahead?"

"I don't know," he replied. "Several miles probably. Unless..."

She was too aware of the pressure of his fingers on her skin.

"Unless what?" she asked.

"Unless there was a major alteration and all I'm picking up is the residual waves."

"Should we go inside and check the sensor?"

His hand dropped away from her arm. "If the laser's used, my ComDev will alert me. Let's walk up the path to the first clearing. The sensor is effective, but it lacks the subjective capacity to feel certain subtleties within the orphic."

They found the path easily in the moonlight. Earl ran out in front, stopping periodically to mark a bush or stick. The higher they got, the stronger the warm trade winds blew until they were looking down on Colin's cottage.

The air seemed clearer on the hill and the night sky twinkled with stars in spite of the moonlight.

"It's so beautiful here and quiet. I can understand why people run away to sea," she said.

"Been there, done that. It gets old."

"Maybe it wouldn't if you had a companion to run away with."

He chuckled. "When somebody's out to kill you, travel companions tend to opt out of touring the world."

What would he do if she volunteered? Laugh, probably. And yet the prospect of spending days and nights alone with him on the sea conjured a swirl of erotic fantasies.

"Are you picking up anything new up here?" she asked.

"I'm not sure. Orphic has a different feel than delphic. Delphic comes in one flavor while orphic..." He paused to find the right words. "Orphic is like food—sometimes the flavors are distinct and obvious like strawberries or lobster or chocolate and there's no mistaking what I'm getting. At other times it's more like a concoction, a casserole or complex dish with spices, herbs, and ingredients whose flavors change when mixed together. Tonight the orphic is a mixed drink—a mojito or piña colada. There's a light sweetness and underneath a kick." He shook his head. "I'm not explaining this very well, am I?"

"I think you're explaining it extremely well considering I have no experience with orphic perception. The only thing I don't get is whether the orphic is good or evil."

"Mostly good," he said. "Good but with a troubling undercurrent of turbulence."

"We can go back and check the sensor," she offered, although she didn't want to leave this spot yet.

"We have plenty of time to sit in front of the screen and wait. It's been a while since I've stood on a hilltop and looked into the night."

She wanted to say something flippant and witty but nothing came to mind. So much had happened between them in such a short time.

"I'm sorry I blackmailed you," she said.

"I'm not," he murmured. "Your methods pissed me off at first but I was going crazy on Fat Dog. I needed to get out of there. The last few days have been quite an education."

"We'll find the laser and you can do whatever you want after that."

"And if we don't? There's no telling the kind of destruction a weapon like that could do and I can't find it with all my goddamned knowledge and resources. Who or what is going to die next while we sit on this fucking island with our thumbs up our asses?"

"You need a drink and so do I. Even if something happens tonight, we'll have to wait until dawn to take Silverbelle up."

He stared into the starry night sky, tension and frustration rolling off him in waves. "Yeah, I could use a whisky. Call Earl."

No sooner had Bodie unlocked the cottage door when

Lex's ComDev blared out Lady Gaga's "Born This Way"—Chantal's self-assigned ringtone. She retrieved the device from her pocket and answered the call. "Good morning."

"Hi. I tried to video you earlier." Like all the French cousins, Chantal's English was impeccable but the accent that used to fall halfway between American and upper-class British now held a distinctly Australian twang.

"We were out." She sat down in a wicker chair on the porch.

"We? As in you and David?"

Lex rolled her eyes. Chantal had a thing for blond men and David was definitely blond, male, and good-looking.

"No, Bodie and me." Saying his name sent a ripple of excitement through her. If there was more privacy, she'd love to tell her cousin about him. As it was, the last thing she wanted was to get all girly about him within hearing distance.

"Bodie? Male and hot?"

"Very." Her cheeks burned in the darkness. "So you got my text with the photo?"

"Obviously."

"I came across the spell this afternoon on a path intersection at the top of the ridge near Spring Hill. Recognize the symbol?"

"Yeah."

"What symbol?" Bodie asked.

She cringed and glanced behind her to find him leaning on the doorframe. "I planned to tell you."

On the other end of the line, Chantal chuckled. "I take it you're talking to the delicious Bodie."

"Hold on," she said into the ComDev before returning her attention to him. "While you were practicing with the energy, I took that walk and found a spell. With everything else going on, I figured it would be more efficient to send a photo to my cousin Chantal first to see if she knew what it was."

His silver eyes were hard. "When were you planning to tell me? Or were you?"

"Yo, Lex," Chantal said. "How about we take this to a vid discussion? I want to see this hottie for myself."

Lex hesitated. Being up-front with Bodie would probably appease him, but Chantal was unpredictable where Lex's love life was concerned and capable of saying something that would make the tension at the cottage even more awkward than it already was. "Fine, but behave," she said into the ComDev.

Bodie hadn't moved. "Well?"

"We're going to video conference this discussion. You'll hear everything I do, okay?"

He followed her inside where she plugged her ComDev into the monitor they'd borrowed from the Ariel and clipped it to the side where the camera would pick up her image to broadcast to Australia. She sat down and waited. Within a couple seconds, Chantal's tanned face appeared on the screen with the interior of a canvas safari tent in the background.

"Hi, Bodie," Chantal said. "So, are you and Lex friends or what?"

"Merely scientists with a common interest," he replied. "How about you two start at the beginning."

Lex took a deep breath. "I followed the road that runs along the ridge at the center of the island to a crossroad near Spring Hill. Someone had constructed a spell there and since indigenous magic isn't my forte, I snapped a picture and sent it to Chantal to see if she knew what it was."

"I want to see the photo," he said.

A couple of taps on her ComDev and the photo shared the monitor's screen in a new window alongside Chantal's transmission.

He drew in a sharp breath. "Fuck."

Chantal frowned. "You recognize it?"

"Do you?" His voice was gravelly and his knuckles grazed Lex's back when he grasped the back of her chair.

Something had upset him and her impulse to protect him surprised her. She directed her attention to Chantal. "The square was white linen," she said. "Do you know what the symbol means?"

"It wasn't drawn in blood, was it?" Chantal asked.

"No. Ketchup, I think, or hot sauce. Is that important?" She propped herself on her elbows on the tabletop, not trusting herself not to lean back into Bodie.

"Could be. The symbol is a protection against possession by evil entities—spirits, demons, and so forth—used in African-based practices such as Vodoun, Santeria, Macumba. Usually it would be drawn in charcoal and a personal item of whoever is to be protected would be placed within the circle of salt. At dusk, everything would be folded into the cloth and it would be buried."

"Buried anyplace in particular?"

"That depends on whose magic it is."

Lex sensed her cousin was holding back information. "And if the symbol was drawn in blood? What would that mean?"

The chair creaked with Bodie's weight and the heat of his body radiated on her back.

On the other side of the Earth, Chantal let out a long sigh. "But it wasn't so why would that matter?"

"Just tell me."

"I know the symbols but the specifics of the magic aren't

my area of expertise. Someone at the Durand library should be able to research the spell for you. All I know is blood binds the person doing the spell and whoever he's protecting."

"Binds how?" Bodie demanded.

"I don't know," Chantal replied clearly exasperated. "Why do I think I'm missing something here? Would you mind sitting down so I can see you?"

He ignored her request. "I know the symbol. Maybe you recognize the others." He stepped closer and turned the inside of his right forearm toward the camera.

Lex looked down at the tattoos he'd hidden from her before. There were three symbols—the protection symbol from the spell was closest to his wrist and two other characters were evenly spaced in a line toward his elbow. Each was delicately drawn in black and about two inches in diameter.

"Where did you have those done?" Chantal asked, her voice unsteady.

"I didn't."

"Then how did you get them?"

When the muscles in his arm tensed, Lex thought she might know the answer and laid her fingertips on his bicep. "If you want answers, you're going to have trust us. Please sit down."

He hesitated.

"Please. Chantal's a Protector as well as an anthropologist. Nothing we discuss will go beyond the three of us."

He pulled a dining chair over next to her and sat down, lifting his arm and staring into the camera. "So translate if you can, Miss Durand."

On the other side of the world Chantal's eyes widened and she gasped. "Oh my god! You're a revenant!"

22

The hair stood up on the back of Bodie's neck "What are you talking about?"

Chantal frowned. "That you're a revenant."

"What's that?"

"You don't know?" Chantal asked.

A buried memory shimmered under the surface. "Know what?"

Lex's lips were pressed into a tight line, her gaze glued to the monitor.

"That you died and came back to life," Chantal said, a touch of sympathy in her eyes.

"Of course I *know*. I was shot—multiple bullets in the chest. Mark rushed me to the emergency room where I flatlined and they revived me."

Both women shook their heads in unison.

"I should know if I was shot," he snapped.

"We're not disputing that," Chantal said. "But the medical staff didn't revive you. Whoever brought you back did it with extraordinary psychic power."

"Bullshit." And yet he'd awakened almost two weeks

later in a room in a private Durand-owned hospital in upstate New York, not Boston General. Still he'd never questioned Mark's version of his resurrection.

Lex's warm hand closed over his icy one. "What color were your eyes before you died?"

He pulled away. "Brown. The doc said the change was the result of trauma, like someone's hair turning white overnight."

Chantal nodded knowingly. "A Durand doctor?"

His chest tightened, constricting his breathing. How could he have missed the obvious inconsistencies? What else had Durand lied about? "And the tattoos?"

Chantal planted her elbows on the table in front of her. "Hold them up again."

He held his forearm to the ComDev camera lens.

She stared at the screen for several seconds before she replied. "The first symbol is obvious. Revenants are susceptible to possession by spirits, ghosts, and sorcerers so your guardian gave you a blood protection enhanced with his own power."

"Prevent possession?" He laughed bitterly. "Sure makes me feel better. And this guardian? Who's that?"

"Whoever used his power to bring you back—Mark most likely," Lex said.

He stiffened. Not Mark. Anyone but that S.O.B.

"Possibly Adrien," she continued. "Revenants are rare and surrounded by myth, even among the Durand. Only an extraordinarily powerful psychic can pull a soul back into a body and return it to life."

Revulsion churned in his gut. "Mark can bring people back to life?"

Chantal shrugged. "I have no idea. Why would he want you alive badly enough to risk his own life to save yours?"

Easy answer to that one. "He wouldn't."

"Maybe you should ask him," Lex said quietly.

He pinned her with his most withering glare. "We're not that close."

"Why not? Seems like he's one of the few friends you have besides me."

The suggestion he and Mark were friends was ludicrous for so many reasons. Durand had insisted on complete secrecy regarding Jack's work so only a leak at DT could have led the government goons to his door. Sure, the guy showed up in time to rush him to the emergency room, only to wipe out Jack's life, all his money, possessions, everything without so much as a "Do you mind?" Jack was killed off and Bodie was born. Durand had given him a new name, tattooed crap on his arm and set up his identity before his head was even clear of the morphine.

Lex turned to him. "I say we send Chantal close-ups of the ink so she can discreetly research the symbols and the specifics of the spell on the hill. And that means no posting the tats on a Durand board for input."

Chantal wrinkled her nose and set her mouth in a pout. "Why not?"

Bodie remembered Adrien's warning of a security leak. "Adrien told us to stay clear of DT for a while. No hurry on the research. I've had these for three years. Another couple weeks won't make any difference."

"Gotcha." Chantal nodded and leaned back in her seat. "Nice meeting you, Bodie. If you ever get to Australia, look me up. You both should come visit. Lex's other boyfriend was *ordinaire* and rather dense. You're a big improvement."

"Bodie's not my boyfriend," she sputtered. "We're scientists working on a problem of common interest."

Chantal winked. "Sure, sweetie. Whatever. Got to go. Cheers." And the screen went dark.

With exaggerated flourish, Lex retrieved her ComDev and reconnected the monitor to Bodie's laptop. Her hands fumbled when she snapped photos of his tats and sent them to Chantal. Good. She was nervous. Exactly where he wanted her. Now it was time for some answers.

"Have you known all along that I'm a revenant?"

Her expression resigned, she settled into her chair. "Since you took off your sunglasses in the Talos that first day. The silver eyes were unmistakable."

"You mean you know other revenants?" The word sounded ominous to him.

"Only one and before you ask, he's never spoken of what happened or what it's like being a revenant. Asking is taboo. He wears tinted contact lenses except on rare occasions with family."

"So he's a Durand."

"Yeah." Her fingers picked at the case of her ComDev until she caught him staring at them and stilled. "Chantal and I've told you what we know. Your eyes turn silver and you're susceptible to possession. You can see ghosts and spirits and they're generally extremely hostile toward you because you came back and they didn't. Whatever psychic abilities you had before you died are seriously ramped up. That's all I know." Her gaze never directly met his.

"How was I brought back to life? What did this *powerful psychic* do to me?"

She met his glare. "I don't know. He pays a price, too, but I have no idea how that works either."

"Try again. The truth this time."

Color rose in her cheeks and fire flashed in her eyes. "That is the truth! Do you really think the Durand are so

196

irresponsible we'd make that kind of power available to just anyone? Aside from the Durand Sentier, only a handful of Protectors have ever had that knowledge."

"Go on."

She took a deep breath, her breasts rising under the snug tank top. "There are legends of revenants among the Navajo, Pitjantjatjara, and Shalamov but I've never heard those confirmed. The Dissemblers generally favor death over resurrection, but for a good reason—who knows what they'll do?"

"Just like your brother."

Her eyes narrowed. "Whatever grudge you have against Mark is your business. Just remember—he could have let you die."

Teeth clenched, he felt his anger rise. "He got something out of it or he wouldn't have brought me back."

"So what? Get over it and move on." She shot to her feet and he followed so quickly her hands flew to his chest to keep from falling into him.

She glared up at him and slowly withdrew her hands. "If I was in your place—alive instead of dead—I wouldn't be bitching about the details."

Adrenaline coursed through him. "You have no idea what I've been through. I lost everything and now someone's blown up my boat. Even the clothes on my back are borrowed from your brother. And you expect me to be grateful?"

She didn't flinch. "After we find the laser, we'll get you another boat if that's what you want. Or a house. Or a fortress."

"We? No way your brother's going to control where I live or what I do ever again."

"I have resources of my own. Considerable resources

from my share of Durand Tech. I'll help you and you won't have to deal with Mark if you don't want to."

"I don't want your charity."

"Reparation. Not charity." Standing, their faces were close. Her voice dropped and softened. "You helped me. Let me make things right."

Her eyes flicked to his mouth and her teeth grazed her bottom lip.

His body responded with a surge of need. "Why would you do that?"

"Because the Dissemblers probably found you in Road Town because they were watching me," she said. "I owe you a new boat."

"We'll see. The laser's still out there. Until I find it..."

"*We* find it."

He couldn't argue with her anymore. His nerves were raw with frustration and having her in his airspace was making it worse.

Her breasts rose and fell with every warm breath. Her skin smelled like honeysuckle soap and sea breezes, and her lips, full and pink, parted slightly mere inches from his. He desperately wanted to kiss her. All he had to do was drop his head just a little.

He jerked back. "Unbelievable."

"What?" Her startled expression told him she'd expected to be kissed. Fat chance he was falling for that again.

He shook his head. "We find the laser and I'm gone."

"But I'll—"

He raised his palm at her and headed for his room. "I don't care. I'm done."

"Bodie. Don't you dare walk away from me."

Yeah. He dared. He shoved the bedroom door open and slammed it behind him. His pulse pounded in his ears and *revenant* echoed in his head. And Lex had known all along and said nothing.

His hands fisted and itched to punch something. When had his life spun so far out of his control? He paced back and forth in the dimly lit room. The laser was his concept and his responsibility and once it was dismantled, the Durands were out of his life for good. Unfortunately, all he had left was this weird revenant shit, some creepy tattoos, and a price on his head.

There was a knock on the bedroom door.

"Go away," he growled.

The door opened and Lex came in.

He glared at her. "Get out."

"We need to talk, Bodie."

"We talked. I'm done being lied to and manipulated."

Slowly she approached him. "I never meant to hurt you."

She came closer and he raised his hand to stop her. The muscles in his arms quivered with outrage. "This isn't *hurt*, princess. This is royally pissed off."

"I know. I'm sorry."

The pain in her eyes almost convinced him she was sincere until she took the final step toward him and rested her hand on his chest. He grabbed her wrist, yanked her hand away and held it roughly between them. Her pulse throbbed wildly against his fingers but she didn't flinch.

"Trust me, you want to use the door. Now."

The pink tip of her tongue moistened her lips and sent a charge of lust to his groin. "Or what?"

"You won't like it."

Her eyes darkened and a smile played at the corners of that lush mouth. "I'll take that risk."

Teeth clenched, he tried to ignore his raging hard-on. He

let her wrist go. "You've got five seconds to change your mind. One. Two. Three..."

She studied his face and didn't move.

Was he really going to do this? "Four."

Uncertainty flickered in her eyes and was replaced with challenge. "Five," she said.

The last of his restraint dissolved. His mouth came down on hers and she drew a sharp breath. If she pushed him away, he'd let her go. But she leaned into him instead and opened her lips to his kiss. Her tongue tasted like wine and honey and within a moment she slid her arms around his neck and kissed him back. He devoured her mouth, every part of him responding to the sweetness of her, to the way she pressed herself along his body. He needed more—skin against skin. To touch and taste every glorious inch of her until she was mindless with the pleasure he gave her.

His arm went around her and lifted her off her feet. Without breaking the kiss she wrapped her legs around his hips and pressed her heated sex against his erection. He groaned deep in his chest, his hands cupping her firm ass. God, she felt good—firm and soft at the same time.

Her teeth grazed his lips and her tongue dueled with his, driving him crazy. The luscious scent of her filled his head and he couldn't stop himself from taking what she offered—her mouth, her body, passion he'd never wanted before.

He laid her on the bed and pulled the tank top over her head. The vision of her full breasts barely contained in a yellow lace half-bra nearly undid him. His hands trembled as he slid her shorts down her hips and his breath caught at the sight of the matching thong—a tiny lace confection that didn't so much cover her sex as point the way to the heat he wanted to sink into and claim for his own. His cock kicked against the zipper of his shorts, impatient to be in her. Mind over body, he fought for control.

Straddling her, he slid his hands slowly up her body and down again. Her skin was like velvet under his calloused palms. Her chest rose and fell more quickly as she stretched beneath him.

"I've wanted to feel your hands on me," she said.

Exactly what he'd wanted. Badly. Her nipples pebbled under the sheer fabric of her bra and he bent to tease them with his mouth and his teeth then pulled down the cups to give him access to naked flesh. Her skin was so soft and sweet against his tongue.

Lex moaned and arched her back to offer herself to him. "More."

His pulse spiked. She didn't have to ask twice. He removed her bra and gave her breasts the attention they deserved then nuzzled his way down her stomach to the fragile thong. The piece of lace was all there was between his mouth and her heat. Brute force would remove the barrier but he couldn't destroy the pretty little thing because it was hers. Instead he drew it slowly down her legs and tossed it on the floor. Gently nudging her thighs, he swallowed hard as she opened herself to him. His heart pounded. His for the taking. And yet he wanted much more from her than a fast fuck. He met her eyes and her nostrils flared.

"Undress so I can look at you," she said.

Without breaking their connection, he yanked his shirt over his head and dropped his shorts.

Her gaze slid down his body and her breath caught when it landed at his hips. She reached out to him. "I want to touch you."

Catching her wrists, he held them over her head in one

hand and stretched out next to her on the bed. "Not if you want this to last more than five seconds. First let me..." He almost said "make love to you" and caught himself. He'd never used those words in his life. "Let me take care of you."

Before she could protest he covered her mouth with a searing kiss. His free hand slid up the soft skin over her ribs to caress her breast and then snaked down to stroke her sex. Wet and hot.

She moaned into his mouth sending a charge directly to his cock.

"Is this what you want, princess?" Shifting, his mouth moved to her breasts. She opened further to him as he stroked and teased her with his fingers. Her hips jacked off the bed against his hand.

"God, Bodie, don't stop!"

Flushed, lips parted, eyes closed, her face stunned him with its beauty. Her chest rose and fell in quick succession and the pulse at her neck pounded. He leaned his mouth close to her ear. "We're just getting started."

The musky scent of her arousal was making him crazy. He released her wrists and slowly made his way down her body, kissing and licking her hard, flat stomach. God, he loved the way her body moved beneath his hands and mouth like she couldn't get enough of his touch. And the soft purr of pleasure deep in her throat nearly undid him.

Every cell in his body craved her. Settling between her legs he gazed down on her possessively. At this moment she was his—naked and aroused—and the need to make her come roared inside him.

He bent his head and swirled his tongue around sensitive flesh. He didn't think he could go slowly now, and he didn't want to. Her muscles stiffened and she gasped. That was when he felt the delphic swirling around them, lifting his awareness of his body and hers beyond anything he'd ever imagined. Their hearts beat in unison, blood pumped in the same ebb and flow, their nerves surged with the same electrical impulse. She moaned and the sound echoed in his groin.

He smiled, his eyes never leaving hers when he swept his tongue where it would give her greatest pleasure.

Her hips lifted off the bed. "Oh, God."

Without breaking their gaze, he pinned her hips with his hands and made love to her with his lips and tongue and teeth, memorizing her response to everything he did to her to learn what drove her higher.

"Come for me, sweetheart," he murmured. "Let me feel you."

A moment later, her body bucked and convulsed, shuddering again and again while he worked her to draw out the orgasm.

"Bodie! Please," she panted. "I need you in me."

Her words shattered the last of his control and his body took over. He moved up and over her and with a single stroke he entered her to the hilt. She was hot and wet and tight around him, and his hips began to move. Her legs went around his waist and she caught his rhythm. With each powerful stroke he claimed her and she claimed him. Sweat ran down his chest, making the skin between them slick. His orgasm was barreling down on him but he wouldn't let himself go.

The delphic churned around them as if it were alive. Sensation magnified a hundredfold until he'd swear he was inside Lex's skin, not just her body. There was no boundary between them, nothing to mark where he ended and she began. A corner of his brain knew she was projecting what she felt to him and he wanted to share what he felt with her.

Their combined pleasure overwhelmed him, but he wanted every bit of it.

Her hands clutched his shoulders, holding on to take him even deeper. Another stroke and another, he thrust into her until she threw her head back and cried out, taking him with her. Powerless over their combined senses, he barreled over the edge with a roar that shook the windows and rocked his world. His release went on and on with an intensity he'd never felt before. Under him she held on, moving her hips in the perfect tempo to draw out their pleasure.

Finally spent, he went still, dropped his head to the pillow next to her cheek and rested his weight on his forearms so as not to crush her. His chest pounded and his breath came in shallow pants. Her rough breathing matched his and her legs held him in place deep inside her. He was still hard, and, hell, that wasn't changing any time soon.

As his pulse rate slowed, the delphic gradually calmed and their psychic connection dissolved, leaving behind an unfamiliar tenderness.

"I like the way you make love," she said softly against his ear.

He lifted his head and brushed her lips with his. "Back at you."

23

Oxley stared at the tall, dark-haired man looming behind the Boss and clenched his hands to still the trembling. The Boss was intimidating. The other man took scary to a whole new level.

The alarm indicating an approaching boat sounded well after midnight and had just as quickly gone silent. The security cameras had all shut down simultaneously. No supply boat was scheduled for the night. He and Henri had waited for several minutes listening. The walls of the bunkers seemed to close in on them, the claustrophobia Oxley struggled to keep at bay crying out that they could be trapped. The fear in Henri Sardou's eyes mirrored his own growing panic. In silent agreement they'd clambered up the stairway and out into the night.

Instantly he'd recognized the change in the atmosphere, a chilling fog descending on the island although there was no visual indication of the cold heaviness that filled his lungs. And then he saw the boat, no, the black mass of a submarine at the edge of the pier and two men standing in the moonlight waiting.

The Boss had called out to him and he'd exhaled in relief. Now with the Boss and the stranger standing in front of him, Oxley re-evaluated his situation and decided he was in deep shit.

"We're here to observe the next test of the laser," the Boss said.

Oxley tried to clear his throat and found his mouth had gone dry. "Of course. I need to replace the lens first. Would you like to go down to the lab? Can Henri get you a drink while you wait?"

"We'll watch you change the lens," the tall man said.

That voice. It filled Oxley with awe and fear. He stared at the stranger, mesmerized. Now that his eyes had fully adjusted to the night he could see that the man was younger than he'd first appeared—late thirties, early forties at the most. His dark hair was long and pulled back from a high, unlined forehead. He wore a black long-sleeved shirt and fitted trousers that looked to be from a different era. So who the fuck was this guy?

"That's not your concern," the man said. "You may call me *Senhor*."

The Boss barked a quick laugh before he caught himself.

Senhor glanced at him, a dark brow arching, before returning his attention to Oxley. "The lens? You have one hour. Do not waste it."

Something inside Oxley had shifted and clouded his thoughts. He shook his head to clear it, not very successfully. "Sure. I'll get the lens and be right back."

He hurried to the bunker and took the steps two at a time. Henri sat at a computer, his attention glued to the screen.

"Do you know who that man is?" Oxley asked.

Henri shook his head violently and said something that

sounded like an incantation in rapid patois. Right, he didn't know the guy and that was why he was scared shitless.

Without pressing the issue, Oxley found the lens and headed back for the surface where the Boss and Senhor squatted next to the laser portal. He slowed. Why had these two come here now? In all the time he'd been on the island, the Boss had only visited three times—all in the first year. To show up unannounced with this fierce companion at such a critical time in the project didn't bode well. Then again, the other tests of the laser had gone perfectly. There was no reason this one wouldn't too.

He knelt next to the aluminum portal cover and cranked it open with a hand crank. The light from his mag-light reflected off of the shattered lens. Now for the tricky part, removing the crystal without dropping shards into the laser itself. He took a clean piece of cloth from his pocket and was about to extract the crystal when a flash of light temporarily blinded him. When he blinked, the crystal was gone. "What the f...?"

"Install the new crystal," Senhor ordered. "You're trying my patience."

Working quickly, Oxley set the lens in place and adjusted the tiny clips that held it firmly. "It's ready for the test," he said and stood up.

"Good. You will now show us how the equipment operates," Senhor said. "Your target is Fallen Jerusalem in the British Virgins."

An island? "I'm not sure it's ready for a land mass."

Senhor turned the full force of his glare on Oxley. "I haven't invested three years and millions of dollars to fuck around with whales and dolphins. You do what I say or I replace you with someone who will."

The hackles reared on Oxley's back. Who the hell did

this asshole think he was to threaten to take away Oxley's breakthrough work? Replace him? No way. He wasn't stupid enough to record all the details of his invention in his records. Key pieces existed only in his mind and as far as he was concerned this Senhor could go fuck himself.

With a quick glance at Senhor, the Boss stepped back. "Fool."

The pain hit every cell of Oxley's body at once and he screamed in agony. The blood froze and then boiled in his veins. His brain throbbed as though it would explode and his skin crackled. Through the pain he saw Senhor's face, expressionless, and he threw himself at the man's feet.

"Please. I'm sorry. Make it stop," he pleaded.

"Why should I?"

"I'll do anything you want."

A low, otherworldly laugh echoed in the darkness.

He was about to die. He wanted to die.

THE FUNNY THING WAS, Oxley didn't mind sharing his brain. It was a little weird at first but not driving for a change allowed him to sit back and watch the show. Sure, the Other asked a lot of questions but Oxley kind of liked the camaraderie. Okay, it wasn't exactly a cozy kind of sharing but it sure beat being dead.

Change of plans, the Other told him. *There's a dive boat off the coast of Anegada just here.*

Oxley watched his own finger point to a flashing dot on the monitor screen. Weird.

Pay attention, the Other roared.

"Yes, sir." Oxley's reply echoed off the hard surfaces of the bunker. Glancing around, he located the Boss through an archway lounging in a chair in what passed for a living room. No Henri in sight. "What do we use for coordinates?"

With no effort on his part, his fingers danced across the keyboard and he recognized the target as a cell phone. Very cool. He suddenly had control of his hands again.

Give us a demonstration of the laser.

Oxley felt a rush of panic. He'd never collected the energy on his own before. Henri had always been there with the majik to guide him and help him focus it. Without Henri, he didn't have the power to make the laser work. "I need to call Henri," he said.

No, you don't. The power will come as you need it.

Right. How was *that* going to work?

A spear of fire rammed through his head and his cry filled the bunker.

Never question me, his brain-mate roared.

"Please. I won't," he sobbed. Had he not been sitting, he would have collapsed on the floor. And then the pain dissolved as quickly as it started. He took a deep breath. "I may need some guidance."

Proceed. You'll have all the power you need.

24

Dawn glowed through the open curtains. Lex pulled the pillow over her head and rolled over. She tried to drift back to sleep to resume the luscious dream. Bodie's scent, earth and his distinctive musk, saturated the pillow and sheets and made her want him again. She reached for him but he was gone. Her eyes sprang open and she jerked into full consciousness. She was in Bodie's room, in his bed, and all alone.

A sharp buzzing went off somewhere then stopped. The heavy thumping of bare feet on wood and some colorful profanities triggered her memory. The sensor had picked up something.

She spotted her shorts and tank on the floor, grabbed them and dressed on her way to the door.

Bodie sat in front of the laptop in gym shorts squinting at the screen. "Come see this."

She crossed to the table and stood behind him. The hybrid map showed the same area they'd looked at the night before. Now a sharp purple line bisected the screen from a point northeast of Anguilla to the reef southeast of

Anegada. At the north end of the line was a blood red spot of orphic.

"Is the purple line the laser's path?" she asked.

"Yeah. The sensor records intense delphic energy in purple since that color can't exist in orphic. The beam only flashed for a few seconds but the scanner picked it up as we'd hoped." His fingertip went to the line's origin in what looked like open water and he zoomed in on a tiny island. "Know this place?"

"It looks like Sombrero. Nobody lives there. It's just a rock with an unmanned lighthouse, lizards, and a lot of boobie and noddy guano."

His head came around. "*What?*"

"Seabird shit."

He chuckled. "So how about we go take a look?"

"There's no beach, just steep cliffs that drop fifteen, twenty feet to rocks and rough water. We'd need a helicopter to land and I don't have one of those handy."

"We could fly over and see what's down there."

"If we saw something, we couldn't land." Her ComDev would tell them if there were any humans on the island, but if they waited until Victor arrived, he'd be able to do a telepathic scan and find out who was down there and what they were up to. "My cousin Victor should be here later today. Maybe we should wait for him?"

"Why?"

Tricky question to answer without revealing Victor's abilities. "Another set of eyes."

He rolled his eyes. "Try again."

"He also has a helicopter license."

"We're wasting time. While you're flying, I'll go online and try to find out what the target was."

"Fine. Get dressed. We can drop Earl off with the Ariel crew on our way out."

Thirty minutes later, they'd showered, dressed, and were ready to head for Silverbelle. Lex's ComDev played David's ringtone. She answered it. "What's up?"

"I just got a call from the Aurora," David replied. "Mike and Dante were on a night dive last night with the Argos crew on a reef south of Anegada and now the boat's disappeared. No communication, nothing, just vanished."

A heavy dread dropped in her stomach and she had to sit down. "Vanished? Do you know when the last communication with the dive boat was?"

Bodie's head came up and his eyes widened. She had his full attention.

"Midnight or so. Our guys had had a few beers and called in to say they were spending the night. When the Aurora sent a Zodiac for them this morning, the Argos was gone—no radio or cell response."

"*Merde*. What about a search party?"

"We called the Marine Police and the Aurora is searching the area. They could use you and Silverbelle."

"Absolutely," she said, although she doubted there was anything to find. "We'll be at the dock in fifteen minutes."

"You're not taking him." Not a question.

"If you mean Bodie, yes, I am taking him." Out of the corner of her eye, she caught Bodie's half-smile. "We'll stay clear of the authorities." With that the smile faded.

"Lex, the truth, are you all right or are you in some kind of trouble?" David's voice was full of concern. "Do you need help? Just say yes if you do."

"No." At least not the kind of trouble David meant. The danger the delphic laser and the Dissemblers posed fell in a category way beyond David's definition of trouble. "Bodie has Durand Tech equipment that could help in the search. We'll stay in touch with you and the authorities until we find the Argos."

The likelihood the dive boat would reappear the way the dolphins had was only a little bit more positive than it disappearing like Poseidon and the whales. She couldn't worry yet about how being sucked into the red orphic spot might affect the minds of the people on board.

"I'm expecting my cousin Victor sometime today. I'll text him to hold tight with the Ariel if I'm not back."

"We're not going anywhere. Chuy's still out there and the team wants to observe the rest of the pod for a few days. "

"Good idea. I'll be in touch." She tapped END and set her cell back on the counter. Behind her Bodie was already packing up his electronics. Taking a deep breath, she turned around.

"A dive boat disappeared off the south side of Anegada with two of our crew aboard," she said. "The marine police and the Aurora are out looking for it."

"Exactly where the laser hit. A direct assault this time," he said grimly. "As long as they stuck to whales and dolphins, they flew below the radar. Picking a good-sized boat full of humans as a target means they think they're undetectable."

"Or unstoppable. So what do we do?"

"We check out the origin to see if the laser equipment is still there and keep the sensor scanning for a blip that would indicate the boat popping back into this plane. Even if the boat reappears, the divers who went over may be dead, alive and crazy, or even just gone."

A knot in her chest tightened. "Who would do something like this and why?"

He zipped his canvas bag. "Sick fuckers."

She shuddered.

He pulled her into his arms and kissed her softly. "It's going to be all right. We know where the laser originated and we're going to stop them."

"I can't help but feel this is personal," she said. "I think someone's targeting the Foundation using our electronics to aim that laser. First the trackers on Poseidon and the dolphins, now perhaps the crews' cells. The Ariel or Aurora could be next."

He hoisted the strap of his bag onto his shoulder. "Then we have to find them before they strike again."

LEX EASED off the control wheel and flipped to electrical power. The engine noise died and Silverbelle leveled off.

"Are you sure you want to do this?" Bodie asked. "Get caught with me and you'll be in big trouble."

"I'm a very highly trained soldier, remember? Besides, I like you in one piece."

"You don't owe me anything, Lex."

"Look, if this is about last night, I know the difference between mind-blowing sex and a relationship. As hot as you are, Bodie, when the current crisis is over, I understand we'll go our separate ways. Neither of us has to explain or look back."

He peered at her over his sunglasses. "Hot, huh?"

Warmth crept up her cheeks. "Like you don't know it. Jesus, my point is..."

"Got it—mind-blowing sex, no strings attached. Anything else?"

"That's it." She turned back to the view out the windshield. "Picking up any color anomalies?"

"Nothing in the ocean between Anguilla and Anegada. Without a baseline map, it's hard to tell about the islands. There are always yellow shadows here and there, even an orange spot now and then. We need to concentrate on what we know—that someone on Sombrero has a Delphic laser and has no moral issue with using it on humans."

"Should we let Adrien know about the missing divers?" she asked.

The muscle in his jaw tightened. "He's your boss, not mine. What if he tells you not to go to Sombrero?"

"He wouldn't do that." Still, she couldn't chance him telling her to wait for Victor. "Okay, we don't call him yet, but if we find the laser he needs to know."

Although Bodie nodded, she got the feeling he wasn't totally on board.

Ten minutes later, a flat white rock with a lighthouse appeared on the surface of the Caribbean.

"There it is," Lex said. "Doesn't look like much, does it?"

Binoculars pressed to his eyes, he scanned the island as the seaplane approached it. "How low can you get?"

She was already taking the plane lower. "A hundred feet or so. I'll circle around so you can check it out." Not that there was anywhere for someone to hide aside from the lighthouse. The structures from the nineteenth-century mining operations had been long since washed away by hurricanes.

The glare of the sun reflected off the white phosphorous surface, making the island seem to glow. Even with her high-tech sunglass lenses, it was nearly impossible to pick out any details.

"Not exactly a garden spot, is it?" Bodie said. "The lighthouse looks abandoned. No doors or windows, just stone and concrete with a metal roof."

She banked the plane to come around for another pass.

"Look. Down to the left," he exclaimed. "There's a square white panel of some kind almost flush with the surface. Six-by-six at least. What do you want to bet it's a hatch?"

"A hatch to what?"

"A bunker of some kind. We need to land and check it out."

"How's that supposed to work? If I land in all this chop, we'll smash up as soon as we get close to the rock cliffs. And how do you expect to climb the faces without any equipment?"

"You land and keep the seaplane off the rocks while I swim to shore. There's got to be some erosion or a rough section somewhere. Fly the perimeter and let's see what we've got."

"We've got coral, rock and heavy currents," she observed. "You'll be ripped up and carried away before you have to worry about climbing any wall."

"How did they do it? Helicopter?"

"Too noisy and high profile if they wanted to keep this place secret. Boats make more sense except for the tricky landing issue. Maybe they had a temporary dock of some kind and took it with them."

Using her ComDev he scanned the island for human life forces. "It's deserted."

"Damn. We're too late."

"Yes, but they were here as recently as this morning. I need to see what they left behind."

And she didn't want to wait in the plane while he went exploring. Unfortunately, without a secure mooring or a safe place to anchor, she couldn't risk leaving Silverbelle.

"I don't have a good feeling about this. Just because you saw some square board in the guano, doesn't mean there's anything under it. We could be risking the plane and your life for nothing. Victor will be here later today. Between his helicopter license and formidable powers of persuasion he can convince the authorities to let him borrow one of the police copters and bring us back before nightfall."

"Are the authorities going to look the other way when I hop in and buckle up? Don't think so." He tucked the sensor into the bag behind her seat and picked up the binoculars again. "These people used my theories to develop their weapon. Nobody else will see what I can. I need to be the one who goes in."

How many times had she gone into an unknown dangerous situation? Dozens. And yet this time felt different. Sure, Bodie was more than capable of taking care of himself, but she wanted to be there in case he needed her.

As they circled the island, she studied the edge where it dropped into the sea. "I'm not cool with this."

"Take that cannon of yours, will you? I've got waterproof bags in the back."

"Who would I shoot, an aggressive booby? Better it stays with you in case we have visitors. There are probably surveillance cameras watching us."

This situation just kept getting better.

"Whoa," he said. "Can you come around again? I think I see something in the water where that flat rock stands up on the edge."

She spotted the landmark and brought the plane around and down for a close look. Sure enough, the sunlight glinted off a metal object in the deep blue water.

"There," he said. "There's something under the surface next to the cliff face. It could be a dock."

"Or a boat. Wrecks still happen out here. I'll take us down and you check it out." Now that they'd found *something*, a surge of adrenaline pumped through her. She landed the seaplane on the choppy surface and glided to within twenty meters of the rock cliff. From the water, the face looked to be about fifteen vertical feet of crumbling limestone and coral —not as long a drop as other parts of the island but steep and treacherous enough to discourage casual visitors.

Bodie pulled his shirt over his head and folded it. "I'll take whatever waterproof pouches you have, a crow bar, rope, life preserver, and the small Berretta."

"In the back. Help yourself. I'll keep Silverbelle off the rocks."

He got out and climbed back in the rear door to pack up what he needed. She handed him his ComDev, shirt, and a towel which he dropped into one of the bags before securing all the items in a mesh dive bag.

His eyes locked on hers and she saw a tenderness there that kicked her in the chest.

He pulled on a dive mask and was gone.

As soon as Bodie hit the water, the current tossed him toward open sea. He kicked as hard as he could and shifted the nylon strap of the dive bag so he could use his arms more effectively. Nevertheless, he didn't seem to be making much headway. The life preserver restricted the movement of his left arm until he pushed it over his shoulder to hang off his back. *Come on, man, you're a good swimmer. Focus and use your full body strength.*

Arm over arm, kicking hard, he finally caught his rhythm. Then it was less than a minute until he looked down on what he'd spied from above—a modern structure not five feet under the surface. When he stood up on it, he was only chest deep in water. So far, so good.

Ducking below the surface, he checked out the platform. The island side appeared to have a collapsible section of pipe and wood stacked accordion style. Steps? There must be some control mechanism. He stood and examined the wall of stone. It didn't make sense to have the controls underwater where they'd quickly corrode.

Searching the wall, he looked for any oddity in the rocky surface. Someplace reachable from a boat would be most likely. A couple feet above the waterline he saw it—a coral block that looked a little too even. The sharp edges bit into his fingers as he gently tugged on it then, when it didn't budge, yanked harder. The block released with a pop and *hello, baby*, he was looking at three simple switches. And, what do you know, someone had left the key in the center one.

"Abracadabra," he muttered and turned the key. A motor hummed softly in the wall but the dock didn't move until he threw the two toggle switches. Slowly the platform rose out of the water and steps unfolded upward until they were almost even with the surface of the island.

Hoisting his bag back on his shoulder, he donned his shades, tied the life preserver to the frame of the stairs and began climbing. The morning sun blazed down on his head and shoulders drying the salt water on his skin. At the top of the stairs he paused to pull on his shirt and survey the stark landscape before him. With so much white, the island appeared to be lit from within, and the metallic odor of baked bird shit assaulted his nose. Even with sunglasses, the glare softened details and made it difficult to bring them into focus. Great place to hide out. Lex was certain there was no one on the island. He hoped she was right. Otherwise his ass was in deep trouble.

Using the lighthouse and the dock to get his bearings, he searched for the raised square he'd spotted from above. It had been halfway between the lighthouse and the shoreline south of where they'd landed. Pulling his baseball cap lower on his forehead, he paced out what felt like half the distance to the island's only structure and turned right.

There it was. Ten yards away a painted square rose from a plane of pale guano. His ComDev buzzed and he answered.

"Nice trick with the dock," Lex said. "Find anything else?"

"Not sure."

"What are you waiting for?"

"I'm talking to you."

"Put me on speaker and tuck the ComDev into your shirt pocket. I'm dying to know what you found."

"Yes, ma'am." As he strode forward, he described what he saw. His new psychic shield gave him a sense of safety he didn't understand. "This is a weird place. I can feel *espectros* nearby but they're concentrated on the other side of the island."

"There was a slave uprising there in the 1800s. Just stay with the program."

The *program* now lay at his feet. He bent to tug on one side. "It's a metal lid." One edge was hinged. He lifted the opposite side and the hatch opened easily, revealing industrial metal stairs that descended into darkness. A rush of cool air hit him from the hole.

"Bingo!" he said. "There's an underground bunker. I'm going down."

"Be careful. It could be booby-trapped."

No shit. "Roger that." He pulled a flashlight from the dive bag and the pistol from its waterproof pouch. He tested the first step before giving it his full weight. It didn't move. When his foot hit the third step, the lights went on below.

"A-fucking-mazing," he breathed and clattered down the rest of the stairs.

"What? Talk to me."

"It's a bomb shelter on steroids." He quickly passed through the rooms to be sure he was alone, while assuming the place was under surveillance by hidden cameras. "Two bedrooms, two bathrooms, a living room, kitchen, and mission control. Furniture is still here but looks like the tech stuff was ripped off the walls and packed up in a hurry." A lot of tech equipment from the number of dangling wires.

"So the laser did originate there?" Lex asked.

He opened the door to what appeared to be a storage closet and found it empty except for some wires, a couple two-by-two boards and an assortment of screws scattered on the floor. "Our data says it did but I don't think we'll find much to prove it."

Surveying what was left of the tech center of the operation, he wondered how many people had worked there. In spite of the multiple workstations, there were only three chairs—sleek high-tech chairs on wheels.

"So what do you think of our little home away from home?" a disembodied voice asked.

Startled, Bodie whirled around. A workstation sat on a counter in a dark corner of the room. As he watched, the monitor came to life and a man's face and shoulders appeared—an albino who looked vaguely familiar.

"Left in a hurry, didn't you?" Bodie asked.

"Who are you talking to?" Lex asked.

"Some guy on a monitor. I'll explain later."

"Too bad she has to wait in her seaplane," the man said. "Although I'm glad we can have this little talk just between us, Jack."

Goosebumps rose on his skin at the use of his real name with such familiarity. "Do I know you?"

On the screen the ghostly thin lips narrowed to a sharp line. "You're still an arrogant bastard, aren't you?"

Still? Creepy, angry, and not a fan. Bodie tried to remember where he'd seen the guy before. If he was the one who had built the delphic laser, most likely their paths had crossed at Princeton. Yeah. He vaguely remembered a pale nerdy guy who used to sit on the edge of late night, beer-induced arguments between the young turks of the science and math departments. "You were at Princeton, weren't you?"

"The great Jack Wilson," the man sneered. "So much potential pissed away while I've made discoveries that will change the world."

"The delphic laser." He noticed a red light blinking on a tiny camera attached to the monitor. He rolled up one of the chairs and parked it in front of the screen. "I abandoned that line of research for a reason."

"Hit a wall, did you? Or wait, did that wall hit you?" the guy chuckled. "I enjoyed the photos, by the way. Looked like you took a shitload of lead. Even the pros pegged you for dead."

Who the hell was this guy? Bodie tried to remember his name. A strange one, something starting with an O? Orville? Oakley? Oxley. Shit, that was it. He was sure he'd never known his last name but it wouldn't be hard to track down an Oxley at Princeton.

"So how did you get recruited to the Dark Side, Oxley?" he asked.

The white face pinked noticeably. "So you do remember me." He smiled. "A top secret government agency approached me and offered labs, equipment, personnel—anything I wanted to develop the Disruptor, or the delphic laser as you called it."

"And they gave you this hip bachelor pad in the middle of the Caribbean. This place must be quite the hit with the local babes."

"Fuck you, Wilson," Oxley snarled.

Bodie fought a smile. Nevertheless, there was a more serious issue to deal with. Behind Oxley he made out what looked like the inside of a luxury villa. "I like your new digs. Looks like you've come up in the world."

"Everything I want at my disposal," Oxley said. "House on the beach, gourmet food, servants, first class lab. You should try it sometime."

"All on the American taxpayer's dime?" Bodie asked.

"Yo, we've got company," Lex hissed. "Local gendarmes. Stay put."

Before he could reply, her call clicked off.

Oxley chuckled. "You heard the lady, Jack. Wouldn't want you arrested just when we're getting reacquainted."

Bodie knew Lex was more than capable of taking care of herself, but leaving her to deal with the authorities alone felt wrong. On the other hand, being wanted for questioning by the BVI authorities didn't exactly make him an asset.

"Don't worry, it's just the Anguillan version of the Coast Guard," Oxley said.

"You've got cameras."

"Everywhere." Oxley leaned into the webcam and the image fish-eyed, distorting his face grotesquely. "I'll let you know if she takes off and leaves you."

"Let's talk about the Argos. Is it coming back?"

A flinch ticked the guy's cheek near his left eye. "I guess you'll find out."

The asshole didn't know, he'd bet on it. That meant his control of the laser was limited to disappearing things. "So you're still in the testing stage."

"Oh, we're functional." A quick shifting of the eyes. "But I don't want to ruin the surprise. Just between us, if you play your cards right, you'll have a front row seat."

Another attack, but where? He needed more info. "Come on. At least a hint."

Oxley shook his head. Behind him, a man stepped into the room through a glass door. The intense outside light threw him into a silhouette that filled the doorway and obscured his features in darkness.

"Who's your friend?" Bodie asked.

Oxley whirled around. "Shit."

As the figure approached the camera it dwarfed Oxley. "Leave us now," a voice deep ordered.

When Oxley glanced quickly back at the monitor, the webcam caught the fear in his eyes. His lips pressed together tightly, then with a quick nod he vacated his seat and scurried out of sight.

The man moved into the light. His angular features sharpened and there was a strange sheen to his skin that couldn't be from any reflected light. His long black hair was pulled tightly back from a gaunt face and secured behind his head.

Bodie recognized him instantly. They'd only met once, on a crowded train from Princeton into New York, but that hour was etched in Bodie's memory like it was yesterday. The man had been nearly as tall as Bodie and a commiserative shrug in the tight space had prompted a conversation.

He'd introduced himself as Narciso Valmor, a Brazilian businessman. "Well, well. Look who it is."

The man smiled coldly. "I'd looked forward to seeing you again, Joaquim. The news of your death grieved me."

"I'll bet." If Oxley was working for the government, then this guy probably had a hand in ordering his murder. "So who are you? And don't waste my time lying."

"My name is Tolian. Perhaps you've heard of me."

"Sorry. Doesn't ring a bell. Should it?"

"In your association with the Durand—Mark Durand in particular—my name might have come up. You made a grave mistake declining my invitation to dinner that evening and meeting with him instead. He was using you from the beginning and I was your only avenue of escape."

"Really." Even through the monitor, the dark intensity of Tolian's stare made him uncomfortable. "Is that why you had me assassinated?"

Tolian scowled. "Not me, incompetent *camponeses*. The last thing I wanted was for you to be killed, leaving me with no one but that sniveling albino to continue your work."

"He didn't continue my work, he perverted my theory and created a dangerous weapon. I would never have done that."

"You would have done whatever I told you and believed it to be your own idea—just as you did for Mark Durand. Durand had you build his sensor. I would have gotten my Disruptor."

"The sensor was my idea," Bodie snapped. "Not Mark's."

"For a brilliant man, you're very stupid, Joaquim. Don't you know that Durand is a master telepath? From the first time you met, he knew everything you were thinking. He manipulated your thoughts and perceptions to his own ends without you ever knowing. And when the *tolos* shot you, he used his psychic power to bring you back to life as a revenant so you could continue to serve him."

"Bullshit." And yet too much of what Tolian said he already knew to be true. But did that mean that even his thoughts weren't his own, and hadn't been since their first meeting? Tolian was screwing with his head.

"Think back," Tolian continued. "He has answers before you know you have questions and you've never wondered why because he didn't want you to."

Bodie bristled. "Twenty-four hours after I arrived in Road Town someone boarded my boat looking for my equipment. Was it your people?"

"How can you be sure Durand wasn't behind the Talos sinking? Maybe he sent some poor unsuspecting fool onboard knowing the boat would blow up and you'd be at his mercy again. He's killed men for his own gain before."

As much as Bodie didn't like Mark Durand, the guy would have no reason to blow up a boat he'd outfitted himself. Lex had told him the intruder was a Dissembler— the enemy of the Durand. Why would she lie to him? On the other hand, she must know her brother had been reading his mind for years. While she was being so damned honest and helpful, she'd left out that critical bit of intel.

"Okay, for the sake of argument, let's say Durand did set me up," Bodie said. "Who are you and what do you want?"

Tolian's slow smile turned Bodie's stomach. "I'm the Hi'aiti'ihi' Sentier, Adrien Durand's counterpart for the Brazilian Source. I'm sure you know where that is. It is after all your motherland."

"I'm American. Never even been to Brazil."

"Hi'aiti'ihi' energy is in your blood. Your mother returned to Brazil many years ago. A formidable priestess and still a beautiful woman, if a little high strung."

"My mother is dead." Bodie didn't know if this was true literally, but the murderous witch had been dead to him for over twenty-five years and that made it true. He sensed this Sentier's manipulation and turned the subject away from himself. "So what does a Sentier do?"

"I command the *Guardiões* who fight the Durand aggressors in their mission to control the world's resources. The Durand empire has infiltrated every government, industry, and culture on earth, taking what they want and brainwashing the *camponeses*—or as they call them, *ordinaires*—into believing their activities are altruistic. We fight for freedom and self-determination."

Bodie was getting a few too many ominous vibes from this guy to buy the "freedom and self-determination" line. The back of his neck prickled. "So you're the good guys?"

Tolian's chuckle held no humor. "There are no *good guys*, Joaquim, only the choice of which bad guys' interests most closely align with yours. I can give you complete freedom and unlimited resources to pursue whatever research and inventions you wish. You can come and go as you please, live as you want, where you want."

"And what do you get in return?"

Tolian shrugged. "We can work that out."

"What do you want?"

"I'll pay you well to perfect the laser and I'm sure we can negotiate a satisfactory deal for the sensor you invented for Durand Tech. After that—it's up to you. You'll be a very rich man."

"What guarantee do I have that once you have the laser and the sensor, you won't kill me?"

"I don't waste resources. You have a technical genius that won't stop inventing and your ability to sense psychic energy will make you one of the most valuable of my *Conselheiros*. We both benefit."

Bodie knew the *benefit* would be stacked in Tolian's favor. Lex had told him the Dissemblers used mind control. It was safe to assume Tolian was as powerful as he claimed Mark was and would use that power to his own ends. If Bodie's new shield really did protect him from psychic intrusion, both Tolian and Mark were in for a surprise. Was he ready to trust Lex's assurances or was she just another cog in the Durand machine?

"I need some time to think about your offer," Bodie said. "How do I contact you?"

"Give me your cell number and I'll send you instructions."

Bodie shook his head. No way was he giving this guy his ComDev code. "No. I'll contact you."

Tolian's mouth thinned but he recited a string of numbers. "Don't think too long. I've promised Oxley another target at midnight, a big one this time, and I wouldn't want you to miss having a front row seat."

"What kind of target?"

"I've been torn between the Ariel and the Aurora. Have a preference?"

"Neither."

"Of course, you're right. One call from Ms. Durand and the boats would be evacuated and the demonstration wasted. No, we should go for the grand gesture—a cruise ship would be much better."

Thousands of people. "You can't be serious."

Tolian's expression turned stony. "I can be whatever I choose. Decide, Joaquim. I'll expect to hear from you in one hour."

Bodie's pulse jumped. He needed more information. "Where are you? How do I get there?"

Tolian shook his head. "I'll send a boat for you. Or better yet, Miss Durand can deliver you and you can deliver her."

"Where?"

"One hour."

25

Mark watched as the doctor tucked Luke Benally's bandaged arm under the crisp white sheet. The rear of the Gulfstream mid-flight wasn't the best place to tend to a critically injured man, but Luke was still alive, on his way to the trauma center in Houston.

"How is he?"

Mark turned to Tanner Hays, the Protector on the other bed. "He'll make it."

Luke would live, but his arms, hands, and legs had been brutally crushed by the drug lord who had held the two Protectors in his dungeons for the past three weeks.

"Thanks for carrying him out," Tanner said. "I couldn't have done it."

Mark patted his shoulder gently. "Yes, you could have." It wasn't true and they both knew it; Tanner had been beaten so badly his back oozed from the lashes and he could barely walk. His face had fared no better judging from an eye swollen closed, a broken nose, and a nasty cut down his cheek between his eye and his jaw which had festered with infection.

Tanner's fingers closed around his wrist. "You risked your life to get us out of that hellhole. The Mexicans would have killed us, but the Dissemblers just kept up the torture knowing when to let up before we died."

Mark closed his hand over Tanner's. "It's over. Get some sleep. We'll be in Houston soon."

Mark went back to the front of the plane and eased into a cream leather seat. A hot shower had cleaned off the grime and the bandage on his shoulder took care of an inconvenient knife wound he'd acquired along the way. He threw back a shot of tequila to ease the pain but it failed to burn the guilt from his gut. It didn't matter that Luke and Tanner had volunteered to infiltrate the cartel, he'd sent them in there and they'd never be whole again.

He wished he could sleep. Instead he turned on his laptop and pulled up his messages. They were prioritized and the one at the top was from Adrien. *Call me immediately.* It was eight hours old. He knew Adrien disapproved of his second-in-command taking on the riskiest missions. His cousin also misunderstood Mark's need to constantly push himself. If there was some other way to keep the darkness under control, he wouldn't need the adrenaline rush. There wasn't. Besides, they both knew Mark's deadly gift was the reason he survived against impossible odds.

He quickly scanned down the list. Four messages from Lex, two from Bodie, all variations on *Call me ASAP.* Not a good sign. A five-hour-old S.O.S. from a key Protector stationed in Somalia caught his attention, a life and death crisis that would have to be handled with paramilitary intervention. The violence in Africa had escalated, fueled by a new wave of Dissembler recruits. Adrien would have gotten a heads up on that Mayday and handled it already, which brought him back to the top message on the list.

His ComDev buzzed and he answered it. "Hey, I was about to call you."

"How'd the mission go?" Adrien asked.

"Everyone got out alive."

"Good."

Although they had few secrets, Mark rarely burdened the Sentier with details. The big-picture Protector strategy was clear and they'd discussed the growing drug violence in Mexico as well as the likelihood Dissemblers were involved. Both accepted Mark's willingness to cross the line when necessary, even if Adrien preferred the moral high ground.

"And you left the head honcho and two Dissemblers dead by stroke, huh?" Adrien said.

"The Dissemblers will make sure the local police never hear about the deaths but Tolian will recognize my handiwork."

Adrien didn't comment. Although the Durand Sentiers and the Brazilian Sentiers had been enemies for centuries, the hatred between Mark and Tolian was personal.

"Bodie thinks he's figured out the disturbance in the Caribbean," Adrien said.

As he related his conversation with Lex and Bodie, Mark pulled up a map of the islands showing the current location of Lex's ComDev and the tracer in Bodie. "Any idea why my sister's floating off a rock in the middle of nowhere?"

"None," Adrien said. "Last we talked, Bodie was setting up his sensor to constantly monitor the Caribbean. He must have picked up laser activity."

"I'll call her." He studied the screen of his laptop. Lex wasn't moving and neither was Bodie. "I'll get back to you after I talk to Lex."

"Do that."

Mark tapped the screen of his ComDev and listened to the ring tone.

"I'm kind of busy here," Lex hissed.

"Doing what?"

A choking sound preceded her reply. "Mark?"

"Yeah. Where are you and what's going on?"

Her voice came through in a rough whisper. "Off Sombrero Island trying to get rid of the Anguillan Navy so Bodie can come out of hiding. Just a sec. Hey, guys, really, I'm fine. He'll be back any time now with the guano and we'll be off. No need to wait. I'll radio if there's any problem."

After a few seconds of silence he took for the ship's reply, Lex called to them, "Thanks. See you guys around." She cleared her throat. "Thought they'd never leave."

"Guano?" he asked.

"Sombrero's uninhabited except for about a million birds. I told them one of my team went ashore to gather guano samples."

"I talked to A," he said. "Any sign of the laser?"

She brought him up to speed on the Argos and why they'd come to Sombrero, including the conversation she'd overheard between Bodie and Oxley. "I told Bodie to hold tight until I called back. He's probably doing some techie thing in that bunker waiting on me."

While she talked, Mark searched his database for "Oxley, Princeton." Results came instantly. Hard worker, ambitious, smart but not brilliant. *Ordinaire*, therefore controllable. The guy had worked for a division of the National Geospatial-Intelligence Agency before dropping out of sight nearly three years ago—not long after Jack Wilson's death. Dissemblers infiltrated most of the government's covert operations so Cowan's defection to the dark side was a logical progression.

"Bodie needs to find that laser," Mark said. "When he figures out where it is, contact me and I'll send in Protectors to seize it."

"Like a military operation? How do you plan to keep a conflict on that scale under the radar? No. We've come this far, we'll go in."

"This is too big for you, and Bodie isn't equipped to fight Dissemblers."

"So we're supposed to watch from the sidelines? Bodie will recognize the laser if he sees it. You have to send us with the team at least."

"No, and that's a direct order."

Her silence vibrated with rebellion. "I'm a Protector, too, and First Order Durand. Are you telling me I'm not strong enough to face these Dissemblers?"

"Finding the laser is dangerous enough. You'll do as ordered, is that clear?"

The plane bumped down on the runway, jolting his shoulder and sending a bolt of pain through his body. He grunted and gritted his teeth.

"Is that clear, Lex?" he repeated before he realized the line was dead.

26

"Sorry about that," Lex muttered and tossed her ComDev on the passenger seat. There was no way she was going to tell Bodie to find the laser so a swat team of Protectors could steal it from him. They were going to find it together and bring it back together. If Mark didn't like it, he could fire her.

She started the electric motors that controlled the propellers on Silverbelle's pontoons and headed for the dock. Tying up might be tricky with the current and surge jostling the seaplane, but she'd managed worse and the dock looked sturdy. As she glided toward the structure, Bodie appeared at the top of the stairs.

"Be careful," he shouted down to her.

Like she hadn't figured that out. The seaplane bobbed in the waves a few yards from the pier, its wing coming precariously close to banging on the wooden platform. If she could get the front of the pontoon close enough, he could come aboard without having to risk another swim. He clamored down the metal steps and stuffed the waterproof bags into the net dive bag as he crossed the dock.

"How close do I have to get for you to jump?" she called to him.

"Six feet? Closer would be better."

"Get ready." She took a deep breath, eased forward and prayed the plane wouldn't be tossed into the platform. The surge lifted the stern, then the bow, rocking the plane so violently the front propellers popped out of the water. For a split second she lost the ability to steer.

The seaplane shuddered with the impact of Bodie's 240 pounds landing on the pontoon. "Go," he shouted.

She slammed the propellers into reverse and backed into open water while he side-stepped to the passenger door and climbed in.

"Nice driving," he said. "I wasn't looking forward to the swim back out."

"So what did I miss?"

He fixed her with an odd stare. "What makes you think you missed anything?"

His tone held an edge. Something was wrong. "You went on shore and I didn't. What was in that bunker? Who is this Oxley guy? Did you find anything that could lead us to the laser?"

He glanced away and she recognized the stubborn set of his mouth. She wasn't going to let him hold out information on her. She turned on the electric propellers on the pontoon and steered Silverbelle away from the dock.

"Bodie, we can stay here all day but I'm not taking off until you fill me in. Your choice."

"You tell me something first."

"Okay..."

"What kind of psychic abilities does Mark have? Besides raising me from the dead?"

Shit. "One of the most basic rules of the Durand is that

no one is permitted to reveal anyone else's abilities, even to other Protectors. We only know what we witness, need to know, or are told by the person himself or herself."

"I need to know."

"Why are you asking me this now?"

"Answer my question. How hard is that?"

Impossible. "I don't have the authority to discuss Mark. You'll have to ask him yourself."

His laugh rang with bitterness. "But that confidentiality only goes one way, doesn't it? He told you everything there was to know about me, didn't he?"

"No, actually. He told me he thought you could help find the whales and said you were in Fat Dog. That's it. He didn't tell me you were a revenant, or about any of your history together.

Oh, and he said you were a genius," she added. "He didn't mention you were also an unreasonable son-of-a-bitch."

"Better unreasonable than a liar."

"I never lied to you!"

"Lies of omission. Same thing."

"What the hell are you talking about?"

"Mark has been reading my mind and controlling my thoughts ever since we met. Want to deny it?"

Her heart stopped and her throat closed until she couldn't breathe. Who was this Oxley that he knew all about her brother? "No, I won't deny it and I won't confirm it either. I can't. Where did you hear this?"

He folded his arms across his chest. "Sorry. You don't talk then neither do I."

"I can't." A wave lifted the seaplane and she adjusted the controls to keep from burying a pontoon.

"Bullshit."

She bit her lip and turned to look out her side window. Why did their relationship have to come down to a choice between family duty and honesty? At least with *ordinaires*, she'd known from the start she could never even tell them about her own abilities. With Bodie she'd shared who she was and stupidly forgotten the larger Durand factor.

She turned back to face him. "You have a shield now. No one can read your mind or emotions, control your thoughts, or project any psychic directive on you. I also gave you the means to use your ability to direct energy. If you want to blame me for doing my duty to the Protectors and my family, go ahead."

His expression remained stony. "You expect me to forget all the ways your brother used me?"

"I expect you to work with me to find the goddamn laser before this Oxley guy uses it again." He flinched and she took that as a good sign. "We steal it or destroy it—your choice—and then you can go on your way."

"Steal it," he said. "I want to see how it works before I dismantle it."

"Fine."

"And you don't tell Mark what we're doing."

"He just called. He told me to help you find the laser so he could send Protectors for it."

"Son of a bitch. So I'm on my own."

"We're on our own. I told him no Protectors. We'll find it and you'll decide what happens to it."

"You told your brother no?"

She shrugged. "Not exactly. He gave me a direct order and I hung up on him."

He ran his hand over the top of his head. "Christ. He'll kill us both."

"What happened in there? What aren't you telling me?"

"I have work to do if I'm going to locate the laser. Where's the closest island we can set up the scanners and laptops discreetly?"

"I'm part of this, Bodie. My ass is on the line right along with yours. Either tell me what happened in that bunker, or I'll drop you off in Road Town and let you take your chances with the authorities. Your choice."

She squinted at the horizon to the north and spotted the Anguillan cruiser heading back in their direction. Damn. They needed to get out of there and fast. With a flick of a switch, Silverbelle's engine came to life. "The coast guard's on its way back. We're going to have to fight somewhere else."

She taxied the seaplane across the chop until it had enough speed to rise from the water. When it reached 1,500 feet, she leveled off, switched to electrical power, and considered her options. They couldn't return to the BVI as long as the authorities were looking for Bodie.

She glanced at him in the passenger seat where he bent over his handheld sensor in rigid concentration.

"Head south," he said. "You sure there aren't other seaplanes in this area?"

"Pretty sure. There's commercial service between St. Croix and St. Thomas but that's it. Occasionally a yacht shows up with a helicopter. Why?"

"I was wondering how Oxley got off Sombrero and how far he might have gotten since the laser attack if it took an hour to dismantle and pack up the equipment."

"In these seas, a cigarette boat could make it to Anguilla in an hour, then he could catch a plane from there," she said. "There aren't many commercial flights but a small private prop plane could get in and out pretty easily without calling attention."

"So in four hours, he could be anywhere."

"Only if the operation was well organized and heavily funded. Logistics in this part of the world tend to be a challenge which is why I have Silverbelle. If the guy's already settled in, my educated guess would put him within one-hundred-fifty miles of Sombrero. Two-fifty max."

"Wherever he was, it wasn't his place. It seemed tropical, expensive, and established. A house on the beach with a lab. Definitely not a hotel."

"Okay. That's something to work from, I guess. Anything else you remember?"

He shifted in his seat but didn't look at her. "After you hung up, Oxley's boss showed up wanting to chat. I met him years ago on the train to New York when I was going to the city to meet Mark."

Lex's stomach dropped. "Do you know his name?"

"When we first met, he introduced himself as Narciso Valmor. Ever heard of him?" He glanced up and she felt his gaze on her.

She thought for a few seconds. "Name's not familiar."

"What about Tolian?"

The blood froze in her veins. Not Tolian. Anyone but Tolian. "He's the Hi'aiti'ihi' Sentier, the Commander of the Dissemblers. Does this Valmor work for him?"

"Valmor is him, or so he said. He knew a lot about your brother and Adrien—that they're telepaths and Mark has been using mind control on me for years. Is that true?"

"Okay. Yes, they're telepaths but no one used you. They're the good guys."

He snorted. "Tolian also wants me to come work for him."

"You can't! He's pure evil."

"That's what he said about Mark and the Durand. I'm inclined to at least keep an open mind about his offer."

"Mark never asked you to do anything morally wrong, did he?"

Bodie shrugged. "Who knows how his people at Durand Tech altered my discoveries to his ends? He used me."

"And Tolian massacres anyone who gets in his way—men, women, children. Imagine the worst, most powerful spells and magic a Santeria priestess can do then multiple that by a thousand. And Tolian doesn't need props—he can do those things with his mind."

He flinched but didn't reply.

She had to make him understand. "His mission is to create chaos through fear and violence so his Dissemblers can step in and take control. Wars, drug violence, oppression, genocide, mass murder—that's what they do."

He turned from her and the muscles in his clenched jaw twitched. "Where are we going?"

"Bodie, I'm telling you the truth. Look at what Oxley did to the Argos—twenty-six people gone. That was just the beginning."

"Where are we going?" he repeated.

Railing at him wasn't going to change his mind, only facts and hard evidence would do that. She studied the screen on the dashboard. The British Virgins were out of the question. Ahead lay Prickly Pear Cays and Anguilla, and beyond that St. Martin and St. Barts. Ideally, she preferred to take the seaplane down in protected water with a sandy beach and good anchorage. Silverbelle was far from inconspicuous, so a remote cove would work to their advantage.

"It depends on how fast you want to get there. Prickly

Pear Cays is about thirty miles, Ile Tintamarre's about forty, and St. Barts is sixty," she said.

"Prickly Pear will do. Is it inhabited?"

"A couple beach bars for the day-trippers."

"Fine." He focused his attention back on his sensor screen.

She remembered the disturbance he'd felt the night before. "Last night when you sensed the odd orphic on the hill, could it have been a person?"

"A week ago I would have said no. After finding the red orphic in the dolphins, I have to say it's possible. The problem is, how would a human absorb the energy?"

"Dissemblers use majik along with their psychic abilities to control *ordinaires*. You've seen majik yourself, so you know a powerful wielder can manipulate the physical as well as paranormal world."

"So?"

She took a deep breath. "I sense majik and majik residue as a smell and even a taste, sort of like how you sense orphic and delphic. When a Dissembler is nearby, his energy taints the air and vibrations around him so a Protector knows when he encounters the enemy."

She had his attention now.

"If this majik changes energy in any way, why don't I feel it?" he asked.

"Are you sure you don't? You can distinguish blue orphic from green or yellow or orange. Maybe we just have a different baseline perception of the same thing."

He nodded. "Possible, I guess."

Encouraged, she continued. "Okay. So maybe if you track subtle trails through the orphic, we can figure out where..." She almost said Tolian, then reconsidered. "Where Oxley and the laser went."

"What do you think I've been doing?" he asked, then softened his tone. "You fly and I'll do my job."

She nodded. Her gut told her he was holding out on her and unless they worked together there wasn't a chance in hell they'd find the laser and make it out alive.

27

Lex set her leather bag on the table where Bodie was already working. The sea was choppy so most of the day-trippers had passed on a boat excursion to Prickly Pear Cay today. Two hundred US dollars had secured the back section of the palm-thatched pavilion, lunch, and a heavy-duty extension cord for as long as they needed it.

"What can I do?" she asked.

"Boot up your laptop and the other monitor. I need a bigger screen and the time-lapse orphic progression to compare with current data."

She did as he asked then settled on the bench across from him. Her ComDev buzzed—Mark's particular buzz. Every Protector and sisterly instinct told her to answer his call but she didn't. Glancing up, her gaze locked with Bodie's. Neither of them moved. What seemed like an eternity later the buzzing stopped and she released the breath she'd been holding. He returned to his work and several seconds later a musical note sounded to tell her Mark had sent her a text. Did getting a message qualify as contact? She was going with *no* on that.

Don't do anything stupid.

A little late, bro. Almost everything she'd done since Bodie showed up in Road Town had been stupid. Still, she couldn't regret any of it. And she'd stick it out with him until he had the laser and left her. She deleted the text.

BODIE TAPPED out a text message on his ComDev. *I'm willing to negotiate.* The device would obscure the source of the text while allowing Tolian to reply.

Within seconds the response came back. *You and the sensor here before sunset. I'll send transport to pick you up.*

Getting on Tolian's boat with the sensor didn't sound very smart, but he couldn't put Lex in any more danger. *What about the cruise ship?*

Up to you. There will be a demonstration. Bring me the sensor and you can pick the target.

Maybe for this test, but it was just a matter of time before a lot of people died. The only way to stop Tolian for good was to destroy the laser. *Target Sombrero Island.*

As you wish. Where will my boat pick you up?

North beach of Prickly Pear Cay.

2 hours. Be there.

An order or confirmation? Probably both. He plugged his ComDev into his laptop and tried to trace the origin of the texts. After a few minutes of bouncing around the world, he gave up. Maybe Durand Tech could trace the messages but he was on his own and intended to keep it that way.

"Tolian?" she asked.

"A boat will be here in two hours."

"What are you going to do?"

"Find where the laser is before then."

The screen in the middle of his improvised network showed the orphic energy for a radius of two-hundred-fifty miles around Sombrero Island. He had run his scans beginning the previous afternoon in time-lapse progression and studied all the fluctuations that might indicate a flow of negativity. The yellow trail between Anguilla and Sombrero had faded by dawn and other pockets of yellow and orange on land corresponded with towns and cities where he expected some degree of violence and vice.

The problem was there were too many square miles to scan and too many variables that affected the energy. He decided to eliminate Puerto Rico and the U.S. Virgin Islands, not because Oxley couldn't be there, simply because there was too much orphic activity to detect any changes that might be significant. Transportation was the next factor he considered. He'd checked the commercial flights out of Anguilla and found they were mostly to nearby islands. If Tolian planned for him to be at the next laser demonstration, then a boat and perhaps private plane were the obvious options. He shrunk his radius to a hundred miles and re-ran the scans beginning with the moment the Argos disappeared.

"There's got to be a clue here," he said in frustration.

She cleared her throat. "I was thinking. The laser uses delphic, not orphic, right?"

"Yeah, why?"

"The primary ability of a Sentier is to channel and control the delphic of his Source."

Now she had his attention. He leaned back in his chair. "Okay."

"What if we're looking for the wrong energy? You're looking for a change in the orphic but Tolian's all about delphic and so is the laser."

"But the scanners picked up the yellow trail from Anguilla to Sombrero a few hours before the laser was used."

She shrugged. "I'm not saying there's no relationship between the Dissemblers and the orphic change. I'm guessing their presence is responsible. I'm just suggesting it could be more productive to track Tolian by his delphic footprint than his orphic."

"It's worth a try. Otherwise I have to get on that boat."

Pain crossed her face. "You aren't seriously thinking of defecting."

The more he considered, the surer he was that agreeing to work for Tolian would be delivering himself into a form of slavery, even ignoring his moral objections to how the laser had been used so far. Going back to work for Mark Durand might not be an option, but neither was signing on with the Brazilian Sentier.

"I'm going to stop any further misuse of my intellectual property and if I survive, I'm washing my hands of both sides—the Durand and the Dissemblers. It's your war, not mine."

"It's everybody's war even if most of the world doesn't know it."

"Then we better get back to work." He re-started the scan history and angled the screen for her to see. "I'm going to filter out all the blue and green orphic and enhance all delphic energy over fourth degree."

The map changed colors from a muddy mix of shades of yellow, orange, and brown to waves of lavender, pink, and purple.

Lex scooted her chair closer. "The purple is delphic, right?"

"Yup. The only color orphic can't be."

"And delphic energy is stationary, right?"

"Right. Unless someone is messing with it. I'm filtering out the baseline map of delphic so we can see if anything's new."

Most of the purple faded away. Not all of it. His pulse spiked. He clicked on satellite view, zoomed in on the deep purple spot, and stared at the screen for several seconds. A complex came into focus not a hundred yards from the water on the south shore of St. Barthélemy, aka St. Barts, aka the Caribbean playground of the ultra-rich.

"Not exactly a Third World location," Lex said. "Think it's Tolian?"

It made sense. Oxley had mentioned a beach and lab. No one would notice private planes, yachts, or expensive speedboats, and privacy was almost a religion among the wealthy. "I guess I'll find out."

"*We'll* find out." She began packing up her gear.

He synced the coordinates of the compound to his ComDev and shut the lid of his laptop. "I can't let you come."

Her eyes widened. "Can't *let* me come? Are you kidding?"

"It's too dangerous."

"I'm a Protector. You won't have a chance in hell of getting in there and back out alive, much less with the laser, without me."

She was probably right but it didn't matter. Putting her life in danger wasn't an option. Even without Mark's threat, the possibility of Lex being hurt or killed because of him wrenched his gut. "I can take care of myself."

Her body stiffened and trembled with outrage. "Against Tolian and a bunch of Dissemblers? You'd never even heard

248

of the Sentier or the majik wielders until a couple days ago. I've trained all my life to fight them."

A fierce surge of protectiveness stunned him. "Too bad. Tolian told me to bring you. He wants you under his control. If you walk into his trap, he'll have a weapon to use against the Durand. Not to mention what he could do to you."

She scowled at him and shook her head. "This isn't my first mission. I can handle it."

"No."

"Suit yourself." She stood up and piled the plates. "The way I see it you have two choices. You can sit here and wait for Tolian's goons to come for you, or we can take Silverbelle and go to him. Me, I like to have my own ride when it's time to go home. But if you're going over to the dark side, guess that won't be a problem."

"I'm not going over to the dark side. All I want is to stop any further use of the laser and there isn't much time."

"How do you know?" She planted her fists on her hips and pressed her lips into a tight line. "Let's have it all."

"The next demonstration comes at midnight. A bigger target this time. At first he threatened the Ariel and Aurora, then upped the target to a cruise ship."

"The laser can do that?"

"I don't see why not if it took the Argos."

She reached for her ComDev and tapped the screen. A moment later David answered.

"Evacuate both the Ariel and Aurora immediately," she barked.

"Why?" David asked.

"Just do it. Put everyone up at the best hotels available on my credit card and make them stay there until I give the all clear." Her voice was calm and authoritative but a faint pink in her cheeks and neck betrayed her anxiety.

"Does this have anything to do with Flynn?" David asked.

"No. We got wind of a terrorist threat and I want to be sure our people are safe. I'll be in touch." She clicked off before David could press for specifics, and blew out a deep breath. "I don't trust Tolian not to take out my boats just for the hell of it. If they're on his radar, they're vulnerable. So how do we find out which cruise ship?"

"We don't. We find the laser."

"Then we better get going." She hoisted her leather equipment bag on her shoulder. "I'll go pull up anchor and motor to shore to pick you up."

"When the boat arrives and I'm gone, he'll know we're coming."

"Probably," she said with a smile. "Doesn't change a damned thing."

AN HOUR later they approached the entrance to Gustavia harbor. Huge motor yachts floated amongst sailboats and powerboats. A three-masted ketch—wooden hull and all the latest rigging—caught Bodie's eye.

He whistled. "Talk about serious boats. Maybe I'll replace the Talos with one of these babies."

If he lived that long. They'd discussed strategy during the flight and agreed that dropping onto the beach in front of Tolian's compound might be heavy on moxie but made them sitting ducks. A more subtle land approach under cover of dark was their best chance, which gave them a couple of hours to get into position.

Lex eased Silverbelle into an open space of water between two oversized powerboats and flipped on the motors to the pontoons. The propellers slowed and finally stopped but not before half the eyes in the harbor were on them.

"Hey, Lex!" a young man in a blue uniform called from the deck of one of the yachts.

"Let me guess," Bodie said, "One of your boyfriends."

"Jealous?" she asked with a grin.

"Don't get sidetracked before we get the laser."

"Me? I'm all business on a mission. Even you couldn't distract me."

"Good. So where're you parking this thing?"

She pointed to a low floating dock where several open speedboats were tied up. "We'll pull in there and I'll flash my passport to Henri. You have a passport?"

"Courtesy of Mark. What about customs?"

She peered at him over her sunglasses. "Not for me. You? Maybe."

"So the weapons...?"

"Can you lug the leather dive bag without looking like a hit man?"

"Very funny."

When she climbed out of the cockpit, two young men hurried to take her tote—which held the sensor—and helped her onto the dock. Her gushing thanks that followed drew the two far enough away for him to rearrange the guns, slip a couple grenades into a side pocket, and stuff towels around the weapons so they didn't clink against each other. When he finally lifted the bag out of the back compartment, Lex and her fans had already reached the open-front building with the *Customs* sign hanging from its roof.

Nobody along the pier paid any attention to him, not even the immigration official who was much more interested in chatting with Lex in French than scrutinizing the passport her porter presented. As long as all eyes were on her, he was invisible.

"Anton, cher," she drawled, switching to English and producing her ComDev from her tote. "We're staying with Bodie's uncle on the south shore. Could you tell us the easiest way to get there?" Two taps called the satellite map up on the screen. She held it out to the dapper West Indian who had stamped their passports.

The young man traced a line along the shore. "The best road is here. It is smooth and well maintained."

She pointed to a route over the hills. "What about this one? It looks more direct."

Anton shook his head. "It is paved to the Hotel Bel Soleil, then it gets rough. Some gravel, some dirt, and only a little paving. The shore road is better."

Lex squeezed his hand. "Thanks. The shore road it is then." With a flirty wiggle of her fingers, she took off down the harbor side road, not even looking to see if Bodie was following. He swore under his breath, shifted the heavy bag on his shoulder and trotted after her.

As soon as they turned into a deserted alley, he said, "Quite a performance back there."

"You're not in jail and you still have your arsenal. That *performance* served a purpose."

"Hey, I'm not giving you flack. I guess I'm thanking you."

Her smile warmed something in his chest. "Ahead is the long-term parking lot for people leaving the island by boat or plane. If there's an attendant on duty, we're screwed. If not, pick the sturdiest SUV you can find and hop in like you own it. I'll meet you at the gate and let you out."

"What about keys?"

"They're usually left in the car. Try the floor, the glove

box, above the sun visor. Just be quick. The longer you take..."

"The more likely we are to be caught."

They reached the end of the alley and a parking lot with about fifty cars and SUVs—mostly Mercedes, BMWs, a few Porsches, and a Bentley—all high-end makes. He couldn't imagine the owners leaving their keys in these vehicles.

"Now move," she said and took off toward the gate.

It only took him five seconds to pick out the silver Range Rover and another one to open the driver side door. Unlocked. He shook his head then threw in the bag. A swipe across the floor on the driver's side located the keys. Even in his wild high school days, he'd never stolen a car. His hands began to sweat. What the hell was he doing?

He glanced out the side window and saw Lex wave to him to hurry. Adrenaline rushed through his limbs. They needed to stop Tolian from using the laser. Everything else was unimportant—even an arrest for grand larceny. The key turned easily and the engine roared to life. He shifted into drive and headed for the gate.

Auto theft was now officially on his resume.

"I THINK my fillings have shaken loose," Lex grumbled.

He veered the Range Rover around a hole so long and deep it could qualify as a trench. "I'm doing the best I can. You're the one who wanted to take the scenic road. This is the longest three miles I've ever driven."

She checked her ComDev sat nav. "Only a quarter mile farther."

"That's what you said a half mile ago."

The front wheel ran over another large rock that tipped

the Range Rover to a precarious angle before it slammed down into a dip in the dirt track. Only the seatbelts kept them from being tossed around the cab. The physical punishment had gotten old in the first mile and wasn't getting any better.

If it wasn't for the sunshine and the turquoise sea in the distance, he would have sworn he was driving through the northern tundra. "For a tropical paradise, this place sure is barren and bleak."

No trees or leafy foliage covered the ragged hills, only prickly scrub, rock, and sandy gravel. And to make things worse, the road, pitiful as it was, dead-ended twenty yards ahead.

"We're here," she announced and bounded out the door to a cropping of boulders at the edge of the steep drop at the end of the track.

He surveyed the hills around them, all too aware that the drive this far had been the easiest part of their undertaking.

Using a huge rock for cover, Lex flipped her sunglasses to the top of her head and focused her high-tech binoculars on the scene below. "Not a bad set-up."

He crouched next to her. A luxurious villa compound sat perched on the hillside a hundred-fifty feet down the steep rocky incline. Thirty feet beneath the main house a white beach met the cliff. The enclave was built like a fortress. Thick stone walls surrounded by cactus and bayonet plants would keep out any riff-raff or casual thieves if the terrain didn't do the job. The layout allowed for security cameras, lights, and motion detectors to alert the inhabitants if an intruder managed to get inside.

"Hand me your ComDev," he said.

She did and he opened the app that scanned for life

forces. The screen came up as all static. "I'm not getting a read on how many people are down there."

A crease lined her forehead and her lips pressed together tightly. "Nothing?"

"There seems to be some pattern but not anything distinct."

"This place may be under some kind of psychic bubble that's scrambling individual energy. You picking up anything unusual?"

He opened his senses to the villa below. "Concentrated delphic with swirls of yellow orphic. Explains why we picked this place up on the sensor. So you think Tolian's inside?"

She shrugged. "Good chance he is."

"We still have to go in for the laser."

She nodded behind her binoculars. "Do you have any idea what it looks like? How big it is?"

"No, but Oxley does, and he and Tolian were together a few hours ago. If they could move it, and have it operational by tonight, the thing can't be too big. We find Oxley and we'll get our answers."

"Two guys just came out of the flat-roofed building closest to the back wall. They're having a smoke. The L-shaped building to the right could be a garage for a fleet of tanks."

"Can I have a look?"

She handed him the binoculars and sat back on a flat rock to give him a better view.

He squatted next to her and studied the structures as she spoke. She was right, the garage had a military look about it. The smokers both had dark hair and tan skin—neither was Oxley. "So did this Protector training of yours include covert operations strategy, because if it did, now's the time to speak up."

When she didn't answer, he put down the binoculars and turned to her. She stared at her ComDev, her brow furrowed in an expression of concentration. "There are two life forces in the hill behind the house."

His pulse picked up. Maybe they'd get lucky after all. "Another bunker. So all we need to do is get into it and force Oxley to turn over the laser."

"Without alerting Tolian or his Dissemblers. Not knowing the layout of the compound, we're heading in blind. Tiptoeing around searching for the entrance to the bunker and hoping not to get caught isn't much of a plan."

"If you've got a better one, let's have it."

Mischief danced in her eyes. "You could chuck some of your grenades into the main house and we could shoot anyone who ran out."

"You're crazy."

"He's Tolian. All the odds are in his favor. He's as powerful a psychic as Adrien *and* he's a master of dark majik. Given the chance, I'd shoot him without hesitation."

"In cold blood?"

"Where Tolian is concerned, Durand blood is never cold."

"So we play it by ear. Not a happy prospect." He turned his attention back to the compound. Without a plan, they'd need as much information as they could get before going in. There was a flat area behind the back wall with a gate wide enough to drive a car through. "Think that's a helipad?"

"Could be. The wind shears make landing in these hills difficult but not impossible. There's no dock off the beach and a shore drop here isn't ideal because of the coral heads out there."

"So Tolian's men would probably arrive by car through the front gate."

"Probably." She glanced at her ComDev. "Five-ten. Sunset is in ninety-five minutes. We can assume he knows we landed in Gustavia and is waiting for us. If he sent someone to Prickly Pear for you, we have some time before they get back here. We know there are at least four people in there now—the two smokers and the two in the hill—and the concentrated delphic is probably Tolian. Five-to-two isn't bad odds but I'd rather wait until dark to climb down this hill."

She'd changed into long pants and hiking boots on the way from the harbor. He was still in shorts and boat shoes, not having anything else to wear. Climbing down the hill in the dark didn't excite him. On the other hand, any cover was better than no cover.

"Fine," he said. "You keep watch out here. I have a couple of downloads and some fine-tuning to do on my ComDev before we leave."

"What about the sensor? Are we taking it with us?"

The million dollar question he'd been struggling with since Sombrero. "Do we have a choice? The sensor or thousands of lives—even if it just buys us some time, it's worth giving it to him."

"Is it? He'll destroy lives with the laser, if not tonight, tomorrow or the next day. What advantage will the sensor give him in the long run?"

"None if I set it to wipe clean in six hours. It's got the same auto-destruct feature as our ComDevs. I'll just set it to blow at a specific time instead of activating the fingerprint and voice code lockout the ComDevs use."

She nodded. "Good plan. In six hours we'll be gone or dead."

He trudged back to the Range Rover, reviewing his mental to-do list and wishing they could just drive back to the harbor and fly away. The wind kicked sand up into his eyes and he swore. Why would anyone pay megabucks to live on this god-forsaken side of the island?

He looked around and saw nothing but jagged hills. No other villas or houses of any kind, only the ruin of a sugar mill high on the next hill overlooking the compound—a point that appeared to be the island's tallest peak. Of course the plantation owner would have chosen the highest elevation for his windmill, which was now a round stone tower crumbling against the darkening sky. Tolian had chosen his remote location well.

THE SQUIRT-GUN ICON on his ComDev screen flashed twice, confirming the final app was programmed and functional. Bodie smiled. He'd made improvements to the standard Durand Tech apps and installed a couple handy ones of his own.

"Ready?" Lex asked.

Standing on the other side of the open window, her dark hair was pulled back from her face in a ponytail and her skin glowed with excitement.

He took her face in his hands and kissed her gently. "Let's do this, babe."

They half-crept, half-slid down the steep hillside to the back of the compound. She'd tucked tranquilizer pistols and the Beretta in the oversized pockets of her bush jacket. His backpack was loaded down with all the weapons he could carry and the sensor cushioned in the front panel. Not much fire power to attack a well-defended compound, but better than nothing. When they reached the bottom, they took cover behind a line of yucca plants.

Leaning into her ear, he spoke softly, trying to ignore the familiar honeysuckle scent of her skin. "I can send an interference signal with my ComDev to freeze the images on the surveillance cameras covering the helipad entrance. We'll have ten seconds max before the cameras auto-reset. I assume you can disarm the gate."

She grinned and lifted her own device. "Standard Protector enhancement. Just say when."

"On three we run for the gate. One, two, three." Together they rose and tore out across the helipad. Just as they reached the gate, the first couple notes of David's ringtone sounded. Lex swore under her breath and cut them off.

"The gate," Bodie whispered sharply.

"One second...."

They didn't have a second. His heart pounded. They were out of time.

The lock clicked and she yanked the gate open far enough for them to slip through then eased it closed. Silently they ducked between a tall hibiscus bush and the cinderblock perimeter wall. He took a deep breath and slowly let it out.

"Sorry," she whispered. "Calls still override my apps. I haven't gotten around to downloading a fix."

"At least put it on vibrate so your social life doesn't get us killed."

She flicked the switch on her ComDev and slipped it into her breast pocket. "See anyone?"

"No." The compound was quiet. No alarm had sounded and no one came outside to investigate. His skin prickled from the odd blend of delphic and orphic shimmering around them. This delphic had a distinctive taste and smell much different from the neutral energy he'd always experienced before. He reinforced his shield but the energy cocktail still set his teeth on edge.

"Picking up anyone in there?" he asked and pointed to the long narrow building to their right.

"Yeah. ComDev's not blocked here. Interesting. Two people. First floor at the other end."

Silently they passed the huge open walls, careful to use the lush foliage as cover. Sure enough, at the far end of the building two dark-skinned men sat in front of a big screen TV engrossed in a soccer match.

"This is too easy," she said. "If they turn around distract them."

She tiptoed into the room and raised the tranquilizer gun. Pop, pop. Both men slumped in their armchairs. Two down. Bodie joined her in the lounge and they rearranged the Dissemblers so from the outside path they appeared to be watching the screen. A quick search confirmed this building was guest quarters—living room, kitchenette, four bedrooms and baths. If access to the bunker was here, it was well concealed.

"There's nothing in there," she said as they stepped out into the shadows of the courtyard. "Tolian's the ultimate control freak. If the research is important to him, he'll regulate who comes and goes from the lab. I can't see him putting the entrance in the garage or an outbuilding."

"So we go in the villa."

She hesitated. "It's too quiet."

Creepy quiet, but standing outside speculating wasn't getting them any closer to Oxley or the laser. His ComDev could read high concentrations of metal and electronics. He tapped the app and slowly scanned the villa. The device detected electronic activity in what he guessed was the main living area and a combination of metal and electronics in the wing toward the back closest to the hill.

"This way." He stepped out of the shadows and raced across the open courtyard. The back of the villa was open to the night, the vast kitchen with its monstrous stainless steel appliances empty and dimly lit. He cursed softly. "So much for fancy apps. Let's look around anyhow."

He started toward the front of the villa and she caught his arm.

Her hand was cold and her grip firm. She leaned into him and pointed toward a thin line of light on the far wall. "There's another room behind that panel. What about surveillance cameras?"

He flashed his ComDev in a 360-degree arc, watching the screen. "None in the living quarters but what do we have here? Bingo. Cameras and alarms dead ahead. Good going, princess."

Freezing the camera images, he motioned her to stand back. Sure enough the wall of the pantry slid open revealing an elevator.

"It could be a trap," he said.

"Could be. If Tolian knows we're here, he's biding his time catching us. We may have enough lead to locate Oxley but we need to move fast."

He agreed. The open kitchen made them easy targets. "Stand back." Drawing the pistol from the holster under his jacket, he pushed the call button and held his breath. The motor hummed quietly as the car rose and the doors opened. Empty. They got in and he pushed the *B* button. The seconds it took to descend felt like an eternity. When the door opened, they raised their weapons and braced themselves.

The man who stood outside the elevator door stared at

them in surprise. Lex shot him with the tranquilizer gun before he uttered a sound.

"You're quick on the trigger," Bodie said.

"He's a Dissembler. I'm a Protector. If I'm not quick, I'm dead."

They stepped into the corridor and Lex pointed toward a door to their right. "The other person is through there."

"Stay behind me. If it's Oxley, he and I have business."

Slowly he opened the heavy steel door. Beyond was a modern electronics lab, and at a workstation facing the wall sat the pale, white-haired figure of Oxley Cowan. He turned slowly in his chair, a smile spreading on his face when he recognized them.

"You're early, Jack," he said. "And you brought Miss Durand."

Bodie's grip tightened on the cool steel. The little weasel was going to tell him what he wanted to know. He took two long strides and aimed his pistol at Oxley's forehead. "Where's the laser?"

"Still a bully." Ignoring the Beretta, Oxley stood and approached Lex, hand extended. "Since Jack has no manners, let me introduce myself. Dr. Oxley Cowan."

Lex pointed her tranq gun at his chest. "I don't care. We're here for the laser."

He smiled. "Of course you are. What Jack couldn't invent himself, he's going to steal."

Bodie grabbed him by the shoulder and whirled him around. "Only a madman would build a delphic laser, much less use it. I don't know who's crazier, you or your master."

"I have no master," Oxley snarled. "I'm the greatest scientist of our time—far superior to you—and my invention proves it."

Bodie crossed his arms and shook his head dismissively.

"Really? I'm not seeing it. So you built a laser that can zap dolphins and dive boats. Nasty weapon but not a scientific breakthrough. Any kid with a credit card and an internet connection can put together an *invention* that blows things up."

Oxley's pale face pinked. "I do not blow things up."

"Semantics."

"You're a fool. You want to see *semantics*? I'll show you *semantics*." He pulled out a chair, sat down in front of a large monitor and started tapping angrily on the keyboard. A moment later a diagram appeared on the screen. "My design is pure genius."

A low whistle escaped Bodie's lips. The schematics were so simple and efficient he had to admire the design. But something critical was missing. "Impressive. Where does the concentrated delphic come from?"

A rosy flush rushed up Oxley's pale neck and face. "That's classified."

Bodie grinned. "Classified? From who? From you?"

"Of course not!"

Lex lowered her gun. "You can't work the laser on your own, can you? You need Tolian's power to make the laser work."

Oxley glared at her. "I don't need anyone."

She turned to Bodie. "He's lying. He stinks of majik but he's *ordinaire* and can't control any significant delphic on his own."

"Bullshit," Oxley sputtered. "I was the one who sent those goddamned whales into oblivion."

She stepped toward him and Bodie caught her arm. On second thought, he released her, seeing the benefit of letting her beat the intel they needed out of the obnoxious twerp. She caught Oxley by the throat and his eyes widened.

"Patience isn't my strong suit," she said. "Answer Bodie's question. Where does the concentrated delphic come from?"

"It doesn't matter. You can't control it anyhow."

Bodie gestured to Lex to let him go. "Then why not tell us and prove how inadequate we are? Or better yet, show us how it works."

Oxley rubbed his neck and glared at Lex. "I'm not telling you shit."

"Wrong answer." Lex landed a quick blow to the side of his head and momentarily stunned him. "Want to try that again?"

Oxley rubbed his ear and glanced from her to Bodie.

"Show us the laser and how it works or we can go for round two," she said.

Oxley's thought process played out on his face. Was he more afraid of the pain Lex inflicted or Tolian's anger? He sucked in a breath.

"It only gets worse," Bodie told him, and noting the trembling of the guy's hands, added, "She's really good at this."

"I might as well tell you. You can't control the energy and he'll never let you out of here alive." Oxley cleared his throat. "They do it with some kind of majik. Tolian can do it with his mind alone."

"Tell us exactly how the integration between the psychic manipulation and the technology works," Bodie demanded.

Oxley barked out a nervous laugh and dropped back into the chair in front of the workstation. "It's genius and totally beyond anything you ever imagined."

The monitor transformed into a picture showing a design in three dimensions. The laser itself was remote to the controls—installed in the ruins of the sugar mill high on the hill behind the villa. It was the ideal vantage point to hit any target within a two hundred-seventy degree radius. But Bodie still wasn't seeing how the energy got from a human source to the laser.

"We're wasting time," Lex said. "Let's just destroy the damned thing and get the hell out of here."

Cowan shuddered and his expression transformed into a cold mask. When he spoke the tenor of his voice deepened and held the hint of an accent. "You're too late, Miss Durand."

Lex swore.

The delphic energy in the room took on a rancid tang that sent a wave of nausea through Bodie's gut until he consciously blocked it. "What is it?"

She readjusted the gun in her hand. "Dr. Cowan isn't alone, are you?"

"How perceptive. Surely you didn't think Joaquim's little tricks with the security system would allow you to enter undetected."

The hair stood up on the back of Bodie's neck. "Where's the laser itself? Show us where it is or you're a dead man."

A deep voice filled the room. "Shoot him if you like. He's dreadfully annoying."

Oxley fish-mouthed his objections then froze, entranced.

Bodie and Lex turned in unison to face the newcomer, hands on their ComDevs and weapons at the ready.

Tolian filled the doorway. Almost as tall and broad as Bodie, he exuded power and menace. Even from twenty-five feet away, Bodie's stomach roiled from the tainted orphic energy vibrating off the man's body, charging the air.

"Who will operate the laser if he's dead?" Bodie asked.

Tolian's smile was hard and cruel. "I can, Henri can,

although he may not be available for our evening demonstration thanks to Miss Durand's stun gun. Dr. Cowan grossly overestimated his own contribution and never could operate it on his own."

Bodie glanced at Lex who stared at Tolian in silence. Her stillness worried him. Her ComDev hit the floor with a crash that startled their host and reminded Bodie to lockout his own device. In Tolian's hands, an operational ComDev could be a formidable weapon against the Durand.

"Put your weapons down. They're useless against me, as Miss Durand must know."

"Only if you can stop us pulling the trigger," she said. "And your telepathy can't penetrate our shields."

"Yes, I noticed Joaquim had acquired the defense. Does your brother know his asset has been compromised? Inconvenient but not an insurmountable problem. Once we have an agreement and return to Amazonas, I'm sure Joaquim will see the benefits of joining our side. "

Bodie swallowed hard to control the churning in his gut. "We will never come to an agreement. I want the laser. It's my intellectual property."

Tolian laughed. "Oh, Joaquim. You have no idea what we can do together—you with your science and me with my..." He thought for a moment. "Me with my many talents. I control power the Durands have coveted for centuries. My disciples live and die for a chance to possess just a taste of what I'm offering you."

Beside him Lex stiffened. "Bodie wants no part of your foul, disgusting majik," she spat. "I'm glad I'm the one to stop you."

Bodie saw her pull the trigger of the tranquillizer gun and watched a dart fly out from the barrel. But it never reached its mark. Instead, it fell to the ground at her feet.

"Oh, my," Tolian sneered. "My majik seems to have neutralized your little gun. Joaquim, if you're planning to shoot me too, please get on with it so we can go back to the house and have a drink and a bite to eat. You must be hungry after your wait on the hillside." A flip of his hand and Oxley sputtered back to life.

"Aren't we going to get a tour of the lab?" Lex asked.

But the Brazilian Sentier had already started down a long corridor, toward the villa. "Later," he said, then paused. "Come, Alexis, walk with me and tell me about your Foundation."

She stalked past Bodie and Oxley, who then followed close behind. "No."

Tolian gestured for her to go before him. "Then I insist you do the honors and pick out the cruise ship for our evening entertainment."

28

"I brought you the sensor," Bodie said. "In return, you promised not to use the laser on a cruise ship."

"Did I?"

"Yes, and you need me to unlock it and turn it on."

"I'd expect no less." With a sweep of his arm Tolian gestured for Lex to proceed up a well-lit stone staircase.

Her Protector training kicked in and she memorized the details of the route. No door between the corridor and the stairs, no security cameras, no light switches. Every cell in her body recoiled from the foul energy and stench of majik rolling off Tolian. If there was no way to take him down with conventional weapons, how would they stop him and get to the laser?

The entire villa opened to the outside, a testament to Tolian's confidence in his abilities to secure the complex. If there were security cameras, they were well hidden. Automatically she noted possible escape routes.

"Before we discuss business, we'll have a toast, Oxley," Tolian said with a smile. "Please open a bottle of Dom Pérignon and serve our guests."

"Prisoners," she muttered.

"You did break in to steal my property," Tolian said. "But I'll overlook that detail. After all, you *were* invited."

A cork popped and she flinched. Out of the corner of her eye, she saw the pale scientist shakily pouring champagne into four flutes. Even if they got Oxley alone, Tolian would maintain control of him. She glanced at Bodie, who hadn't moved from his stance, staring out at the sea.

Balancing the tray of glasses, Oxley offered the champagne to her and she shook her head.

"I insist," Tolian commanded. "Joaquim, join us."

Bodie turned and silently strode across the room, his face stony and cold. Having distributed the flutes, Oxley hung back from the group until Tolian waved him forward. Tolian raised his glass. "To the brilliant mind behind the evening's show. A genius that will be remembered for turning the course of history when I finally bring Adrien and Mark Durand to their knees."

"Fat chance," she muttered.

Tolian ignored her and smiled at Bodie. "Welcome home, Joaquim. Together we will destroy the Durand and make the world bow to us."

Before Tolian's champagne reached his lips, Bodie's glass shattered to the floor, shards and champagne raining in all directions.

"Fuck you," Bodie growled and stepped toward their host. "The only reason I'm here is to keep you from murdering innocent people, you son of a bitch."

Rage engulfed the Sentier's face and Bodie flew backwards into the air, overturning an armchair when he landed twenty feet away.

Before Lex could rush to his side, Tolian trapped her arm in a steel grip and stopped her. "I'm no longer amused by either of you. If you need a demonstration of my power, so it shall be."

Bracing on the chair, Bodie pushed himself to his feet. "Let her go and I'll give you whatever you want."

Tolian pulled Lex closer, his fingers biting into her bicep. "You'll both give me whatever I want starting with your Durand communications devices."

"They're locked and can't be unlocked for at least an hour." The S.O.B.'s grip was strong and cruel. She braced herself to bear it. "If we try to bypass the timer, the hardware self-destructs."

Fingernails digging into her flesh, he lifted her to her toes. "Our genius can override the lock-out, can't you, Joaquim?"

"No, but we can discuss our trade while we wait. I'm willing to give you the sensor and in return, you dismantle the laser."

"Dismantle the laser? No one agreed to dismantle anything. Why should I? I can take the sensor away from you any time I want."

"But you can't make it work."

Tolian relaxed his grip enough to allow Lex to regain her balance. "Oxley can. He did build your laser."

"My laser," Oxley protested.

Tolian ignored him, but Lex sensed a wavering of confidence in the *ordinaire*. Perhaps she could use the rivalry with Bodie to their advantage. A little fear and anger could go a long way.

"What if Bodie agrees to work for you?" she asked, ignoring Bodie's startled reaction. "Durand Tech gave him access to the latest technology and greatest minds in the world. What are you offering besides this second rate lab assistant?" She nodded toward Oxley.

"I won't..." Oxley sputtered but Tolian cut him off.

"Shut up. You'll do whatever I tell you." The Sentier squeezed her arm harder forcing her to stifle a cry of pain. "I'll do whatever I want. To all of you. Killing you, Joaquim, would be a waste of talent. Sometimes, however, it's necessary to make one's point. And I will relish seeing Mark Durand's face when he learns his precious sister is carrying my child."

Her gut clenched with revulsion as her eyes found Bodie's. The murderous fury there gave her hope and worried her. He was no match for Tolian's power. Their only chance was to outsmart the Sentier—and good luck with that. She shook her head almost imperceptibly to ask him not to do anything rash.

Lifting her glass, she downed the last of the wine. "Now that we've had our champagne, show us your command station. I assume you can control the laser from here?"

"Oxley, raise the controls so Ms. Durand can admire your work."

On a side of the room a large screen rose from an island counter, transforming into a high-tech workstation complete with built-in keyboard and keypad controls. Adrien had a similar set-up in his office in Paris. The irony wasn't lost on her. "Impressive."

He released her arm and allowed her to move closer to mission control where Oxley sulkily stood guard. The scientist keyed a code into the keypad and a map of the Caribbean appeared on the screen.

"And what does this do?" she asked, aware that Bodie had moved closer and behind Tolian. Although Bodie had height and weight advantage, she doubted the Sentier would rely on his own physical abilities in a man-to-man fight. And Bodie would end up dead.

"From here we can watch the world," Tolian said. "Unlike commercial resources, this shows details in real time."

"You tap into government satellites?" Bodie asked.

Oxley wrinkled his nose and scowled at his rival. "We are the government, *Jack*, all the governments."

Lex glanced over her shoulder where Tolian fixed the pale man with a deadly stare. "Your Dissemblers killed Bodie, didn't they?"

"They were overzealous and punished for disobeying my orders. Had he been captured as planned, we wouldn't all be here now. The war would be over, I would control the governments of every country in the world and all the Durand would be in hell."

"Didn't know I was that useful," Bodie said. He moved toward the console. "How do you collect the energy?"

"Ah, that was a problem in the early stages but a little majik solved it," Tolian explained. "A simple spell, really. Something your mother was quite good at. Or don't you remember her spells?"

Bodie flinched.

"Okay," Lex said. "I understand directing delphic, but storing it and intensifying it into a powerful stream. How does that work?"

Tolian smiled. "I won't bore that lovely head of yours with all the technical details when we can simply show you."

"No!"

But Tolian was already instructing Oxley to prepare the system to accept the delphic energy for transmission.

"You see," Tolian explained, "We haven't quite perfected a storage function that enables us to collect the energy and store it until it's needed. Once the delphic is in the device, it has to be projected within fifteen minutes, sooner if possible."

"We're locked on the Disney Fantasy cruise ship," Oxley said. He zoomed the screen in on a huge, brightly lit ship off the coast of St. Martin.

"Don't do this," Bodie said. "I'll come with you and give you the sensor technology."

"You'll do that anyway," Tolian assured him. "Your attachment to Ms. Durand will guarantee that. Oxley, prepare the intake."

Lex watched Oxley execute a few keystrokes and click on a pulldown menu on the screen. She memorized the procedure and noted Bodie doing the same. With any luck they'd get the chance to abort the sequence before the laser fired.

"Now this is the fun part," Tolian said. "Think of it as loading the device." He stood back from them and breathed in deeply.

She'd watched Adrien channel the Durand Source's energy on many occasions and had even learned from him to do it herself. Tolian, however, was thousands of miles from his Brazilian Source and had only the ambient delphic to work with. Like Bodie had on the hill. She wondered if now was the time to tell Bodie to counter Tolian's collection. No, Tolian might hurt him and the Sentier was too powerful to stop with physical strength alone.

Within a couple seconds, she could sense a change in the atmosphere. She glanced at Bodie.

There wasn't any indication of where Tolian was sending the energy but a battery icon on the screen of the monitor began filling.

"Good trick," Bodie said.

"Not a trick, a skill, Joaquim. Once Oxley designed the

holding battery, finishing the laser was easy. You gave him all the data yourself."

"Can I pull the trigger?" Oxley asked eagerly, then turned to Bodie. "Watch and weep, asshole. This is what a real scientist can do if he doesn't let sentiment get in his way."

"Or morals," Lex added.

Tolian turned to her and nodded. "I think we'll let the lady do the honors."

"No. You want to kill people, you do it yourself."

"Oxley. You may proceed then."

With a grin, the pale man moved the cursor over a small shape in the corner of the screen and clicked. A tiny digital clock appeared showing fifteen minutes. He clicked on that and the countdown began.

Her heartbeat kicked into high. Fifteen minutes to get control of the device and abort the sequence. Her mind raced. Bodie turned and their eyes locked. They both knew their options were down to one—to take the Sentier out and prevent the attack.

Tolian chuckled. "In case you're planning to try to stop the firing, you should know that once the countdown starts it can't be stopped or canceled. The laser will hit the ship and all of those precious little *ordinaires* will be propelled into another dimension. You might as well relax and enjoy the show."

Bodie nodded and simultaneously they launched themselves at Tolian. Before they even touched him they were propelled backward into a wall. She hit hard, her head bouncing off the plaster, and the breath was knocked from her lungs. She gasped for air and a crash at the front of the villa shook the entire structure. Stunned, she reached for Bodie and was relieved when her hand closed around his arm. Then she saw the rage on Tolian's face and knew they were about to die.

A split second later, a blast came through the front door leaving a gaping hole.

"Hello, Tolian," Mark said.

Lex gasped.

Her brother stepped through the opening where a mahogany door had been. For a long moment, no one moved. Then Bodie pulled her back against his body.

She looked from Mark to Tolian, chilled by the raw hatred charging the air. Both men were tall and powerfully built but physical strength was irrelevant in their world. The only thing that mattered was psychic power and in that arena she hoped they were evenly matched.

Tolian broke the silence. "Two First Order Durand in one night. I'm honored."

Mark ambled toward his adversary showing neither caution nor hesitance. "This is between you and me. Let Lex and Bodie go."

Tolian glanced down at them and shrugged. "They'll be easy enough to find when I finish you off."

Lex's heart pounded. The Brazilian Sentier and the Protector General squared off. If Tolian won, they were all dead.

"Far away from home, aren't you?" Mark said.

Tolian shrugged. "Unlike the Durand Sentier, I'm not imprisoned by my Source. No one dares challenge me for power and I don't care if the fools fight among themselves."

Mark shrugged. "And yet without your Source, your power is weakened. Are you sure you're up to facing me?"

Hatred flashed in Tolian's eyes. "I can still kill you, Durand." His arm lashed out and a violent bolt of majik flew at Mark.

Lex gasped but Mark flicked his hand and deflected the assault shattering the crystal chandelier over the dining table.

Tolian blinked and stared at him.

"I've picked up a few tricks myself since we last met," Mark said.

Tolian bared his teeth. "Not enough to stand up to me."

A blast of malevolence sent a coffee table flying at Mark and he sidestepped its path before it exploded into a grand piano, sending ivory and wood shrapnel in every direction.

"Fuck," Bodie choked out.

Lex could only stare at her brother in astonishment. His calm was more disconcerting than Tolian's rage.

"You could at least put up a fight," Tolian sneered.

Mark smiled, a silver shadow shimmering around his head and body. "I thought I'd let you warm up first. Just to be sporting."

"I'm going to enjoy killing you, Durand." Tolian raised his arms over his head and the villa began to vibrate.

Lex grabbed Bodie's arm and hopped to her feet. "Come on. Let's make Oxley show us how to abort the attack."

Bodie hauled Oxley to his feet and pushed him toward the hallway. Glass crashed behind them and they began to run, dragging Oxley with them.

"You're going to take us to the laser controls," Lex said. "Or Bodie's going to shoot you."

Bodie yanked the pistol from the holster at his back. "With pleasure."

Oxley didn't argue. "He was telling the truth. The firing sequence can't be stopped."

"We'll see about that." Bodie poked him in the back with the barrel of the Beretta. "Now haul ass. Time is wasting."

When they got to the lab, Bodie sat down at the console

in front of the same image as the monitor upstairs. The countdown showed eleven minutes to go. "How do I get into the commands?"

Oxley shook his head. "You can't. When the sequence is set, the system locks until after the laser fires. He had me program it that way."

"There's got to be a way to hack the timer." Bodie worked the keyboard and mouse hard for nearly a minute then slammed his palms on the surface of the desk. "Fuck."

"You're wasting your time," Oxley said.

The countdown clock read 9:46.

Bodie leapt to his feet and ran for the stairs. "The beam comes out of the projector in the sugar mill on the hill. If I can manually re-aim it…"

She took off after him. At the top of the stairs there was an exit into the compound. When he pushed the door open an alarm blared and floodlights lit up the area like midday. A shot rang out and the bullet whizzed past her head hitting the wall at her shoulder and sending pellets of stucco everywhere. "What the hell?"

Bodie yanked her around the corner of the villa. "You okay?"

"Yeah, but more Dissemblers have arrived." She pulled out her pistol. "Find the way out. I'll cover you."

He shoved a pouch of ammo in her pocket. "Be careful, babe."

"Go!"

She reached in her pocket for her ComDev to scan the compound for life forces before she remembered it was inside. She took a half dozen wild shots in the direction the fire had come from, giving Bodie the chance to duck behind the warehouse.

The alarm went quiet leaving an eerie silence except for

the ringing in her ears. Pressing herself against the wall, she peeked out into the open space. A man shouted in Portuguese and the floodlights went dark. They wouldn't be able to see her but she also couldn't see them.

Assuming Bodie had found the way out, she'd be of more use at the foot of the hill than waiting here to run out of bullets. Pushing off the wall, she sprinted in the direction he had gone, weaving back and forth to evade the new round of shots. Pushing her legs to their limit, she tucked in behind the warehouse and searched the exterior wall for a door. There wasn't one.

On the other side of the compound the gunfire continued. She listened. Automatic weapons of a higher caliber than had been aimed at her had joined the exchange. Had Mark brought Protectors with him? An explosion in the villa shook the ground. She couldn't think about Mark and Tolian now, only about helping Bodie stop the laser.

Darting across the open lawn, she crouched behind a hedge of bougainvillea and saw the doorway not fifty feet away. And under cover.

Then she heard it—a low deep growl. Out of the shadows next to the door the largest wolf she'd ever seen stalked toward her, teeth bared. His coat gleamed like silver in the moonlight and his yellow eyes seemed lit from within.

Lex rose to stand tall and stared him down. "Nothing personal, buddy, but I don't have time for this."

29

Bodie burst through the metal door and out into the night. He took a couple of precious seconds to let his eyes adjust to the moonlight and to orient himself to his location. The passage had dumped him outside the walls of the compound at the base of the hill where the sugar mill stood. The hill was tall, rugged, and steeper than it had looked from the point where they'd left the Range Rover, steeper and rockier.

Twenty yards below he spotted a rough path winding up the hillside and took off for it at top speed. How much time was left? He scrambled up the trail, pushing his legs harder as they loosened up. A rock bit into the ball of his foot through his boat shoes and he swore but didn't slow. Normally the ambient delphic fed him and boosted him when he ran, but here it was thinner than usual.

A gully bisected the trail and he leapt it, sliding in the sand as he landed. Even in the daytime, the path would be treacherous. Now with only the moonlight to light the way, a misstep would land him at the base of the hill and all those families... he willed his legs to move faster.

He recalled the schematics he'd seen of the device on Oxley's computer. There had been a light laser beam as well as the delphic function. Made sense when he thought about it. The delphic had cohesion issues and the light would act as a binder to focus the delphic over distances. That meant he'd see the laser when it fired. The problem was how to disperse the delphic without breaching the fragile membrane between realities and sending himself into darkness.

"Shit." Halfway up the hill and time was running out. His lungs began to burn and he ignored them. His legs ate up the distance but not fast enough. Every second could be the last.

His right foot came down hard and the ground gave under him. He threw himself at the hillside and grabbed onto a scrubby bush as his footing tumbled away. Thorns pierced his palm but he held tight until he regained purchase on what remained of the path. His heart pounded and he gasped to fill his lungs.

Then he looked up and his heart stopped. A red light pulsed on and off in the sugar mill. Time was up.

"No." A beam of light flickered then strengthened. He sensed the delphic intensifying.

"Push it off course," Lex shouted from below.

He focused his mind and willed the energy to move toward the sky. Nothing happened. His heart pounded and his breath ripped in and out of his lungs. He had to stop the disaster, save all those people. In his heart he knew there was only one way.

Concentrating with every cell of his body, he inhaled deeply and pulled the delphic to him. The beam wavered and he drew harder. For an instant the delphic shifted from its path before intensifying in a blazing ray of light.

Fill me, he directed the delphic, imagining the energy forming a vortex from the laser to his body. Light exploded in the night and the energy obeyed with a force that threw him backward. Falling or flying? It seemed an eternity before his shoulder hit the earth. His momentum bounced and rolled him—to his back, his hip, his knee—down the rocky hillside. He covered his face with his arms and felt the skin on his forearm rip on a thorny bush just before his skull hit the ground.

The night swirled inside his head, points of light, clouds of darkness, and the rumble of the earth tottering on its axis. The stillness of his body amplified the sensation of weightlessness. How many bones were broken? Could he move? His brain dismissed those questions as irrelevant and bathed in the oneness of the world around him. Floating above, the scene below him came into focus.

Lex skidded to a stop next to him or what had been him. The corporeal Bodie lay on his back, eyes closed. She knelt next to his shoulder and felt the side of his neck for a pulse.

"Goddamn you, Bodie. You can't die on me."

So he had no pulse. The information only mildly interested him.

She shifted so she could press the heel of her hands into his chest with practiced efficiency—one, two, three, four. "Beat, damn it, beat." He lost count. She knew what she was doing. "Don't you dare die."

His shield had dissolved and left him open to her emotions. The warmth he'd felt when their minds joined on the hill filled him now. Instead of pulling back, he floated closer.

The pumping stopped and she bent over his head. Her lips brushed his in a soft kiss and his mouth tingled to kiss her back. She positioned his chin and breathed into his lungs, filling him with an ache of longing. A tear hit his face and ran down his jaw.

She lifted her head and stroked his cheek. He felt the warmth of her hand, the gentle brush of her fingers on his face. *I'm here*, he tried to say with no voice.

"I love you," she whispered. "Please don't die."

Could he? He felt another presence and looked up toward the villa. No one was there. Then a soundless voice spoke in his head. *Your choice this time.*

His choice to live or die.

Lex returned to working on his chest. Her back rose and fell in an even rhythm. "I'm not giving up on you, damn it. I'll never give up on you."

In a flash of clarity he knew what he was feeling were his own emotions, not hers. That warmth he felt was something tender, protective. Love?

A silver cord shimmered in the moonlight from him to the tattoo on his forearm closest to his elbow. The way back. His choice. Yes, he wanted his life back. He wanted to go back to her. For her.

The jolt of re-entering his body stunned him and pain lanced his shoulder blade. He gasped, gulping in the cool night air.

Lex took his head between her hands and kissed his face —eyes, nose, cheeks, forehead, and finally his mouth, all while crying for joy, murmuring endearments in a jumble of French and English.

He tried to open his eyes but nothing happened. His body felt heavy and numb, and no amount of concentration budged so much as a finger. This couldn't be happening. He hadn't returned to his body to be trapped here as a vegetable. He would have laughed at the irony but that, too, was impossible.

Running her hands over his arms and legs, she gently checked for obvious broken bones or bleeding wounds before stroking his cheek. "Wake up, Bodie. Please, wake up."

"I'm so sorry for everything," she whispered. "You sacrificed yourself for that ship and I know that was what you had to do. But you're alive and that's all that matters."

She took his hand in both of hers and brought his fingers to her lips. The warmth of her breath on his skin seeped through his hand and into his arm like a light illuminating a path in the darkness. His fingers closed over hers and applied pressure.

"You can hear me," she said.

Sensation crept along his nerve ways spreading through muscle and skin in pins and needles until feeling returned with an exhilarating vengeance. He opened his eyes and stared into her lovely tear-stained face.

"Hey," he managed.

Still clutching his hand, she blinked back tears. "Hey, yourself. You scared the hell out of me, Dr. Flynn."

"I scared the hell out of myself." He squeezed her hand. "Thanks."

"For what?"

"For reviving me. For bringing me back." He tried to sit up and she pressed him back to the ground.

"You're hanging tight until we find out if you have any broken bones—specifically neck or back."

"Neck and back are fine. A couple ribs are cracked and my right scapula—wing bone. Otherwise, only scrapes and bruises."

Her eyes narrowed. "You can't know that."

And yet he did. "Trust me. If anything important is busted, you can give me a burial at sea."

"I will, you stubborn idiot."

He pushed himself to a sitting position and this time she let him. His broken ribs shot stabs of pain through his body and he clenched his teeth to control it before climbing gingerly to his feet. "We need to check on Mark."

30

Bodie reached his hand down to help Lex to her feet.

"Are you crazy? You've got broken ribs!" She pushed herself to her feet and brushed her hands on the seat of her pants. "From here on in, you don't do physical labor—no lifting, pushing..."

"This isn't over. We have to go back in."

Dread pooled in her stomach. Her brother was still inside and so was Tolian. If Tolian killed Mark, all their efforts would have been for nothing. The Durand Protector in her knew what had to be done. "Let's do it."

Once back inside they hurried to the kitchen entry and she took the tranq gun and the Beretta out of her pockets and handed him the pistol. As they passed into the hallway she listened for noise that would clue them into what was happening in the front rooms of the villa. The only sounds were Bodie's breathing and the waves breaking on the beach below.

"It's awfully quiet. Too quiet." She opened her senses and concentrated. "There's a powerful force ahead."

"Tolian or Mark?"

"There's no way to tell."

"He could be waiting for us."

Bodie didn't have to use the Brazilian Sentier's name for her to understand. "It's possible." She stopped and put a hand on his arm. "In case I don't get to say this later, I wouldn't trade having met you for anything in the world."

His eyes shone down on her. "Me either." He bent and pressed his lips to hers. "When this is over, I'll do that right."

If they lived that long. "Let's see what we've got."

Cautiously they passed through the long formal dining room and paused to listen. A soft clicking sound was barely audible above the waves.

"The battle's over," he whispered. "Wait here and run if you hear Tolian. I'll try to keep him busy until you get away."

"We go in together."

"No. Let me do this." His jaw flexed and his eyes hardened with determination.

She swallowed her protest. He was willing to sacrifice himself to protect her. She had to respect that. And yet, her duty as a soldier was so ingrained in her, abandoning him wasn't an option. "You go first and I'll be back-up."

"I want you safe. He can only kill me..."

She fought a shudder at the memory of Tolian's threat. "I'll be careful."

He nodded, took a deep breath and stepped into the villa's great room. "What the fuck...?"

Unable to resist, she followed him and stopped dead. "Jesus."

The place looked like a tornado had ripped through it—furniture tossed and broken, walls battered, glass shattered. And in the middle of the chaos, Mark worked at the computer console in front of a cracked but still functional monitor.

A massive weight fell from her shoulders. They were safe and Tolian was gone. "What happened, Mark?"

"A shit storm nobody won," her brother replied bitterly. He turned to them. "Good job, Bodie. Your powers have come along nicely since you left Fat Dog."

Bodie stared at him. "You know what I did?"

He nodded. "Tolian was royally pissed off."

"Where is he?" she asked.

"Gone."

"Where?" she and Bodie asked in unison.

"No idea. We were having a *discussion*," Mark gestured at the destruction, "when Bodie pulled down the delphic. Apparently the son-of-a-bitch had skin in that game and when the smoke cleared, he'd vanished." Mark's voice was steady but she heard the anger and disappointment. She also saw the dark red stain blooming on the shoulder and arm of his shirt.

She moved closer, stepping over what used to be the leg of a chrome coffee table, and Bodie stayed by her side. "You're hurt."

"Old wound re-opened. I'm fine."

Two men appeared at the side door leading to the court-yard. She recognized her cousin instantly. "Victor! What are you doing here?"

He grinned and ambled toward her. "Swat team duty. Mark called me en route to meet him here." He hugged her and kissed each cheek.

"I thought I heard a gunfight."

"Yeah. Three Dissemblers arrived via the beach just as we got here. Are the guys sleeping out back your handiwork?"

"Mine and Bodie's."

Victor extended his hand. "Victor Durand."

Studying him cautiously Bodie took it. "Bodie Flynn." He glanced from her to Mark. "Is this the team that's taking the laser?"

"That's your call," Mark replied. "Do you know how to operate it?"

"Yes."

Mark closed the distance between them and the two men faced off—both tall, muscular, and poised for battle. Lex slipped her hand in Bodie's, taking his side in whatever came down next. Tension hung heavily in the air and Bodie's grip tightened on her fingers.

"Good," Mark said, "because I wasn't getting anywhere."

The muscle in Bodie's jaw tightened. "You're never going to use it. I'll make sure of that."

The shock in Mark's eyes was genuine. "Use it? I want to be sure it's shut down and can't be re-activated by someone else with remote access."

"Then you don't mind if I take a look?"

Mark stepped aside. "Go for it."

Bodie went to the console and began to work.

"There's a guy named Oxley Cowan in the bunker under the hill," Lex said. "He's the one who built the laser. You'll want to question him."

"*Ordinaire*?" Victor asked.

"Yes."

Victor grinned. "Already have him in the guest house."

"Find out what he knows about the Argos, and if he can bring it back," she said.

"Sure. I heard it was missing." He turned to Mark. "Any other orders?"

"Ask him how to pack up the laser equipment. I'll grill

him about Tolian myself. See what you can get out of the Dissemblers."

Victor saluted him. "Will do."

"You didn't happen to see a wolf, did you?" Lex asked.

"He's asleep in the guesthouse. Friend of yours?"

Lex shrugged. "He was a Dissembler guard wolf until recently. Maybe he can catch a ride to Valtois?"

Victor winked at her. "I'll work out the logistics with my brother. Later guys."

When Victor was gone Lex studied her brother. His personal quest to destroy Tolian was no secret and the Brazilian Sentier rarely surfaced outside his Amazon realm. Something about Mark's arrival didn't pass the sniff test. "You certainly showed up in the nick of time."

"Figured you could use some help. It was easy enough to track your ComDevs." He met her gaze, his silver eyes concealed by blue contact lenses.

"Did you know Tolian was behind the laser?"

"*Know*? How would I have known?"

Not an answer. A chill washed over her. A master strategist wouldn't walk into a situation without some idea what he'd be facing. And why come himself instead of sending Victor and his team of Protectors to do the job? Had he set her and Bodie up in order to find Tolian? No, he wouldn't do that. He loved her.

"That should do it," Bodie said. He slowly got to his feet. "There's no way I can dismantle the equipment myself with these injuries. Can your people do that?"

Mark nodded. "No problem. We'll take it to DT and you can analyze it there."

Bodie's eyes narrowed and his mouth tightened into a thin line. "I'm done. Get one of your whiz kids to do it. Or take Oxley back and use mind control on him. That's what you did to me."

Fire flashed in Mark's eyes. "I respected your intellect and understood your abilities better than you did. I never controlled your mind."

Lex stepped closer to Bodie. "Tolian told him you're a telepath and you manipulated him with your psychic abilities."

"Did he?" Mark's voice remained even, but cold loathing vibrated in the air. He addressed Bodie. "I have read your mind. I haven't manipulated it."

"Why did you bring me back to life?"

Mark's face registered surprise. He glanced at Lex and then back to Bodie. "I don't know. I arrived too late to prevent the Dissemblers from shooting you. Maybe I thought I owed you."

Bodie's eyes widened as understanding dawned. "You set me up."

"No, but Tolian targeted you because I got careless. His network turned out to be more extensive than I realized. I now know Dissemblers have infiltrated every branch of government of every major country in the world. Adrien suggested we relocate you somewhere you'd be off the radar."

"Why didn't you tell me about being a revenant?"

"I gave you what psychic protection I could before sending you to Fat Dog."

Bodie held out his forearm ink. "You call this psychic protection? An anti-possession symbol and soul glue? A heads-up on the revenant business would have been nice."

Mark grabbed Bodie's wrist and held his arm between them. "If it wasn't for the *soul glue*, you wouldn't have had the choice of staying or going out there just now. Tolian's a master of possession so this..." He poked the symbol sharply with his finger. "Would have come in handy had he found you before Lex gave you that shield."

Bodie winced but his eyes never left Mark's. Lex was still trying to figure out the soul glue comment. Had Bodie chosen to come back from the dead out there? Before she could process that thought her brother pressed his finger on the center symbol on Bodie's forearm.

Bodie yanked his arm away and hissed. "Jesus! What...?"

"Packs a kick, doesn't it?" Mark unbuttoned his shirt halfway and pulled the fabric aside to reveal the same symbol on the upper part of his pectoral muscle. He then popped one of the blue contracts out of his eye.

Bodie's mouth dropped open and he stared at Mark, speechless.

"We revenants are a small club linked by this." Mark tapped the tattoo before closing his shirt. "In times of extreme peril, we draw from our brothers' power to survive no matter where we are."

"You're a revenant?" Bodie blinked and shook his head as if to clear it. "I don't understand the tattoo link?"

Mark glanced at Lex and back to Bodie. "I'm not sure I do completely either, but we'll talk when we have more time and aren't standing in a Dissembler stronghold."

"How long have you known about this place?" Bodie asked suspiciously.

"Since you arrived. When Lex wouldn't answer my calls or texts we tracked your ComDevs."

"And yet you knew Tolian would be here."

Mark shrugged. "Suspected. I didn't know for sure."

Without warning, Bodie's hands flashed out and he caught Mark by the neck. "You bastard. You used us for bait. You lured that evil piece of shit with your own sister."

"Too much is at stake to ignore the few opportunities we have to destroy Tolian. I always knew where you were and, as Lex pointed out, I got here when I was needed."

"Just barely," Bodie growled, his hand trembling in rage. "Don't expect anyone's gratitude for showing up in your good old time."

Lex laid a hand on his arm. "Bodie, please let him go. Tolian rarely leaves Brazil. I understand why Mark had to seize the rare chance to destroy him."

"I don't."

Mark grasped Bodie's wrists and gently pushed his hands away. "The war with the Brazilian Sentier and his Dissemblers has heated up in the past two years and the Durands are losing ground. Drug violence in Mexico, the bloody conflicts in Africa and the Middle East, terrorist attacks, mass shootings in the United States—all bear the fingerprints of the Dissemblers. Tolian is the most powerful, brilliant, and ambitious Sentier ever to control the Brazilian Source. Kill him and any organization there is now will disintegrate into an internal power struggle that could last for a decade or more."

"Not my problem," Bodie said.

Mark folded his arms across his chest. "Really? You think you can just walk away? Tolian has you on his radar, has for years. He doesn't forgive or forget. Sooner or later he'll come after you. Him or his minions."

Bodie looked to Lex for confirmation. It pained her to back Mark up. "I'm sorry. He's right."

The anger drained from Bodie's face, replaced with sad resignation. "I don't get why he noticed me in the first place. What did he want?"

The question had crossed her mind, too.

The sound of voices drifted in from the courtyard

reminding her that there were still Dissemblers in the compound, as well as Cowan.

Mark glanced behind him at the front door then turned his attention back to Bodie. "A guess? With a mind like yours on board, the Dissemblers might have a chance against Durand Tech. Add your psychic abilities and the misconception that they came from Brazilian genes—you'd make a perfect right hand man."

"I *am* Brazilian, or at least my mother is," Bodie said.

"Brazilian but San, not Hi'aiti'ihi'," Mark said.

San? "You're sure?" she asked.

Her brother shot her an insulted look. "Durand Bio is sure. Really, Lex. Why would you think he's Hi'aiti'ihi'? That's absurd. The San are earth energy psychics. He's almost classic."

"What's San?" Bodie asked.

"The San are the people of the Kalahari in southern Africa," she said, then noticed the frown on Bodie's face and explained. "They're earth people who have an uncanny ability to survive, even flourish, in a harsh and unforgiving environment."

"But I'm not from Africa," Bodie pointed out.

"No," Mark agreed, "but your ancestors were. Probably brought to Brazil as slaves centuries ago and assimilated into the general population over time."

Victor appeared at the courtyard door. "We're ready to move out."

"Load up. We'll be there in a couple minutes," Mark replied. When Victor was gone, he turned to Bodie. "We'll take the laser to DT in L.A. Come with us."

"An order?"

"An invitation."

"I've got no money and no boat, so I guess I don't have a choice."

"Actually you have a substantial balance in a Swiss account—royalties and profits from your share in DT."

"My share?"

"A small share of an extremely profitable company."

It was Lex's turn to feel outrage on Bodie's behalf. "When were you going to tell him?"

Bodie put his hand on her shoulder and addressed Mark. "Doesn't matter. I'm done with DT and with you."

Mark frowned. "Really? I was going to offer you a job. You'd make a damned good Protector—which I'd insist on if you're in a relationship with my sister."

She cringed. "Mark!" Her cheeks warmed with embarrassment.

Bodie turned to her. "Are those his conditions or yours?"

Her heart began to pound. Gathering her courage, she searched his face for some clue to what he was thinking. The vulnerability she saw there lifted her heart and gave her hope. This might be her only shot with him. It was no time to be a coward.

"I have no conditions," she said. "I love you but I won't turn my back on my family or my duty so you can have revenge on Mark."

Hurt filled his eyes. "Is that what you think of me? That I'd use you to hurt him?"

How to answer? She studied the handsome face so dear to her. He had hated Mark for so long and yet something seemed to be changing. Did he really care for her? She had to take a leap of faith.

"No," she said. "I know you wouldn't hurt me."

He took both her hands in his and gazed into her eyes. "Out on the hill I saw you try to revive me. My soul was ready to go but I couldn't leave you. I don't know what love feels like, Lex, but I know I want to be with you, to cherish and protect you. I've never cared about anyone before. Will you teach me how it's done?"

Tears filled her eyes and she blinked them back. "Absolutely."

He gathered her in his arms and kissed her. His lips were warm and soft, gentle at first, then firm, hungry, possessive. The sweet invasion filled her with love and desire and the warm happiness of unlimited possibilities. This was the man she wanted to be with forever and ever, and by some miracle he wanted her, too.

31

Bodie settled into the beach chair to watch Lex and his former assistant Josh in the shallow water of Little Harbor, Earl curled up next to him in the shade. She held the windsurfer board while Josh absorbed her instructions. In the past two weeks the pair had become fast friends.

Josh pulled the sail of the windsurfer out of the water, tilted it to catch the wind and the board began to move. Lex turned and waved at Bodie then gave him two thumbs up. He flashed the okay sign in reply. Grinning, she plowed through the shallow water toward the beach, wet orange bikini clinging deliciously to her curves.

She grabbed the towel on the chair next to his and began to dry off. "Did you see him? It won't be long until he's as good a windsurfer as you are."

"In your dreams, woman."

She pressed a salty kiss on his lips and he wrapped a hand around the back of her neck to hold her in place while he leisurely explored her mouth. He loved the honeysuckle taste of her, the fresh scent of the sea on her skin.

"Want to get a room?" she asked huskily.

He grinned at what had become a running joke since Josh had joined them. "Always."

She dropped into the other beach chair. "I can't believe we're flying to Paris tomorrow."

"Hard to believe we've been here for ten days."

Her tone sobered. "Are you sure you're cool with Mark and Adrien?"

After a dozen discussions with the Sentier and his Field General, Bodie had come to terms with the reality of his new life. Most of it, anyhow. He took her hand and squeezed it, savoring the slim femininity that had given him so much pleasure. "Yeah. I wouldn't have signed on for Durand boot camp otherwise. Sure you won't do a refresher course?"

She slipped on her Ray-Bans. "You know I can't. I've taken off enough time and need to get back to work. Besides, it'll do you good to miss me."

And he would miss her. Four weeks was a long time, even if she promised to visit mid-semester. The possibility that he could ever lose her froze him to his soul. He knew what he wanted. The words were harder to find. He drew a deep breath. "I think it's time you made an honest man of me."

Her mouth dropped and she peered at him over the top of the shades. "Excuse me?"

His heart pounded in his chest and he steeled to plunge on. "I was raised Southern Baptist. You don't expect me to continue *living in sin*."

A slim eyebrow cocked. "Sin? Since when do you care about sin?"

"Since you told me I'm going to meet your family under the Sentier's roof."

She poked him in the arm with her pointer finger. "Do not tell me you're backing out of this trip."

He shook his head. "I don't know. Your parents, aunts, uncles, cousins. That's a lot of Durands in one place. What do you say we get married while we're there?"

She stared at him mouth open, then threw herself into his arms. They tumbled onto the sand, just missing poor startled Earl.

"Yes!" She kissed him fast and hard. "Of course I'll marry you, Bodie Flynn. Paris, L.A., Fat Dog Island. Doesn't matter where."

He ran a hand down her back and over her bottom. "Paris, then." His chest felt like it would burst with his love for her. "I love you, princess."

"And I love you."

32

There had been a time when extracting information from the likes of Isidore Balaskas had been far more dangerous. Adrien Durand hit send on his ComDev and slipped it the inner pocket of his tux jacket, almost disappointed that his mission tonight had been so routine.

A few subtle questions, a telepathic nudge and the Greek industrialist had mentally reviewed his entire arms smuggling and money laundering network. All that had been left to do was tune in and listen. No intimidation. No threat of violence. All so civilized.

A waiter approached with a tray of champagne. Adrien took one. It was a hell of a party and now that his intel had hit Mark's inbox, he might as well enjoy himself.

The fashionable crowd's attire rivaled the dazzling décor of the event's venue—Versailles's Hall of Mirrors. It was hard to imagine Louis Quatorze's extravagant showplace could be even more embellished but the American heiress who organized the event had filled every window with ten-foot flower arrangements on crystal pedestals and lit them with twinkling lights. As if all the mirrors and chandeliers weren't glitzy enough.

He scanned the room to identify any unusual or negative energy. Just the usual petty hostilities—none of them directed at him. He no longer needed his playboy cover, notorious for having more money than scruples. Damn, he missed the intrigue and constant danger. He swallowed the resentment that crept up on him now and then. He was Sentier now, Guardian of the Durand Source. Stuck in Paris for the duration.

"Adrien Durand. I was hoping to meet you." The sultry American voice belonged to a striking woman who had planted herself in front of him.

"Were you?" He attempted to keep his gaze on her face and failed. Large breasts overflowed the low-cut bodice which cinched in an impossibly tiny waist emphasized by more than ample hips and thighs. She couldn't be more than five foot four without the towering stilettos and yet she exuded a huge personality. And clearly assumed he knew who she was.

"You're much better looking in person." Her gaze dropped and slowly lifted back to his face. "And much bigger."

He chuckled. Women came on to him all the time, but this one didn't seem to be flirting, just stating her opinion. "I'm happy I don't disappoint."

She laughed. "Not at all." Her hands skimmed down the skirt of a skin-tight gown with flesh-colored lining that gave the illusion she was almost naked. "Are you enjoying yourself?"

"Not particularly," he admitted. "You?"

She shrugged. "Business is business."

A photographer approached. "May I?"

"Of course." Adrien's companion stepped closer to him and posed while the photographer popped off shots.

Across the room a woman laughed and tossed her head. Adrien froze. She faced away, engaged in conversation with a Russian diplomat. Her straight dark hair glowed as it brushed her creamy shoulders. He tapped her mind and found it shielded. It must be her. Even after all this time, hatred twisted in his gut. How did she dare show her face in Paris? After seven years of being hunted by the Durand and the Shalamov?

"Are you okay?" The American rested her hand on his arm. "You look like you've seen a ghost."

"I should be so lucky. Excuse me." He took a step forward and a pain seared through his hip. He caught himself before he stumbled and breathed in deeply to steady himself. Another reminder of everything Irina Demidova had stolen from him.

The crowd parted as he made his way toward her, unsuccessfully trying to conceal his limp from the curious stares. For once he didn't care. The Russian saw him coming and frowned. Adrien sent a telepathic command—*Walk away. Now.*

The diplomat excused himself and hurried off.

Adrien slowed, preparing to savor the confrontation he'd wanted for so long. An emerald green satin evening gown draped her slim figure and he suddenly despised the color green. "Irina." Her name came out as a growl. She didn't respond.

He stepped closer and spoke in Russian. "Did you think I wouldn't find you?"

Slowly she turned to face him. The breath caught in his throat and his mind whirled in disbelief.

"Excuse me? Do I know you?"

He studied her face, analyzing every feature. The cheek-bones were the same and the nose, but the mouth was different, and the eyes had almost an Asian tilt. The voice was definitely wrong. It didn't matter that this woman was a psychic and probably Shalamov blood. She wasn't the one who had betrayed her people and blamed him.

"Sorry," he sputtered. "I thought you were someone else." His automatic bow was stiff and formal. "Please accept my apology."

He didn't wait for a response. Heading for the exit, he ignored the pain shooting up his side as the adrenaline drained from his body, leaving him suddenly exhausted. As much as he wanted revenge, thankfully this wasn't the time or place he'd have to face her. Maybe Irina would never surface. Maybe she would remain hidden in a new life.

Hopefully she was already dead.

Want more?

KEEP READING for a preview of Adrien's story, MIND SHADOWS.

If you enjoyed Lex and Bodie's story, please consider writing a review on Amazon or your favorite online bookseller. Even a short review is so important to authors and to readers looking for new books.

I hope you'll sign up for my newsletter to get extra scenes, short stories, previews, news and more—including the epilogue with Lex and Bodie's wedding!

www.larkbrennan.com

You can also find me at:

https://www.facebook.com/LarkBrennan/

https://www.bookbub.com/profile/lark-brennan

https://www.amazon.com/Lark-Brennan/e/B0172H0KVW

https://www.instagram.com/larkbrennan/

Keep reading for a preview of Adrien's book — **MIND SHADOWS**, Book 2 of The Durand Chronicles—which will be available October 2019.

MIND SHADOWS

Paris, France

Once again Tate Fulbright checked the number over the shop door against her mother's email on her cell. 42 rue du Bac. They matched. There was no way the tiny garden shop housed "the most amazing collection of Coleoptera and Lepidoptera." She pulled open the door. Maybe someone inside would know where this entomologists' mecca actually was.

Two steps into the dim interior she froze. It was like stepping into another century. The dark wooden shelves and paneling shone in golden light from antique wall sconces. The scent of beeswax polish and lemon oil filled the air.

"*Bonjour*," she called.

No reply. She walked past quaint baskets of old-fashioned gardening utensils and leather gloves to shelves displaying pinafores, straw hats, and wellingtons.

"Hello, anybody here?"

Still no reply. She turned to leave and saw it—a shadowbox with three huge beetles tucked between the shelves. Goliathinis?

A man's voice drifted down a stairway at the rear of the shop. A sign next to the stairs read OUVERT, "open," with an arrow pointing up.

"*Bonjour, monsieur*?" She climbed the age-worn treads of the narrow staircase concentrating on where to place her feet. She kept her eyes down and didn't see the horse until they were muzzle to nose.

"Jeez!" Her voice echoed in the stairwell. Not a stuffed toy horse, but a stuffed *real* horse. She half expected him to snort in her face but he just looked at her through a port-hole in the wall.

Climbing the last two stairs, she gasped. A grand dining room fit for a château was set for an elegant dinner party. Around the fully set dining table stood three zebras, two gazelles, a water buffalo, and a donkey—all stuffed.

The animals looked as though they had frozen midparty when she hit the top step. Friendly eyes greeted her from dozens of animal faces and a strange and welcoming feeling embraced her. Her chest ached. How could anyone have killed these wonderful creatures?

"They all died of natural causes." A man in his twenties studied her from the doorway of a room full of bookshelves.

"Really?"

He smiled. "It's a nonnegotiable condition of taking them." He made it sound like the stuffed animals had been adopted.

"What is this place?"

"La Maison d'Ermonie."

"Is there a collection of insects by any chance?"

He frowned. "You're looking for insects?"

"Yes. I saw the Goliathinis downstairs."

The phone in his hand rang and he glanced at the caller ID. "I need to take this. Adrien's through there." He gestured toward a doorway and answered the call. "*Bonjour, monsieur.*"

She hesitated a moment, then crossed to a set of carved doors that opened to the next room.

"Oh my god," she murmured. It was like staring into the ballroom of the Ark. Stuffed animals—real animals—were everywhere. Hundreds of them. Every species from parrots to giraffes partied together like it was New Year's Eve at Versailles. She reached out to pet a magnificent lion and a wooden drawer slammed shut with a bang.

A man stood in a far corner of the room glaring at her. Her pulse thundered in her ears and she reminded herself to breathe. He came at her, walking with a pronounced limp. The hard set of his jaw and the scowl on his brow took nothing away from the striking impact of his dark hair and startling blue eyes. "What are you doing here?"

"The man out there pointed me in this direction."

"Why?" His expression was stern, his accent not quite British or American.

"I asked about the Goliathinis downstairs."

"You want to buy beetles?" His tone was just short of a sneer. "Who are you?"

Tate just wanted to escape. "My mother gave me this address. She said there's an important entomological collection here. An insect collection."

"I know what entomology is."

"I'm sorry—she gave me the wrong address. I'm leaving."

He nodded once.

"I'm glad I got to see this place," she said. "The animals are..." How to describe them? "They're magical." She turned to leave.

He caught her arm and Tate had the sense of falling. An electrical current flowed from his fingers and shimmered through every cell in her body. The world clicked into high definition with every sense heighted. His breath caressed her face and the scent of woodsy cologne filled her head.

Abruptly, he let go. She tried to read what he was feeling and got nothing.

"Who *are* you?" he demanded.

She straightened her back. "Tate Fulbright. Who are you?"

"Adrien Durand."

"Do you work here?"

"This is my establishment."

"Really?" These wonderful animals belonged to him? "What exactly *is* your *establishment*? Are the animals for sale?"

"No. They can be rented for special events and photo shoots, and were used in films before digital effects took over." His fierce expression softened a little. "Our primary business is the sale of natural specimens: shells, books, maps, charts, and..." He paused. "Insects. We're widely known by collectors for our extensive inventory of rare Coleoptera and Lepidoptera."

She planted her fists on her hips. "And you were letting me leave without telling me?"

"You're still here, aren't you?"

A smartass reply jumped to her lips and died when he smiled. The transformation kicked her in the chest. He was even more handsome when he wasn't scowling.

"Would you like to see our *bugs*, Ms. Fulbright?"

She nodded.

His hand swept in the direction of a door on the far side of the ballroom. "This way. Be careful you don't trip over anyone."

Anyone. She smiled.

Carefully, she stepped over the small creatures and around the large ones. Why was this room in such chaos? She followed him warily. He was tall and well built, and his clothes were expensive. She tried to sense his emotions and again got nothing. Not possible.

He frowned at her. "Where did you come from?"

"Indiana."

"All the way from Indiana just to see our collection?"

"No. I'm here on business. The pharmaceutical company I work for has a booth at the international convention. My mother's an entomologist who studies African beetles. She gave me this address and insisted I come by while I was in town." *Stop explaining.* The guy made her nervous.

"What's your mother's name? Maybe I've heard of her."

"Dr. Margaret Fulbright, but she isn't famous."

"And you share your mother's interest?"

"When I was little I spent a lot of time in her lab at the university. Bugs are in my genetic makeup."

Adrien stood aside so she could enter the room ahead of him. "Our collection."

She froze and stared around the room. "It's amazing."

Tall glass display cases stood symmetrically along the walls and walnut lateral files were lined up in three rows in the center of the room. Thousands of insects—butterflies, moths, beetles, dragonflies, and dramatic exotics—were displayed in framed boxes inside the glass cases and on every exposed bit of wall.

"Unbelievable," she breathed. "And so beautiful." Beginning with the closest display case, she studied the carefully arranged specimens.

Adrien stood back and watched her. He'd been reading her thoughts since she arrived and nothing contradicted the obvious—that she was a tourist who'd wandered into his world. As she studied the butterfly exhibits she recited the Latin names in her head. What was a powerful empath doing here and why didn't she have a shield? She paused and stared at a rare Asian butterfly, trying to recall its name.

"*Papilio elwesi*," he said. "That one's from China."

"It's lovely. There are a lot of these I don't know. I guess I'm better at bugs than butterflies." She hadn't even questioned how he knew what she was thinking. "They're natural art, aren't they?"

"I've always thought so."

She passed from one display to the next until she got to the beetles. He liked the way she studied them as though they were jewels in a showcase at Cartier.

Dissembler spy or not, she was clearly middle-class American. Her blonde hair curled unfashionably to her shoulders, but it was natural and suited her. Too many angles prevented her from being classically beautiful, and yet she was far from unattractive.

Empath, he reminded himself. And an animal telepath. At worst an enemy, and at best an American tourist with a great ass he was never going to touch.

"I don't see any Goliathinis," she said. "Are the ones downstairs the only ones you have?"

"No, the unmounted specimens are over here."

He crossed to one of the huge flat file cabinets and opened the second drawer, where six Goliathinis rested under glass.

Tate came to stand next to him, close enough that their arms just barely touched. "So many." She studied the insects for a full minute. "I'd like those three. In a box like the one downstairs. If they aren't too expensive." A rosy flush bloomed on her cheeks.

The heat of her arm near his felt too intimate, the softness in her eyes too vulnerable. "They're not expensive and the boxes are premade," he said curtly. "I can show you what we have and you can choose one."

"I hope I'm not taking up too much of your time."

Her teeth grazed her bottom lip and her golden eyes gazed into his. He pulled out of her mind. No way he was listening to those thoughts.

Once again she was attempting to tap into his emotions, but unlike her, he had a shield—and a lifetime of experience using it.

He stepped back. "Let's go pick out a box for your Goliathinis."

Her smile wilted as he led her through the ballroom to the reception area. The sooner she was gone, the better. What had passed between them when he touched her was out of his control, and nothing in this place could ever be out of his control. That was who he was and what he was.

"Thank you," she said. *You and this enchanted place are what I'll remember of Paris.*

His instincts went on high alert. She sensed too much. "Would you like to have lunch?" he asked. "Victor can assemble and wrap the Goliathinis."

"I wish I could. I'm due at the convention center at one."

"Tomorrow, perhaps? Here at twelve thirty?"

Her eyes lit up and he was rewarded with a lovely smile.

"I'd like that." She stroked the horse's neck on her way down the stairs. "It was nice meeting you, Maurice. *Au revoir*, Mr. Durand."

His reply lodged in his throat. "Bye," he managed as she disappeared down the stairs.

When the door below closed he whirled on the horse. "Maurice? How the hell did she know your name?"

The horse's ear twitched. *A good guess?*

"I don't think so." He turned so he could address the room. "What's going on here?"

Louis, a huge African lion, replied. *Don't you like her?*

"I don't even know her. And anyone showing up here with empathic abilities that strong is suspect. What if she's a Dissembler?"

She isn't, Maurice replied. *She's completely untrained and unguarded. You know that. You were in her head the entire time she was here.*

"Forget it. I'm not looking for a woman." Especially an empath.

The llama replied, *Tate is different. She felt us. She likes us.*

"That is not *good*. Even if she isn't a spy, someone sent her here."

Victor appeared in the doorway. "So who was the empath?"

"Some American tourist," Adrien snapped.

"What's your problem?"

He's taking her to lunch tomorrow, a cheetah confided.

Victor grinned. "Really?"

Adrien groaned. "You're on my side. Humans stick together."

"She looked pretty hot to me—in a wholesome sort of way."

"Drop it. What do you have for me?"

Victor handed him a list of names with dates and times on it. "Everyone's coming except Chantal. She called to say she broke her arm."

"Broken arm, huh?"

Victor nodded at the list. "We'll have a full house as it is."

Adrien shoved the paper in the pocket of his jeans. "Should be interesting."

"The camera crew is due at two o'clock to plan the video shoot," Victor said. "In the ballroom."

"Then let's go put it in order."

They entered the ballroom and Victor leaned against the wall, awaiting directions.

Adrien crossed to the center. He stood among the stuffed animals and breathed deeply, focusing on tapping into the power of the Source below. The energy swirled and pulsed until the air crackled. Soon the power surged through him, growing, pounding, expanding until it filled his body and mind with light. Slowly he lifted his arms.

The energy flowed from the Source through him to the Guardians, pure spirits who had taken possession of the stuffed bodies over the past three centuries.

The animals began to move.

ACKNOWLEDGMENTS

So many people have supported and encouraged me on this writing journey and I thank you all! Special thanks to Cheryl Stoy and Sarita Oertling who read my very first tome and still wanted to read the second. Thanks to my critique partner and literary midwife, Sarah Andre and all my writer friends—especially Jo Anne, Kay, Sharie, Nicole, Kim and Colleen--who have been there with their encouragement and support through all the ups and downs.

I also want to thank Becca Stumpf for believing in the Durands so long ago and Randall Klein for everything he taught me about writing.

ABOUT THE AUTHOR

Lark Brennan's love of reading, writing and travel has led her to a string of colorful jobs and a well-worn passport – as well as several years spent sailing and diving in the Virgin Islands. Her travels have inspired her romantic suspense series, The Durand Chronicles, which takes place in some of her favorite destinations--the British Virgin Islands, Paris, Glacier National Park, New Orleans and Scotland.

Lark dreams of one day moving to the South of France, and in the meantime lives in Texas with her husband and two adorable canine "children."

For more books and updates visit:
www.larkbrennan.com

 facebook.com/LarkBrennan

 instagram.com/larkbrennan

bookbub.com/profile/lark-brennan

Made in the USA
Coppell, TX
25 January 2024

28208016R00194